D1029752

FRENCH AND ENGLISH

Also by Richard Faber

THE VISION AND THE NEED
BEACONSFIELD AND BOLINGBROKE
PROPER STATIONS

— En Angleterre, les petites filles sont très jolies... mais trop souvent fouettées.

Cartoon found in a Seine bookstall

RICHARD FABER

FRENCH and ENGLISH

FABER and FABER
3 Queen Square London

First published in 1975
by Faber and Faber Limited
3 Queen Square London WC1
Printed in Great Britain by
Butler & Tanner Ltd, Frome and London

ISBN 0 571 10727 3

CONTENTS

Oxford English Dictionary

Anglomania: *A mania for what is English, an excessive admiration of English customs, etc.*

Gallomania: *An unreasoning attachment to France or French customs.*

Larousse (1866 Edition)

Anglomanie: *Admiration exclusive, exagérée de tout ce qui appartient à l'Angleterre . . .*

Gallomanie: *Admiration passionnée pour la nation française.*

INTRODUCTION

THE FRENCH and the English are both too different, and too similar, not to find each other surprising. There would have been less friction between them if they had been less, or more, alike. More alike, they would feel more immediately at home with each other; less alike, they would have had less reason to compete. There are people in both countries who relish what is most exotic in the other: this makes for a kind of affection, if sometimes at the cost of respect. The affection may be enough to keep a holiday friendship going; but it rests on too unreal a basis to survive much wear and tear. More prosaic, work-day relationships face the opposite danger. Here, on familiar ground, the temptation may be to overlook the differences, rather than to romanticize them.

Perhaps this explains the element of tension and uncertainty, the undercurrent of danger, that makes the Anglo-French relationship so fascinating. When estrangement is at its greatest a sense of shared values can intervene. When all is smooth there can be sudden reminders of unshared prejudices. Sympathy, politeness, affection, even a taste for the exotic help; but, like most relationships, this one has always thriven best on mutual respect. Not that respect has always been expressed, or even felt, in practice. At times the two peoples seem to have co-existed cheerfully on a basis of mutual contempt. Yet, under the contempt, there has usually been an awareness of having developed civilizations of different texture, but roughly equal weight. When one of the two nations has been politically eclipsed by the other, it has been able to keep its self-respect by reflecting on past triumphs, on its artistic or scientific achievements, or (if all else fails) on its talent for *douceur de vivre*.

There cannot be any two neighbouring countries, elsewhere in the world, which have been on roughly equal terms for so long, have fought so frequently, have exchanged so many civilities, have had so much social and intellectual intercourse, have traded relatively so little with each other and have preserved such distinct identities. Over the centuries something like a miracle of balance has been achieved between them: alternately repelling and attracting each other, they have each managed to keep their essential qualities intact. The result is a unique relationship, soured by many wrongs and sweetened by many benefits, an extraordinary medley of resentment, esteem, disdain, warmth, liking and distaste.

One of the most striking features of this relationship has been a widespread and persistent ignorance of life in the other country, except in the relatively small circles of Frenchmen who have known England well and of Englishmen who have known France well. Burke wrote that he was 'astonished considering that we are divided from you but by a slender dyke of about twenty-four miles, and that the mutual intercourse between the two countries has lately been very great, to find how little you seem to know of us.' Educated Englishmen of his generation were perhaps a shade better informed about the French; but their knowledge seldom went deep and the vast mass of their countrymen had the most elementary notions of life across the Channel. Two centuries later a former French Ambassador at London* could write: 'One has said and resaid it and for my part I have never ceased to repeat it: there are no two neighbouring countries which know each other so little.'

Almost as striking as this mutual ignorance has been the sense of entering a completely different world traditionally experienced by passengers arriving at Dover or Calais. Halèvy tried to put this in perspective, in 1912, by pointing out how insignificant the contrast must seem to an Asiatic traveller from Calcutta or Peking. But he nevertheless described the sensation as one of 'dèpaysement radical'.

The modern traveller, especially by air, is likely to feel a less abrupt and exciting sense of transition. Modern technology makes everywhere for greater uniformity and airports are particularly obvious instances of this. But, even at airports, sharp contrasts between French and English manners and expressions are still visible and audible.

* M. René Massigli in *The Times* Saturday Review Column for 17 July 1971.

Perhaps it is a good thing that these contrasts should be preserved. Perhaps it is important that both France and England should keep their own peculiar qualities in as much of their native purity as possible. Perhaps nothing contributes more to this than the ignorance of both peoples about each other. If there has been so successful a balance between the two nations, perhaps the great object should be to perpetuate it. Perhaps we should cherish, not weaken, the obscure instincts of self-preservation which have hitherto kept the scales weighted on both sides.

Yet each people has such an enormous fund of complacency about certain—if not all—aspects of its civilization, that the danger of any really extensive proselytism, or loss of identity, seems rather remote. Insofar as the danger does exist, it may not be wholly alarming. One can think of French habits that could happily be imported by the English, and vice versa. But in fact the usual fate of such imports has been to suffer such a sea-change that they become triumphant expressions of the genius of the importing, rather than of the exporting, country. Good communications need not corrupt manners very far. Differences of climate, of education and of temperament seem likely to survive the most uniform world civilization and to provide an inexhaustible supply of fuel for local prejudice.

What does seem inevitable is that better communications will build up an increasing stock of half-truths and of superficial experiences, that will need to be corrected by deeper knowledge if they are not to cause pointless friction. An Englishman can get to know and like France, and a Frenchman can get to know and like England, without thinking the less of his own country and without losing the capacity to look through its eyes.

All of this is academic against the current economic and political background of Western Europe. If the enlarged European Economic Community survives (or even if not) there must be practical co-operation between its members in all sorts of fields. Successful co-operation between French and English will need more understanding between them, not so much in the good periods, but in the bad. At the very least it will be essential to keep some stubborn prejudices in their place.

This process of greater understanding will not always come easily. Writing in *Le Monde* in late 1971, André Fontaine referred to '. . . this great country, so near to France, so linked to her history, and yet at the same time in so many aspects so remote . . .' E. M. Forster told the authors of *Mésentente Cordiale* (an Englishman married to a Frenchwoman)* that 'he believed the two peoples cannot understand, but can only love, each other.'

But there are, after all, solid bonds as well as barriers. A French historian writing between the two World Wars† attributed the cordial alliance between the two countries in the First World War to 'certain intellectual and moral affinities stronger than the apparent dissimilarities . . . a common conception of what the good life ("la vie digne d'être vécue") should be, a common scale for evaluating ideas and merits, a common ideal of greatness and civilization.' In the eighteenth century Lord Chesterfield claimed that 'true wit, sound taste, and good sense, are now as it were engrossed by France and England.' Nobody could dream of making such a claim today; but there is a sense in which French and English intellectuals still use a common language.

E. M. Forster's comment raises the question of what 'understanding' another people involves. How far is it ever possible? Do we understand our closest relations or, for that matter, ourselves? At best the condition of understanding another person is never absolute, never excludes the possibility of surprise, and can never be reduced to a simple formula. Usually it is an instinctive, not an articulate, state of mind.

When we say that we 'understand' other people, we seldom pretend to analyse their actions in detail, to read their inmost thoughts and expose their most deeply buried impulses. However self-analytical, we have difficulty in reading, and explaining, ourselves in this way. The most that we usually mean is that we are not mystified: we have experienced behaviour of this kind before and we know what sort of reactions to expect. Understanding in this sense is the result of regular contact. It can be improved by keen observation; but it basically depends on familiarity and it is not very easily communicated to others. It can sometimes be deepened by accounts of what others have experienced, but must primarily be got through personal dealings.

In this sense an Englishman who has lived some time in France, or read much French literature, may cease to find any strangeness in what he experiences there. He either feels that he under-

* Legrand and Grant, *Mésentente Cordiale* (1952).

† Georges Ascoli in the preface to *La Grande-Bretagne devant l'opinion Française au XVIIe siècle* (1930).

stands the French, or—what perhaps comes to the same thing—he no longer feels the urge to understand them. He may like or dislike, but he is no longer disconcerted or bewitched. He may not be able to explain; but what happens has ceased to surprise him. In time he will probably find that he stops liking or disliking the French altogether, except as individuals. The sense of contrast may return to him after an absence in his own country; but for most of the time the categories of 'French' and 'English' will cease to count for him—provided, of course, that he has not come to the point of finding his own countrymen exotic.

It would be impracticable for more than a small minority of French and English ever to feel so much at home in the other country. Perhaps this is just as well. The foreigner may lose the feeling of strangeness without ceasing to be strange himself. It would be a pity, too, if the 'love' that E. M. Forster talked about, the magic of what is strange and unattainable, were totally to be superseded by more humdrum feelings. The Anglo-French relationship has often been pictured, or caricatured, as a stormy love-affair. According to one French writer* France has always been for the Englishman 'like a capricious mistress, whom he wants to strike at the very moment that he loves.' (It must be a tribute to the charms of Marianne, rather than to the virility of John Bull, that the active and passive roles in this partnership have seldom been pictured in reverse. Some Frenchmen have maintained that the English are not rational enough to be genuinely masculine.)

But at bottom even the most bewildered stranger knows that nationality is only one, and not the most basic, of the things that divide human beings. Where there is no language barrier, an Englishman and a Frenchman of the same profession or tastes are likely to have a good deal more in common with each other than with uncongenial compatriots. 'I cannot help remarking, that the more we investigate what are called national characteristics, the more we find that they are in fact exterior garbs, varying in appearance, but covering similar feelings, foibles and weaknesses.' This was the conclusion of Sir Charles Darnley, Bart., an imaginary English traveller in France, in *London and Paris*, a series of comparative sketches published in 1823. It is the conclusion of most travellers who stay long enough to lose their

* Charles Bastide, *Anglais et Français au XVIIe siècle* (1912).

first, sharp, impressions. The early generalizations, commonplace or brilliant, may be true enough in their way; but sooner or later they cede to a sense of reality that is more complex and less distinct.

Personal experience, whether at first or second hand, develops a kind of understanding and perhaps the only kind that is really useful in practice. But of course it does nothing to *explain*. In a more intellectual sense it is only possible to understand another people through historical, social and geographical knowledge. The possibilities of accumulating explanatory information about France and England are clearly limitless and different people are likely to find different bits of information illuminating. In any case most people in any country manage quite comfortably with a very imperfect knowledge of their own national history and constitution. But it would be difficult to take an intelligent interest in French politics without having heard of the French Revolution.

It is easier to exhort the English and the French to greater understanding of one another than to suggest what exactly they should do about it. Nevertheless, in spite of the inevitable limitations, in spite of the impossibility of ever attaining to a state of complete 'understanding', the more people ready to grope towards it, whether on a practical or on an intellectual level, the less risk of fatal misunderstanding there will be. No doubt we should not be too optimistic; whatever happens, a good deal of misunderstanding is bound to continue. But we can try to eradicate the silliest and most offensive generalizations; to bring the two national images up to date (in not too simplified a form); and, given the need for closer co-operation, to resolve on both sides of the Channel to put up with a great deal from each other that we do not understand.

The anonymous author of *London and Paris* described his object as being: 'To combat national prejudice by showing, in the correspondence of two Gentlemen of equal character and respectability, how very differently the same objects appear to natives and foreigners. . . . The trouble of the Editor will be amply repaid, should the perusal of these letters tend, in however small a degree, to soften those antipathies which have so long divided the two wisest and most powerful nations of modern Europe.'

Gentle appeals of this kind have often been made by English Francophiles and French Anglophiles—and, after all, they have not been wholly disregarded. Antipathies remain, but far less virulent than in the worst periods of the past. There is something depressingly cyclical about Anglo-French relations; but the general progress of the cycles does seem to be towards better information and greater mutual tolerance.

My own aim in this book has not been to try to explain the French to the English (or vice versa) but, by drawing on a selection of representative French and English writings, to convey an idea of what the two peoples have thought of each other, and incidentally taken from each other, in the course of their dealings. Nobody, pursuing this aim honestly, could contrive to give an overwhelming impression of sweetness and light; and I have sometimes had to dwell, more than I might have cared, on traditional feelings of enmity between the two peoples. But, if sweetness and light have not always prevailed, neither have dark and bitterness. I hope that, if this study shows anything, it shows how enormously complex the Anglo-French relationship has always been: how wrong it would be to suppose that, even historically, the predominant feeling of French and English for each other has been one of simple aversion. One conclusion which certainly emerges is that, though there have been some constants in the relationship, there have also been several variables —and this may suggest that even the most rooted prejudices can in time disappear. But perhaps the most striking impression to stay in the mind is the extent of the reciprocal debt. No two countries in any continent or epoch can have owed so much to each other, on such an equal footing, over so long a period of time.

Although this book pretends to an Olympian detachment, its author is English and Francophile. My English patriotism may be responsible for some distortions, while other passages may suggest a touch of wistful sentimentality about Anglo-French relations. A further drawback is that, although I lived for a time in France and have often travelled there, I never did so as a child or adolescent. Consequently, my knowledge of English life and literature, however limited, goes much deeper than what I have learned of France. There is an imbalance between my French and English sources, though I have tried to correct it where I could.

A number of other apologies seem necessary. The scope of the book is very wide—much wider than my qualifications to tackle it—and my treatment has had to be very selective. Since my aim was to write for a general public and since I wanted to give as representative a picture of Anglo-French relations as I could, I thought it more useful to cover a wide canvas patchily than to work in detail over a smaller one. Even so, I have barely touched on scientific and commercial exchanges and only very selectively on scholarly and artistic ones. My idea being to bring out how the two peoples have viewed each other, some types of political, fashionable and literary exchange seemed more relevant than technical contacts with less human interest and confined to more restricted circles.

The chapters in this book, taken separately, are obviously inadequate as specialized accounts of Anglo-French contrasts and contacts. But I hope that, read together, they give an idea of what the two countries and peoples have meant to each other at different times. They concentrate on the seventeenth, eighteenth and nineteenth centuries, because there is too much modern, and and too little medieval, evidence. But I have had no fixed period in mind and have sometimes blundered into the present day. I have only handled events as pegs for personal impressions. The method is a patchwork one and the quilt is meant to be seen as a whole.

Throughout I have used the word 'English' in contexts where I would normally write 'British'. This is partly in order to conform to French usage, but also because the English were not British—and certainly not Scottish—at many points of Anglo-French history. What appears as 'English' in these pages may often include an important Scottish, Welsh or Irish contribution; but the French have usually found these contributions difficult to distinguish. It is typical that R. L. Stevenson, travelling on his donkey in the Cévennes, should have been addressed, and should have responded, as an Englishman. On the other hand I have avoided the special relationship between France and Scotland, the 'auld alliance', since this was something exclusive to the Scots and clearly identifiable as such.

I have not given the detailed references that would be expected in a work of scholarship; but I have tried to indicate in the text (or in the bibliography at the end) the sources on which it is based. I have hesitated whether or not to translate French quotations. On the one hand readers may prefer not to skip too much from the one language to the other; on the other hand some

French passages do not turn well into English and many lose their flavour. Horned by this dilemma I soon gave up any attempt at consistency.

Professor Seznec of All Souls College, Oxford, was kind enough to give me some ideas for reading, when I started on this book. My friend M. Alain Pillepich helped me more than I can say by allowing me to pick his brains and borrow his books.

'Cher enfant . . .' says the angelic Mme de Mortsauf in Balzac's *Le Lys dans la Vallée*, racked by a less than angelic jealousy of Lady Dudley: 'La France et l'Angleterre ne sont-elles pas toujours ennemies? Madeleine sait cela, elle sait qu'une mer immense les sépare, mer froide, mer orageuse.' What follows is a series of more or less agitated crossings.

ONE

Wars and Peaces

WHEN I WAS a small boy we used to play a game called 'French and English'. Whether or not it has survived the Second World War, it had certainly survived the First World War and a generation of the *Entente cordiale*. It has always seemed to me rather typical of the Anglo-French relationship, both in the way in which it perpetuated centuries of rivalry and because, as far as I can remember, only the most narrowly patriotic among us minded being drafted, or enlisting, under the French colours.

It is by now over 150 years since the English and the French were last at war with each other and, during this time, they have fought on the same side in three great conflicts: the Crimean War and the two World Wars of this century. Perhaps, by this time, there are not many Frenchmen or Englishmen who would consciously think of each other as hereditary enemies. But traces of the habit persist, at least at a certain level of consciousness.

Until well into the nineteenth century the hostility was more or less explicit. Byron, himself Francophile, wrote sarcastically in *Don Juan*:

> . . . . they betray
> Their country; and as traitors are abhorr'd
> Who name the French in English, save to show
> How Peace should make John Bull the Frenchman's foe.

The continuance of anti-French feeling of this kind, just seven years after the Battle of Waterloo, was human enough. Some Englishmen, who had the future on their side, were already taking a more enlightened view. The anonymous author of *London and Paris* (published in the same year as *Don Juan*) makes the Marquis de Vermont, an imaginary French traveller to London, write to his English correspondent in Paris:

I shall conclude by expressing a wish, in which I am sure you will cordially join, that as England and France, during a long succession of many centuries, wasted their treasures and their blood in a silly and wicked contest for military superiority, so may the only struggle from henceforth between them be to rival each other in the acquisition of useful knowledge, and of those purer morals which are the forerunners of peace and freedom, and consequently, of the improved happiness of mankind.

Sir Charles Darnley replies by recalling that, at a levee 'during the consular government', Bonaparte remarked to a party of Englishmen:* '. . . the two most powerful and most civilized nations on the earth; we mutually deserve each other's esteem; and we ought to unite in cultivating peace, literature, and the fine arts, and by so doing to form the happiness of mankind.'

Yet neither of the two old Adams was capable of being regenerated overnight. In 1830 Tennyson could still publish a rousing catch, in his most true-blue manner, casting the French as the national enemy:

For the French the Pope may shrive 'em
For the devil a whit we heed 'em:
As for the French, God speed 'em
  Unto their heart's desire,
And the merry devil drive 'em
  Through the water and the fire.

Twenty years later his imprecations against Louis Napoleon breathed muted, but still lusty, defiance.

Even after the Franco-Prussian War of 1870 there were Frenchmen enough whom a whiff of *Perfide Albion* would drive into apoplexy—as popular reactions to the Fashoda incident, and earlier African squabbles, amply showed. For that matter Proust's butcher-woman (in *Sodome et Gomorrhe*) advocated a war with England because she could not be disabused of the belief that the English, as well as the Prussians, had fought the French in 1870:

As my sister was just explaining, since this war that the English made against us in '70, we are being ruined by the commercial treaties. After we've beaten them, we won't let a single Englishman come into France any more without paying three hundred francs as an entry fee, just as we have to pay now to go to England.

* J. G. Lemaistre was one of this party (at the Tuileries, after the Peace of Amiens, in 1802). He recorded that Bonaparte spoke 'with a smile which is peculiarly his own and which changes a countenance usually stern into one of great mildness.'

I have read somewhere that, in real life, a Breton peasant lamented to one of Proust's friends at the beginning of the First World War that the fight was not against the English: 'Ah, madame! Si c'étaient les Anglais, on aurait plus de cœur!'

There is no need to recall the diplomatic differences between the two countries, in the Middle East and in Europe, during the inter-war years: unhappy events in the Second World War: or the bias of French foreign policy under General de Gaulle: to make the obvious point that, in spite of many scotchings, the snake of Anglo-French hostility still enjoys a kind of life. Nevertheless, for well over a century, it has not been the beast that it used to be. Even if war were still a thinkable instrument of policy in Western Europe, it would be difficult to find modern Englishmen or Frenchmen who could seriously contemplate using it against each other. The myth (and the reality) of Anglo-French hostility has on the whole succumbed to the myth (and the reality) of *Entente cordiale*.

The tradition of Anglo-French hostility was of course as ancient as it was sturdy. Kipling was a passionate Francophile who spoke in 1920 of the English conviction that the French 'were the only other people in the world who mattered' and said in 1927 to an audience which included Maréchal Foch:

> I am sure that, as the actual memories of the war itself recede into the background of the years, we in England have come more and more to realize the patience, endurance and goodwill of that great Ally with whom we entered into the War . . .

But in 1913 he had celebrated the centuries of Anglo-French rivalry in coloured, yet moving, verse:

> Where did you refrain from us or we refrain from you?
> Ask the wave that has not watched war between us two!
> Others held us for a while, but with weaker charms,
> These we quitted at the call for each other's arms.
> From each other's throat we wrenched valour's last reward—
> That extorted word of praise gasped 'twixt lunge and guard.
> In each other's cup we poured mingled blood and tears,
> Brutal joys, unmeasured hopes, intolerable fears—
> All that soiled or salted life for a thousand years.
> Proved beyond the need of proof, matched in every clime,
> O Companion, we have lived greatly through all time!

During those 'thousand years' the French and English did not spend so much time actually fighting each other as one might suppose. The Hundred Years' War, from the middle of the fourteenth to the middle of the fifteenth century, left an impression of perpetual conflict. But, of the period between then and the Battle of Waterloo, rather under a quarter was in fact spent at war. Seeley, referring in 1883 to Anglo-French rivalry in the eighteenth century for the possession of the New World, pointed out that the two previous centuries had been more peaceful. Of the eighteenth century he wrote:

> ... the whole period stands out as an age of gigantic rivalry between England and France, a kind of second Hundred Years' War. In fact in those times and down to our own memory the eternal discord of England and France appeared so much a law of nature that it was seldom spoken of. The wars of their own times, blending with a vague recollection of Crecy, Poitiers and Agincourt, created an impression in the minds of those generations, that England and France always had been at war and always would be. But this was a pure illusion. In the sixteenth and seventeenth centuries England and France had not been those persistent enemies.

Even in the sixteenth and seventeenth centuries, however, England and France, if not persistent enemies, were certainly not persistent friends. There were treaties and peaces; there were royal marriages and projects of marriage; between the accessions of Elizabeth and William III there was relatively little direct conflict. The Stuart kings adopted, fairly consistently, a pro-French policy. But the moments of really cordial and active alliance were few. One of the most effective was the offensive alliance between Cromwell and Mazarin, in 1655, which resulted in the short-lived English occupation of Dunkirk; but it certainly did not reflect any close sympathy between republican England and monarchical France.

The scars of the Hundred Years' War would have healed more rapidly and completely, had it not been for the religious cleavage that developed in the sixteenth century. The French Chancellor, Michel de l'Hôpital, whose policy was to work for a united and tolerant France, opened his speech to the States-General at Orléans in 1560 by deploring that there was now more love between an Englishman and a Frenchman of the same religion than between two Frenchmen of different persuasions. The triumph of Catholicism in France soon ensured that the majorities in both countries belonged to different faiths and could hate each other with a clear conscience. A passage in Pepys's diary for 30 September 1661 shows how strong anti-French prejudice remained in England, even in the first flush of the Restoration. There had been an absurd dispute in London for precedence between the Spanish and French Ambassadors; it came to blows and the Spaniards got the best of it: '. . . at which', said Pepys 'it is strange to see how all the City did rejoice. . . . And . . . indeed we do naturally all love the Spanish and hate the French.'

English resentment of France in the seventeenth century was envenomed by a sense of being bottom dog. We are used to regarding France and England as equals and no doubt, even in the seventeenth century, there was the sort of equality between them that there always is between sovereign powers. But England was, during most of that century, in a position of marked inferiority. It was in every sense a smaller country.

Even in 1800 the combined population of England and Wales (some 9 million) was only a third of the population of France. In 1700 (when it was about 5½ million) it was under a quarter of it. In other words, it was in roughly the same proportion to the French as that of, say, the Netherlands is to that of Britain today. Scotland had just over 1½ million inhabitants in 1800 and is supposed to have had about 1 million in 1700. The combined population of the British Isles can hardly have exceeded a third of the French population in 1700, or a half of it in 1800.

As these figures show, the disparity tended to diminish during the eighteenth century, because the population of England grew at a faster rate. This was particularly the case where the two capital cities were concerned: whereas the population of Paris seems to have remained more or less static throughout the eighteenth century (it stood at 546,000 in the census of 1801), the population of London, which had been smaller than that of Paris in the seventeenth century, had progressed to 900,000 in 1801. It was not, however, till the end of the nineteenth century that the two countries as a whole found themselves in the same population league. The French population in 1901 had grown to 38½ million, while that of England and Wales stood at 32½ million and the combined population of the British Isles at over 40 million.

There was thus a considerable disparity in apparent French and English power even in the middle of the eighteenth century. Contemporary observers were well aware of this. Bolingbroke thought that France had been left too powerful by the Treaty of

Utrecht. Chesterfield wrote of the advantages that French policy could derive from a situation where nearly 'twenty millions of people, and the ordinary revenue of above thirteen millions sterling a-year, are at the absolute disposal of the Crown.' If the English were not too intimidated by the contrast with their own resources, it was perhaps partly because they had no very clear idea of how great the disparity was; they could also take comfort from their growing economic prosperity and from the tonic effects of their vaunted free constitution. What, after all, were mere numbers to John Bull? Chesterfield noted in 1747 how '. . . that silly, sanguine notion, which is firmly entertained here, that one Englishman can beat three Frenchmen, encourages, and has sometimes enabled, one Englishman, in reality to beat two.'

Throughout the nineteenth century, of course, industrial and maritime England made enormous strides and, where she had formerly entertained (if not too noticeably) an inferiority complex towards French power and luxury, she now began to develop a superiority complex in its place. Even the French were impressed, though often appalled, by the achievements of English industry and by its methodical penetration of the civilized and uncivilized world.

By contrast, when we go back to the seventeenth century, there was really no respect in which, say, the court of Charles II could compare with that of Louis XIV except in the field of scientific and philosophic thought. The two capitals were roughly of the same size, but in most other respects hardly in the same class. Evelyn, in 1652, described Paris as being unrivalled in the world. A decade earlier he had written of French predominance, though in a sourer vein:

> There is scarse a Prince in Europ, but what have been scholars in the French Academys and which by consequence has leaven'd them all, with the mode as well as language of France, and disposed them to an undervaluing of their own Countryes with infinite prejudice to the rest of Europ; the French, naturaly active, insinuating and bold having with their trifles and new modes allmost debaucht all the sobriety of former times, continualy aspiring to enlarge their Tyranny, by all the arts of dissimulation; and tretchery: Tho it cannot be deneyed: that there are many worthy persons of probity, and greate learning among them, who are weary of the intollerable yoake under which they groane.

Groaning or not, the seventeenth-century French set the tone in all the politer arts of life. It was then that the minority of Englishmen, who actively coveted superior polish, conceived something like a real inferiority complex towards French arts and manners: the feeling remained strong in the eighteenth century and there are still traces of it today.

Not that French 'trifles and new modes' began their debauching mission in the seventeenth century. Even in the sixteenth century they had had their English imitators. But the distracted condition of France for so much of that century, the relative weakness of her monarchs and the discord of her religious factions, had combined with the personal splendour of the reigns of Henry VIII and Elizabeth to keep the two countries in a more equal balance. Besides, the memories of English power in France —which Henry VIII tried briefly to revive—were then of more recent date.

Looking back from the seventeenth century, and bearing in mind the relative sizes of the two kingdoms, one wonders how medieval England can ever have cut the figure in medieval France that she did. It was, of course, only possible while France was disunited and so long as the French kings governed effectively only a small part of the country. As things were, the wealth and power of the English kings compared very favourably with those of their crippled French colleagues. Much of them, in any case, they derived from their French possessions. Henry II was, as well as King of England, Duke of Normandy and Count of Anjou and, through his wife Eleanor of Aquitaine, master of a large area in south-western France. The French King said of him that he wanted nothing: 'Men, horses, gold, silk, diamonds, game, fruits: he has all in abundant plenty. We in France have only bread, wine and gaiety.'

The size of the English Empire in France alternately expanded and contracted throughout the Middle Ages. Normandy was lost to it in the reign of King John, but Gascony remained. Some two decades after the beginning of the Hundred Years' War Edward III, at the height of his power, held parts of Flanders as well as a large area covering Poitou, Aquitaine (Guyenne) and Gascony. In the campaign of 1369–75 du Guesclin stripped England of all these possessions, except for Bayonne, Bordeaux and Calais; there were even destructive French raids on the southern English coast. Then the tide turned again. Henry VI, who was crowned in

Paris in 1431, at one time held the whole of northern France, including Normandy and Brittany, together with a sizeable strip in south-western France, including Bordeaux and Bayonne. In another couple of decades, when the Hundred Years' War ended in 1453, all of this had been lost, except for Calais.

Calais itself did not fall to the French until a century later, at the end of Mary's reign. Its loss was a sad blow to Tudor pride. As late as the 1590s Elizabeth was still trying, in negotiations with Henri IV, to recover this jewel for the English Crown. Even the pacific Stuart kings retained the title of King of France as part of their formal style until William III abandoned it after the Peace of Rijswijk in 1697.

English interference in medieval France started because the kings of England were also French magnates. It continued for the same reason (the Plantagenets fearing French designs on their remaining French possessions); but also because of trade rivalry; because Edward III was in a position to satisfy international law by a formal claim to the French throne; and because the English fighting classes needed profit and employment. According to Froissart:

> The English will never love or honour their king, unless he be victorious and a lover of arms and war against their neighbours and especially against such as are greater and richer than themselves. Their land is more fulfilled of riches and all manner of goods when they are at war than in times of peace. They take delight and solace in battles and slaughter: covetous and envious are they above measure of other men's wealth.

It seems to be generally agreed that, at first, the struggle had not the characteristics of a war between nations, in the sense that those words would now convey. It was only later, as wrongs accumulated and the French consciousness of national identity developed, that the English were widely execrated as savage and marauding foreigners. But till the end, of course, there were Frenchmen whose interests lay with the English and areas where the English rule was not harsh. The Duke of Bedford, who acted as Regent in Paris during the minority of Henry VI, seems to have tried to be liberal. The long English presence in Guyenne left no deep resentment. Montaigne, who lived in the neighbourhood of Bordeaux, wrote of the old cousinship between the people of his district and the English nation ('c'est une nation à laquelle ceux de mon quartier ont eu autrefois une si privée accointance qu'il reste encore en ma maison aucunes traces de nostre ancien cousinage') and he complimented the Black Prince as 'celui qui régenta si long temps nostre Guienne, personnage, duquel les conditions et la fortune ont beaucoup de notables parties de grandeur.' The Bordeaux district no doubt profited commercially from the English connection. Perhaps it was not the only district to do so. An article in *Le Monde* for 19 April 1972 reported that the 'Norman movement whose adherents campaign for the reunification of Normandy' had declared itself favourable to the enlargement of the Common Market on account of the traffic that was bound to pass through Norman ports and roads: never, the movement believed, since the Plantagenet Empire, would 'Normandy find itself in such a favourable situation'.

Whatever the compensations of the English Empire in France—and they were no doubt limited to certain districts and classes—the Hundred Years' War left undeniable scars. Jeanne d'Arc created, or others created for her, a potent and enduring myth. Tocqueville, at the age of twenty-three, wrote a letter to a friend from Tocqueville in Normandy, only a short distance from the harbour from which the Normans set out to conquer England. In this letter, although a future friend to England, he had this to say of the Hundred Years' War:

> Then began the most heroic, the most brilliant and the most unhappy time in our history. Such, dear friend, was the first history book that fell into my hands, and I cannot convey the impression it made on me: every event is engraved on my memory, and thence derives that often unreflecting instinct of hate which rouses me against the English. Time and time again when I came to those disastrous battles in which valour was always crushed by superior discipline, I have skipped the pages and left out whole passages to which nonetheless irresistible curiosity would later drive me back.

The Hundred Years' War obscured the memory of the twelfth and thirteenth centuries when there had been frequent Anglo-French intellectual exchanges; when Thomas à Becket had studied in Paris; when the bishops of Winchester had resided in what is now a Parisian suburb (Bicêtre); and when the English, together with the French, the Normans and the Picardians, had been one of the four nations comprising Paris University (the Rue des Anglais remains to show where the English students lived). H. A. L. Fisher, in his *History of Europe*, emphasizes the relative lack of contrast between France and England at that time:

> The Norman Conquest had made of England a province of French civilization . . .
> . . . A traveller passing from one country to the other in the reign of King John would have found no very palpable contrast between the French and the English scene. . . . England he would probably pronounce to be the rougher and richer country. But so indistinct were the spiritual frontiers between these two remarkable peoples that the barons of the Charter did not scruple to invite the heir to the French throne, afterwards Louis VIII, to take the English crown, and that Simon de Montfort, the leader of the national revolt against Henry III, and the great popular hero of English liberty, was the son of the French nobleman who crushed the Albigensian Crusade. To the Frenchman of this period the German was a foreigner and almost intolerable. England was different. Though the commonalty spoke an unintelligible tongue, and for lack of vineyards were driven to a disgraceful beverage, the gentry were of a familiar world and could make themselves intelligible in their provincial French.

No doubt some sense of social/cultural familiarity continued to link the ruling classes on both sides throughout the Hundred Years' War, although the French knights must have had mixed feelings about the rough islanders against whom they were pitted. Ascoli thought that Shakespeare had struck exactly the right note in his *Henry V* when he showed the Frenchmen as being 'full at once of admiration and of disdain for this people'. Chivalry may have done little for the peasant, but it had a softening influence where it applied. Montesquieu comments somewhere on the author of a work about ancient chivalry: 'He attributes to chivalry and the feelings inspired by it the fine actions by French and English respecting prisoners, to the chivalry which flourished in these two nations, while so much barbarity was being practised by their neighbours. I could add that when chivalry came to an end, we fell into the horror of the wars of religion, during which such savage practices were witnessed.'

At least there were some chivalrous actions to remember, a sense of fighting war according to the same rules, alongside the historian's 'disastrous battles' and the peasant's experience of pillage and destruction.

The French never quite got their own back on the English for the Hundred Years' War—but then, in a sense, they had had it already. The last successful invasion of England was, after all, a French one. The Normans, though originally of Germanic stock (like their predecessors, the Anglo-Saxon and Scandinavian invaders of England), were well established in France, had intermarried and were imbued with the French culture of the time. Voltaire in his *Lettres sur les Anglais* regarded the Normans as French; so, in effect, did Taine. The Saxons may eventually have succeeded in absorbing their conquerors, but only after being well and truly conquered. No king of France ever held an acre of English soil; but the French triumph in England was more lasting than any dominion that the English achieved in France.

There were two subsequent occasions when the English felt threatened in their own island by French power. The first was the period of French supremacy during the reign of Louis XIV. For much of this period the threat seemed distant. Louis exercised a kind of patronage over Charles II, but he paid relatively little for the privilege and his direct influence on the actual conduct of English affairs was slight. He seems in fact to have had a low opinion of England's potential importance at that time and to have had no urge to dabble across the Channel more than, as a good Catholic, he need. He did not intervene when William III took the English throne and, after the failure of the Irish expedition, he was careful not to commit himself too deeply in support of the banished James II and his family. William III opposed him stubbornly, but more as a continental prince than as an English king.

Gradually the majority of the English came to see it as being in their own interests to check the European policy of the French monarchy; a joint address of both Houses of Parliament in 1709 referred to the need to prevent 'the ambitious designs of France for the future'. Voltaire at least at one period, saw things in the same light and said that the English were 'acharnés contre Louis XIV uniquement par ce qu'ils lui croyaient de l'ambition'. But the French wars of the late seventeenth and early eighteenth centuries were only intermittently supported by the English nation as a whole; the Tory squires and parsons, whose successors were so firm in the struggle with Revolutionary France and with Napoleon, were often eager for peace. In spite of the Gallophobia of the lower classes, one gets the impression that there was less national animosity in these wars than in those of a century later, just as there was less national animosity in the Napoleonic Wars than in the World Wars of the present century. Louis was playing the game according to rules—his own rules, but ones that could to some extent be understood in England. He never completely lacked admirers there.

Dryden could write in 1693: '. . . setting prejudice and partiality apart, though he is our enemy, the stamp of a Louis, the patron of all arts, is not much inferior to the medal of an Augustus Caesar.' Prior included the following lines in verses addressed to Boileau after the Battle of Blenheim in 1704:

> I grant, old Frend, old Foe, (for such we are
> Alternate, as the chance of Peace and War) . . .

This is a far cry from the total propaganda effort of some later wars and suggests the relatively civilized and detached attitude towards war, as a professional activity, which characterized most of the eighteenth century. The supreme instance is enshrined in the possibly apocryphal story, extremely popular in France, that the French at the Battle of Fontenoy politely invited the English to shoot first: 'Messieurs les Anglais, tirez les premiers!'

Even French assistance to the rebellious American colonies did not spoil the spirit in which the ceremonious, if energetic, conflict between monarchical France and monarchical England was normally conducted. Louis XVIII, when Comte de Provence, composed the following debonair verses in a year of French aeronautical experiments:

> Les Anglais, nation trop fière,
> S'arrogent l'empire des mers;
> Les Français, nation légère,
> S'emparent de celui des airs.

Arthur Young, in the preface to his *Travels in France*, looks back with some complacency on a first-class match between evenly balanced teams:

> It is a question whether modern history has anything more curious to offer to the attention of the politician than the progress and rivalship of the French and English empires, from the

ministry of Colbert to the revolution in France. In the course of these 130 years, both have figured with a degree of splendour that has attracted the admiration of mankind.

It was, of course, another matter when the English became engaged in what turned into a life-and-death struggle first with Revolutionary France and later with Napoleon. Napoleon, after all, was a much more volcanic and unpredictable figure than Louis XIV: there could be no possible question as to the extent of his personal ambitions; and he was at one time engaged in what seemed to be serious preparations for an invasion of England. Many Frenchmen find it difficult to forgive the English for the petty and unimaginative way in which, as they see it, the insular oligarchs blocked Napoleon's vision. But then they have never had to react to an English Napoleon. (Bossuet did indeed describe Cromwell as 'un de ces esprits remuants et audacieux qui semblent être nés pour changer le monde'; but Cromwell entered into treaty with Mazarin and could hardly be represented as even a potential threat to French independence.) They have only had to fear English commercial and maritime predominance.

Yet even the struggle with Napoleon, intensely serious and patriotic as it was, had its graceful side. Anglican clergymen might regard Bonaparte as the devil incarnate; but crowds of Englishmen flocked to Paris in 1802, during the short-lived Peace of Amiens. Ensign, later Lieutenant, Wheatley, who served in the Peninsular War and the Waterloo campaign, wrote in his Journal in November 1813:

> Saw the French Army through a good glass. They were drawn up in line and looked clean and well as far as I can discern. Poor tools of affluent ambitious men! Mere machines of politicians! Another month and many of you will lay low and still for ever. The French people are our common enemy, yet I like them as a nation and I really am of opinion every Englishman does the same in his heart.

Earl Stanhope recorded Wellington, in later life, as expressing great admiration for the French troops under Napoleon:

> I never on any occasion knew them behave otherwise than well. Their officers too were as good as possible. The French soldiers are more under control than ours. It was quite shocking what excesses ours committed when once let loose. Our soldiers could

> not resist wine. The French too could shift better for themselves, and always live upon the country . . .
>
> The French system of conscription brings together a fair sample of all classes; ours is composed of the scum of the earth.

Chateaubriand described the two armies at Waterloo as exchanging steel and fire with a gallantry and ferocity animated by a national enmity of ten centuries: 'Lord Castlereagh, reporting on the battle to the House of Lords, said: "The English and French soldiers, after the attack, washed their bloody hands in the same stream and from one bank to another congratulated themselves mutually on their courage." Wellington had always been fatal to Bonaparte, or rather, the rival genius of France, the English genius, barred the road to victory.'

Throughout these centuries of struggle and uneasy peace national differences would acquire more, or less, of an edge as ideological differences waxed or waned. The Protestant English were deeply shocked by the Massacre of St Bartholomew in 1572 and by the Revocation of the Edict of Nantes in 1685. The Catholic French were equally shocked by the religious somersaults in England under the different Tudor monarchs: Montaigne deplored that, since his birth, he had seen three or four changes in the religious constitution of England. They mourned Mary Queen of Scots, executed in 1587, both as a representative of the Catholic faith and as a former Queen of France. For that matter the English had a bad reputation in pre-Revolutionary France for butchering royalties, only equalled by that of the Tudor monarchs for butchering subjects. The death of Thomas More, who had an international reputation as a man of letters, made a particularly poor impression in France. The regicide theme was as old as the Middle Ages: Charles d'Orléans wrote of the treason of the English to their kings and in 1403, when seven French and seven English lords joined in combat at Montendre, the French reproached the English with the odious murder of Richard II.

When therefore Charles I was executed, the sense of indignant shock in France was only mitigated by a feeling that this was the sort of thing to be expected from the English. The Glorious Revolution of 1688, which forced James II to make way for his daughter and son-in-law, was seen as a disgraceful example of family impiety. Throughout the seventeenth century the inconstancy and insubordination of the English people were bywords in right-thinking French circles.

A century later the right-thinking English were to be no less disturbed by the excesses of the French Revolution and by the executions of Louis XVI and his Queen.

At times, of course, a convergence of ideologies led to a temporary burying of national hatchets either by certain classes or by the two peoples as a whole. In the first dawn of the French Revolution there was a meeting of minds between French and English enthusiasts. After the Restoration of Louis XVIII the English were valued in reactionary French *salons*, if nowhere else in Paris. A century earlier it had been the English legitimists who put their hope in France.

In the sixteenth century, the struggle between Catholicism and Protestantism dominated men's minds. Even after Henri IV decided that Paris was worth a Mass his toleration of the Huguenots made him popular in England. Elizabeth, who had periodically helped the Huguenots, formed an *entente* with Henri against Spain, sent Essex dazzlingly to France to salute him, promised him men and money and gave him the Garter. Henri's peace with Spain in 1598, together with Anglo-French commercial conflicts, ruffled this friendship. It was not in Elizabeth's way to be a lavish negotiator and Henri was not the only French ruler to take the view that one had to pursue a tough diplomacy with the English to get anything out of them. However, under his reign Anglo-French relations remained relatively good. When he was assassinated in 1610 he was greatly mourned by Prince Henry, son of James I, who called him his second father.

It was during this friendly spell that Shakespeare, in *Henry V*, described France as 'the world's best garden' and, in general, did his best for Anglo-French relations. In his rough wooing of the French king's daughter, Henry V says to her: '. . . shall not thou and I, between Saint Denis and Saint George, compound a boy half French, half English, that shall go to Constantinople and take the Turk by the beard?' The French king is made to bless the match:

> Take her, fair son; and from her blood raise up
> Issue to me; that the contending kingdoms
> Of France and England, whose very shores look pale
> With envy of each other's happiness,
> May cease their hatred; and their dear conjunction

Plant neighbourhood and Christian-like accord
In their sweet bosoms, that never war advance
His bleeding sword 'twixt England and fair France.

Where, one cannot help feeling, has one heard this before? Anglo-French history is punctuated by these pious, in retrospect sometimes pathetic, hopes of concord. When Henry VIII and François I ('Those suns of glory, those two lights of men . . .') met glitteringly on the Field of the Cloth of Gold in 1520, Clément Marot expressed the general rejoicing in France:

Bref il n'est cœur qui ne se réconforte
En ce pays, plus qu'en mer la sirène
De voir régner, après rancune morte,
Amour, triomphe et beauté souveraine.

Yet only a short time afterwards, Shakespeare's Duke of Norfolk acknowledges:

The peace between the French and us not values
The cost that did conclude it.

Du Bellay, addressing a sonnet to Mary Queen of Scots in 1558, hailed her as the instrument through which France and England were destined to replace by a durable peace 'the hereditary war which has lasted so long from father to son'. Ronsard, dedicating a volume to Elizabeth in 1565, described the peace established by the Treaty of Troyes as being 'so strong that it has been able to dissipate in two years the resentments and dissensions that so many centuries have fostered and multiplied, almost in the course of nature, to the disadvantage of two such neighbouring and flourishing realms'.

Royal marriages, or engagements, provided obvious occasions for the expression of sentiments of this kind. In the Middle Ages there had been much marrying between the Houses of France and England. Edward I married the sister, and Edward II the daughter of Philippe le Bel. In the period of calm at the end of the fourteenth century Richard II asked the hand of Isabel, daughter of Charles VI. Henry V and Henry VI both made French marriages. The habit continued, if less regularly, under the Tudors and Stuarts. There was enthusiasm in Paris in 1514 when Mary of England, sister of Henry VIII, married Louis XII, though the joy turned to mourning three months later, after the elderly bridegroom's death. (Mary stayed on for three months in the

Hôtel de Cluny, closely watched by the new King, François I, for fear she might be pregnant.) Mary Tudor, later Queen of England, was affianced to the Dauphin when she was two years old and he five months. Elizabeth dallied diplomatically with the Duke d'Alençon for several years; he was received at Greenwich almost as a fiancé in 1579 and rings were exchanged in 1581. But the engagement was unpopular in England and it was broken off in 1582.

The last French queen of England was of course Henrietta Maria, daughter of Henri IV and wife of Charles I. Charles had seen her dancing in the Louvre, before asking her hand, and the wedding agreement was signed in November 1624. All the auspices seemed fair. Buckingham came over to Paris in 1625, scoring a brilliant personal success there; the impression that he was supposed to have made on Anne of Austria suggested to Dumas the plot of *Les Trois Mousquetaires*. The crossing of the Channel was, for once, smooth and Henrietta seems to have been led to expect an idyllic life in her new country. But she had an uncomfortable night at Dover Castle and was disappointed at her first meeting with Charles. In the end the marriage was at least a personal success. Henrietta learned English, bore children and was a faithful wife in adversity. So long as Buckingham was alive, however, he took care to prevent the Queen acquiring too much influence—and he was soon casting himself, unsuccessfully, as the saviour of the French Huguenots at La Rochelle. Buckingham apart, the marriage was nearly doomed, and its popularity in England perhaps permanently affected, by the insensitive way in which the French Court sought to use Henrietta as a spearhead for Catholicism in England. She was initially accompanied by a large suite, including thirty ecclesiastics, as if to protect her from the barbarous and heretical land in which she found herself. In the end, after much negotiation, a smaller suite was reconstituted. But the harm had been done: an occasion that should have promoted Anglo-French friendship had reinforced suspicion.

The way in which Richelieu approached these negotiations appears from his instructions to Ambassador Blainville, when he expressed a classic principle of French policy towards England:

> You will find out by experience that the temper of the English is such that we will always be playing music with them; if we speak

> softly they will speak loud, and because there is advantage in being on top, it would be as well for you to assume now and again such a commanding tone that they cannot dominate it.

It was presumably from his French mother that Charles II inherited his 'black' looks, as well as his grandfather's sense of humour and love of women. His sister, Henriette-Anne, married the Duke of Orléans, brother of Louis XIV, who had notoriously inherited a different taste. But she was loved by Louis XIV, as well as by her brother, and she came in person to Dover in 1670 to sign the abortive Treaty, with its secret clause binding Charles to declare his belief in the Roman Church. Daughter of one Anglo-French marriage and wife in another, educated in her mother's religion and habituated to the French Court, she can have had little instinctive sense of how far her brother's subjects would rally to his 'august example'.

In the nineteenth century, State Visits took over the cathartic function of the royal marriage ceremonies of former times. When Victoria visited the French Royal Family in 1843, it was the first visit of a reigning English monarch to France since the Field of the Cloth of Gold. In 1844 Louis Philippe paid a return visit to Windsor and the expression *entente cordiale* seems to have been coined for the first time. As usual, the cordiality was not entirely free from misgiving. William IV had not been an admirer of the Orleanist monarchy and his Private Secretary had written to Grey, in 1832, that the King 'entertains a prejudice, so rooted, that he cannot help seeking for an *arrière pensée* in every assertion and every measure of the French Government'.* Without going to that extreme the Duke of Wellington wrote to Lord Mahon from Walmer Castle in September 1846:

> There is no individual more convinced than I am of the necessity for peace, and indeed good understanding, possibly even *entente cordiale*, with France, in the existing state of the politics of the world. But the relation should be no other than patent; we ought to preserve our own independent existence, views and national interests; and, above all, we ought to be in such a state of national defence, as that we could at any time speak out upon a case of national interest or national honour . . .

It was to be another sixty years before the *Entente cordiale* of the present century was consecrated. Meanwhile England and her

* Cf. Philip Ziegler, *King William IV* (1971), pp. 224–5.

Queen adjusted themselves, not always gracefully, to successive French regimes. The *coup d'état* which established the Second Empire provoked some strong public reactions in England. Tennyson wrote indignantly, early in 1852:

> We hate not France, but France has lost her voice,
> This man is France, the man they call her choice,
> By tricks and spying
> And craft and lying
> And murder, was her freedom overthrown,
> Britons, guard your own.

Nevertheless Britain and France were soon to be close allies in the Crimean War and, in 1854, Prince Albert accepted the invitation of Napoleon III to visit his camp at St Omer. The following year the Imperial couple paid a State Visit to England. They crossed in fearful fog; but the Empress Eugénie brought the first crinoline to England and the visit was a great success. The return visit to Paris took place only four months later: Victoria succumbed to the charm both of Napoleon and of Paris, which she found 'the gayest town imaginable'.

By the time of the Franco-Prussian War in 1870, there had been some cooling-off in Anglo-French relations. The Prince of Wales, who had hero-worshipped Napoleon III and who was to promote the 1904 *Entente cordiale* as Edward VII, expressed the hope that Prussia would be beaten. But Queen Victoria, while preserving strict neutrality, had Prussian sympathies and so had many of her subjects. It was only as the French fell back that the Queen began to feel sorry for them. She wrote that, whereas people in England were formerly 'very German' in the dispute, they were now 'very French'.

One English 'German', the historian J. R. Green, regarded the war as France's fault and wrote to a friend: 'I hope when the war is over they will just lock up all France—turn it into a gigantic National Asylum and keep every man of 'em in a strait-waistcoat.' However, he wrote another letter at about the same time displaying less determination:

> I am German to the core, but like Joan of Arc I have pity for that *bel royaume de France* . . . France remains, vain, ignorant, insufferable if you will, but still with an infinite attraction in her, at least to me. There is a spring, an elasticity about her, a 'light

> heart' that has its good as well as its bad side, a gaiety, a power of enjoyment, which Europe can't afford to miss . . . with an infinite respect for Berlin I should prefer *living* at Paris.

The Second Empire, whatever its other merits or demerits in English eyes, at least sponsored one of the comparatively rare attempts to liberalize Anglo-French trade. Napoleon III, spurred on by de Persigny and Cobden, and catching the prevailing Free Trade tide, instigated the Anglo-French Commercial Treaty of 1860. It seems doubtful whether, politically speaking, it did him much good at home; attempts to liberalize Anglo-French trade have seldom had an easy passage. The earlier Commercial Treaty of 1786 had flooded France with English goods and brought about an industrial crisis, particularly in Flanders, Normandy, Picardy and Champagne. French exports had of course also improved; cheaper goods had become available for the poor; and French industry had been stimulated to greater competition. But these benefits had been less immediately obvious than the ill effects. Arthur Young, the traveller, had observed the violent hostility towards the Treaty, which collapsed with the outbreak of war in 1793, in Rouen, Abbeville and Lille.

Earlier in the eighteenth century Montesquieu had noted that there was hardly any trade between England and France. The Abbé le Blanc, writing a few years afterwards, declared that the balance of Anglo-French trade was in France's favour, but hoped that French imports from Britain could eventually be dispensed with altogether:

> Nous prenons actuellement beaucoup de Tabac des Anglais, et du Blé dans les temps de disette. Je ne doute pas qu'avec le temps la sagesse du Ministère ne remédie à ces deux inconvenients.

Adam Smith, in *Wealth of Nations* (1776), recalled that it was Colbert who had originally imposed high duties upon a great number of foreign manufactures, with the result that, in the 1670s, '. . . the French and English began mutually to oppress each other's industry by the like duties and prohibitions, of which the French, however, seem to have set the first example. The spirit of hostility which has subsisted between the two nations ever since has hitherto hindered them from being moderated on either side.' According to Smith: 'These mutual restraints have put an end to almost all fair commerce between the two nations, and smugglers are now the principal importers, either of British goods into France, or of French goods into Great Britain.'

Even in the Middle Ages, although England had close trading connections with Bordeaux and Rouen, it was in Bruges and Ghent that English wool was worked up. In the natural course of things, therefore, the bulk of English trade with Europe tended to take a more northward direction.

No doubt there are explanations; but, on the face of it, it is remarkable that for such long periods and even up till our own day, the trade of these two wealthy and neighbouring countries should have been relatively so small. Is it more effect, or cause, of the traditional tendency in each country to see each other as a rival, rather than a partner? One of the main arguments in favour of the 1786 Treaty was that it would break this pattern of rivalry and lead to lasting peace and friendship between the two peoples. This was also Cobden's aim when he promoted the 1860 Treaty. Personally Francophile, he wrote to the French publicist, M. Chevalier, in September 1859:

> . . . I should be glad to see a removal of the impediments which our foolish legislation interposes to the intercourse between the two countries. I see no other hope but in such a policy for any permanent improvements in the *political* relations of France and England. . . . The people of the two nations must be brought into mutual dependence by the supply of each other's wants. There is no other way of counteracting the antagonism of language and race. It is God's own method of producing an *entente cordiale.*

For some years after the death of Louis XIV (the age of the Regency in France) there was a period of peace between the two countries, during which the French began to satisfy a new curiosity about England. In 1716 the triple alliance between France, Britain and Holland was formed; in 1725 there was a defensive alliance of France, Britain and Prussia. The War of the Austrian Succession, the Seven Years' War and the American War lay in the future: Europe was still the centre of the scene and colonial rivalries had not yet come to the fore. But Montesquieu put his finger on the shortcomings of both countries as allies, when he wrote in his *Pensées*:

> It is not at all in the interests of France to form an offensive and defensive alliance with England. The help of France is prompt;

but that of England is subject to the delay and uncertainty attendant on deliberations. It is true that France is more exposed than England, and thus has more often need of help.

Much of this analysis held good up till our own times. It illustrates, poignantly enough, how Anglo-French relations have been perpetually haunted by the same recurring themes.

TWO

Cocks and Bulldogs

PERHAPS FEW PEOPLE would choose to be reincarnated either as cocks or as bulldogs if they could take their pick of all the beasts. But both have their good points and both do, in a way, symbolize their adoptive nations. There is a stimulating cheerfulness about the cock: vain, gallant, vivid and loquacious, he may not be typically French, but he is at least more French than English. There is a comforting independence about the bulldog: with his tenacity and rather aggressive calm he seems more conventionally English than French.

In any event it is as cock and bulldog types that the French and English have tended to think of each other, whether or not they have had these particular symbols in mind. A more offensive comparison used now and then to be drawn between bears and monkeys. The cock crows, but the monkey chatters; the bear is still surlier than the bulldog and less controlled. Hazlitt confessed that, when he travelled in France in 1824, the image of the monkey would now and then spring to mind. Frenchmen who visited England in the eighteenth century found something distinctly bearish in English manners—particularly in the ungracious treatment of foreigners by the mob.

A still further pair of creatures suggested the nicknames which the two peoples have popularly given to each other. The Englishman may be a 'Limey' in some parts of the world: in France he has been a 'Rosbif'. This at least has the justification that most Englishmen eat beef quite often (though it is a question whether modern Frenchmen do not eat more). Frenchmen have been less lucky in England; however seldom they may wrestle with them, they are still liable to be damned as 'Frogs'. Physical appearance apart, nothing is more immediately striking in a strange people than a difference in eating habits. I remember the awe with which

I heard as a child that an aunt of mine had actually eaten frog in France and found that it 'tasted like chicken'. Beef could hardly inspire the French with the same fascinated horror; but they too were in awe of the quantities of it that our ancestors were supposed to, and perhaps actually did, consume.

Shakespeare reflected this awe when he made the Constable of France say of the English, on the eve of the Battle of Agincourt:

> . . . give them great meals of beef, and iron and
> steel, they will eat like wolves, and fight like devils.

He also reflected the contempt felt by the French for the English national drink (as yet unchallenged by tea):

> . . . Can sodden water
> A drench for sun-rein'd jades, their barley-broth,
> Decoct their cold blood to such valiant heat?
> And shall our quick blood, spirited with wine,
> Seem frosty?

Perhaps people do become a little like what they eat and drink. At any rate it is not surprising that both French and English should sometimes have imagined so. The elegant Aramis, in Dumas's *Vingt Ans Après*, tells Athos: 'Je hais les Anglais, ils sont grossiers comme tous les gens qui boivent de la bière.' Another of the four friends, d'Artagnan, gives vent to his feelings after reluctantly agreeing to prolong his stay in England, by describing it as a country where boiled mutton is a treat and people have nothing to celebrate with but beer. Nineteenth-century French visitors found there was all too much celebrating, or self-stupefying, with gin. As to boiled mutton, Montesquieu noted that the common people of London (in about 1730) ate a lot of meat: 'that makes them very robust; but at the age of 40 to 45 they burst'. A century later Michelet associated meat-eating with the red necks and prodigious energy of the English, while Taine wondered whether the prominent teeth displayed by English beauties might not have been inherited from generations of carnivores.

I suppose that, physically speaking, the typical Frenchman has tended to be, for the English, a meridional type: small, neat and dark. But English writers have usually been more preoccupied with French clothes, manners and gestures than with their physique. Although Frenchwomen have had a great reputation in England for elegance and seductive charm, they have not been so noted for beauty as such. Mrs Trollope, visiting Paris under the July monarchy, claimed that she had never met a Frenchman who would not admit that regular beauties were more numerous in England. However, with Mme Récamier in mind, she approved the saying: 'Quand une Française se mêle d'être jolie, elle est furieusement jolie'; a beautiful Frenchwoman, she thought, was perhaps the most beautiful in the world.

One physical characteristic of the French that did strike the English, particularly in the eighteenth and early nineteenth centuries, was an almost scarecrow leanness. By contrast, the English peasantry was more prosperous, better fed and more robust-looking than the French peasantry before the Revolution. This was a matter of fact; but the English exalted it into an article of faith. 'I hate the French,' wrote Goldsmith in 1760, 'because they are all slaves and wear wooden shoes.' A century later Dickens makes the Marquis St Evrémonde, in *A Tale of Two Cities*, look at his peasants and see in them 'without knowing it, the slow sure filing down of misery-worn face and figure, that was to make the meagreness of Frenchmen an English superstition which should survive the truth through the best part of a hundred years.' The superstition was reinforced by the penury of the French *émigrés* in England after the Revolution. The Introduction to *Quentin Durward* describes the writer's aunt as being married to a French 'military scarecrow'—all legs and wings and no body. Edmund Wheatley found the French soldiers in south-western France in 1814 'pretty well dressed but I cannot vouch for their being so well fed, as rumours are so numerous'. But he was a friendly witness and added: 'Their physiognomy is pleasing, I think.'

For the French the typical Englishman has been tall, fair and either beefy or stiff. Dumas makes Mazarin's *valet de chambre* describe Cromwell's emissary as 'Un vrai Anglais, Monseigneur; cheveux blond-roux, plutôt roux que blonds; œil gris-bleu, plutôt gris que bleu; pour le reste, orgueil et roideur.' When the two valets of the four musketeers were disguised as Englishmen, the first presented 'the calm, dry and stiff type of the discreet Englishman', the other 'that of the paunchy, puffy and lounging Englishman'. Between them they must have represented the horse and fish types into which Jules Vallès unkindly divided the male population. Other writers have been more complimentary.

Jules Verne's Phileas Fogg, besides being tall and fair, was 'de figure noble et belle'. For Baron de Charlus the English soldiers in the First World War were 'Greek athletes . . . Plato's young men, or rather Spartans.' Maximilien Misson at the end of the seventeenth century described the inhabitants 'of this excellent country' as 'tall, handsome, well-made, white-skinned, fair-haired, supple, robust . . .' But he, too, was a friendly witness.

Jean Queval found in 1956 that it was becoming harder to identify the English by external appearance alone: 'Le type est en légère régression.' This is probably increasingly true of most European countries, as a result of increasing mobility. But of course it is also a question of manner as well as of physique. People look different when they carry themselves differently. The modern Englishman has lost some of his nineteenth-century stiffness—and perhaps the average Frenchman never gesticulated quite so freely as the English were apt to suppose. Hazlitt, writing 150 years ago, stressed the folly of carrying the abstraction of national characteristics too far: 'All classes of society and differences of character are by this unfair process consolidated into a sturdy, surly English yeoman on the one side of the Channel, or are boiled down and evaporate into a shivering, chattering *valet de chambre*, or miserable half-starved peasant on the other.'

The reputation of English women for beauty in France, though considerable, has been qualified by the criticism that they do not always make the best of themselves, that they tend to lack piquancy and to show a poor taste in dress. Flaubert gives as one of his *idées reçues*, under the heading *Anglaises*: 'S'étonner de ce qu'elles ont de jolis enfants.' In earlier times there were fewer reservations—except that Englishwomen's teeth were supposed to be bad. Perlin, a far from friendly witness, gave sixteenth-century English ladies the reputation of being the most beautiful in the world, with skins as white as alabaster, and described them as gay and courteous. Misson was very complimentary about their great-great-granddaughters. Taine, however, an acute observer of Victorian England, while praising the fresh complexion and good bone structure of Englishwomen, found a certain insipidity in their looks. But he waxed lyrical over the unmarried girls: 'Rien de plus simple que les jeunes filles; parmi les belles choses, il y en a peu d'aussi belles au monde; sveltes, fortes, sûres d'elles-mêmes, si foncièrement honnêtes et loyales, si exemptes de coquetterie.' Jules Vallès, while admiring the beauty of many young Englishwomen, found it ephemeral; their angel faces lost attraction after their early twenties. In every century English complexions have been admired in France. Théophile Gautier was mesmerized by the black hair, red lips and dazzlingly white skin which he gave to an English heroine.

I cannot resist quoting a passage from a review of the *Salon* of 1892, because it sums up what for many Frenchmen has been the ideal—pure, if a trifle flaccid—of English female beauty. The French critic turns to a tranquil composition by an English artist, entitled *Summer*, and contrasts its calm with a Spanish painting which he has just been noticing. He says:

> They are very English and entirely charming with their fair or brown hair, their dazzling complexions and their limpid eyes, these young girls clothed in long bluish tunics. The painter has grouped them in calm attitudes, under a marble colonnade where bronze fountains play their clear waters.

It seems a far cry from Balzac's Lady Dudley, though she too had fine brown hair and was 'si svelte, si douce'. Under her seemingly fragile phosphorescence, however, was 'an iron organization'. Typically English as an Amazonian horsewoman, she was less typically, or at least less conventionally, English as a tigress in love. But then Balzac had given his French heroine, Mme de Mortsauf, exclusive rights over the soul. He left it to Lady Dudley, remorselessly, to represent the flesh.

In the Middle Ages the French either supposed, or teased their neighbours by pretending to suppose, that the English had something diabolic, as well as fleshly, about them: they were alleged to have tails. The story was that St Augustine, preaching at Dorchester, had had fish-tails pinned on his clothes by the inhabitants and had retaliated by a curse which condemned them and their descendants to carry real ones. Thenceforward the English were *coués* or (in Latin) *caudati*. The result was a good deal of innocent merriment at the expense of the English students in Paris. The touchiness of the English on the subject was shown as late as the sixteenth century when English emissaries to the christening of Prince James of Scotland were not at all pleased by some imaginary tail-wagging staged for their benefit by French players in a masque. It is a relief to record at least one Anglo-French myth which (so far as I know) is now extinct.

The physical differences between the two peoples, insofar as they can be generalized, have clearly been influenced by climate at least as much as by diet; and perhaps this would be even truer of the moral differences. It is obvious that the contrast with English complexions and conditions becomes more marked the further south in France one travels. The Abbé le Blanc in the eighteenth century suggested that virtually perpetual fogs helped to explain the English disposition to melancholy; he also noted that in Normandy, which resembled England so closely, the people exhibited the same good sense as the English did.

The effect of racial factors is less easy to assess, though certain racial types are identifiable at a glance in both countries and it is remarkable how, in spite of its Catholicism, Brittany bears a visual resemblance to Wales. Whatever the real importance of race distinctions, the consciousness of belonging to predominantly different races has historically contributed—particularly in the race-conscious nineteenth century—to keeping the French and English apart. Very broadly speaking the French have regarded themselves as a predominantly Mediterranean people and the English as a predominantly Germanic one, more closely akin to the peoples of northern Europe than to the Latin races. Most Englishmen, if pressed, would probably see things the same way. But of course, apart from its extensive Celtic sub-soil, England has been fertilized from time to time by non-Germanic strains. Equally the French have Germanic elements. Both peoples are racially very mixed.

In *Henry V* Shakespeare makes the Dauphin attribute English fighting prowess to the injection of Norman blood:

> O Dieu vivant! shall a few sprays of us,
> The emptying of our father's luxury,
> Our scions, put in wild and savage stock,
> Spirt up so suddenly into the clouds,
> And overlook their grafters?

The Duke of Bourbon gloomily replies:

> Normans, but bastard Normans, Norman bastards!

Whatever its racial consequences, both French and English writers have recognized that the Norman Conquest powerfully and permanently affected the organization of England, thus influencing the English character indirectly, if not directly. It also created a vague, but to some extent enduring, sense of kinship between the French and English upper classes.

The Celtic strain, so widespread and prominent in England through inter-marriage with the Scottish, Welsh and Irish, seems more submerged, or at least less easily distinguished, in most parts of France. The Celts and Druids, who once straddled the Channel, are seldom hailed as supplying a common ancestry to the two countries. But Bossuet, in his funeral address on Henrietta Maria, did trace the origins of the English back to the Gauls. He attributed the English treatment of Charles I to false religion, rather than to natural arrogance: 'Let us not believe that the Mercians, Danes and Saxons have so corrupted in them the good blood that our fathers had given them, that they would be capable of launching into such barbarous proceedings if other causes had not been at work.' (He blamed previous English monarchs for tampering with the old religion and so fostering in their people a licence of thought which was to prove ultimately destructive to themselves.)

Perhaps it is these 'other causes'—the adoption of different religious and political systems—which will appear, in the end, to have most sharply differentiated the two peoples. Diet, climate and race have had direct physical, as well as moral, effects. The influence of system has been primarily on the mind; but it has been deep and pervasive. It may have been partly for racial and climatic reasons that England became Protestant and France Catholic; but, when one recalls that Mary's England was Catholic and that sixteenth-century France had a powerful Huguenot party, it is difficult to feel sure that this religious cleavage was an inevitable consequence of different national temperaments. What is certain is that Catholicism and Protestantism, once firmly established, tended to steer these temperaments in different directions. So did the difference in political systems: the establishment in France of a highly centralized and effective monarchy at a time when the English monarchy was already losing its grip. Different concepts of education developed to meet different religious and political needs.

Balzac suggested that 'Protestantism and Catholicism explain the differences which give to the soul of Frenchwomen so much superiority over the reasoning, calculating, love of Englishwomen. Protestantism doubts, examines and kills beliefs and is thus the death of art and love.' By contrast George Moore, writing as a Protestant Irishman, said that he felt nearer to the French but loved the English with a foolish and limitless passion:

> Dear, sweet Protestant England, the red tiles of the farmhouses, the elms, the great hedgerows, and all the rich fields adorned with spreading trees, and the weald and the wold . . . Southern England, with its quiet, steadfast faces . . . England is Protestantism, Protestantism is England. Protestantism is strong, clean and westernly . . .

If George Moore thought that Protestantism had helped to furnish the southern English with their 'quiet, steadfast faces', Tocqueville had little doubt that the proverbial English reserve was due 'much more to the constitution of the country than of the citizens'. There might be some difference in blood between the French and the English in this respect; but the real difference was one of system. The main cause of English reserve was that, while aristocratic pride was still a very strong force in the nineteenth century English, the boundaries of the aristocracy had become less clearly defined. Hence everyone was afraid that advantage might be taken of familiarity and tended to remain firmly on his guard.

One consequence of French religious and political absolutism was a tendency, in pre-Revolutionary France, towards a polished uniformity of manner. This is what Sterne had in mind when he told the Count de B. at Versailles that he found the French almost excessively polite; if the English arrived at the same polish they would lose their 'distinct variety and originality of character'. Taking some worn, smooth and indistinguishable coins out of his pocket, he added: 'The English, like ancient medals, kept more apart, and passing but few people's hands, preserve the first sharpnesses which the fine hand of Nature has given them—they are not so pleasant to feel—but, in return, the legend is so visible, that at the first look you see whose image and superscription they bear.' Even a generation after the Revolution, Stendhal commented: 'Sterne avait trop raison: nous ne sommes que des *pièces de monnaie effacées*; mais ce n'est pas le temps qui nous a usés, c'est la *terreur du ridicule*.'

Another possible effect of absolutism was the good nature—the readiness to put up with things cheerfully—for which the pre-Revolutionary French were celebrated. Where the father takes all the decisions, the children are free to cultivate charm and good manners. Arthur Young, travelling in France on the eve of the Revolution, was never tired of praising French 'urbanity' and good temper though, like Sterne, he seemed to think that, among people of rank, the urbanity tended to banish originality and vigour of expression. He was inclined to regard this smooth pleasantness of behaviour as an effect of the French system of arbitrary government.

If the French displayed a certain uniformity in the eighteenth century, the English, under the pressures of industrialism and empire, developed a different kind of uniformity in the nineteenth century. Balzac wrote in the 1830s that everything was regulated by law in England; in each sphere there was total uniformity; the exercise of the virtues seemed like the mechanical play of wheels rotating at fixed times. Later in the century Vallès remarked on the 'similitude of physiognomy' and 'monotony of type' which deadened the London street. But the moral uniformity of nineteenth-century England was never totally incompatible with unorthodox behaviour, provided a certain code was observed. Jules Verne's Phileas Fogg is presented as both a wildly eccentric and stiffly conventional figure. In the eighteenth century English eccentricity had been proverbial in France. The young La Rochefoucauld wrote in 1784 of a cousin of his friend Mr Symonds: 'We found in this man the most original character possible, a real Englishman, full of benevolence; he has no politeness; one does exactly as one likes in his house, but he takes no advantage of it, one is at home there . . .' The reputation for originality has never quite died. André Maurois, after the First World War, found that Maurice Baring had 'un côté de fantaisie hardie et presque sauvage, qui était fait pour étonner un Français'.

By no means all Frenchmen have approved of this streak of fantasy in the English character. According to Ascoli: 'This exaggerated individualism is a perpetual surprise and a perpetual source of disquiet for the serious-minded Frenchman, fond of the coherent, not to say of the conventional . . .' The Abbé le Blanc observed in the eighteenth century that there was a wide diversity of English types, regrettably including numerous eccentrics. The English authors, he said, 'reproach us with being all of one piece . . . and yet it is this alleged defect which makes us, if not more virtuous, at least more sociable than the English.'

Diet, climate, race and system have all left their marks. But geography, too, accounts for a good deal. Living in an island and surrounded by the sea the English developed a degree of moral self-sufficiency and a tendency to regard foreigners as excessively foreign. At the same time they lacked the sense of cultural and material self-sufficiency that the French got from inhabiting a more extensive country, rich in more varied produce and at once northern and southern in character. Then again, as a result of their geographical position, the English of earlier centuries were uneasily conscious of being farther than the French from the traditional sources of European civilization. All of this tended to encourage cock and bulldog attitudes.

In spite of their celebrated eccentricity the English have seldom been regarded in France as very lively company. At times they have been reputed a worthy people, at others not. They have often impressed with their practical, intellectual and even poetic, gifts. Occasionally they have managed to export to France their manners and fashions. But they have still not shaken off the reputation of finding it difficult to enjoy life. Although accepted nowadays by the French as a civilized (in some ways a highly civilized) people, they still trail clouds of Nordic barbarity and boredom, of long winter nights and grey skies, about them. Back in the 1840s Théophile Gautier suspected that they were only superficially civilized and knew it: '. . . they realize that at bottom, in spite of their prodigious material civilization, they are only polished barbarians.'

This fits in well enough with the bulldog theme and so does the earlier reputation of the English in France for being an extremely warlike people. English, as well as Scottish, soldiers were recruited by the French in the seventeenth century. Bossuet described England as 'une des plus belliqueuses nations de l'univers'. In the aftermath of the Napoleonic Wars Hazlitt said of his own countrymen that they understood two things: 'hard words and hard blows'. He claimed that the French expressed astonishment 'at the feats which our Jack Tars have so often performed'. He considered the English 'not thin-skinned, nervous or effeminate, but dull and morbid . . . what every one else shrinks from through aversion to labour or pain, they are attracted to, and go through with, and so far (and so far only) they are a great people.' He also noted how 'ten thousand people assembled at a prize-fight will witness an exhibition of pugilism with the same breathless attention and delight as the audience at the *Théâtre français* listen to the dialogue of Racine or Molière.'

Taine gives a portrait, not of the bulldog, but of John Bull himself:

> Lowbrow, no wit, short and brief ideas; those that he has are those of a merchant or a farmer. In return he reveals good sense and energy, a fund of good humour, of loyalty, application, tenacity, in short that consistency of character that enables man to prosper in life and to render himself, if not lovable, at least useful. . . . There is better than that in England; but one will not make too much of a mistake in taking this type and those that resemble it to paint the aptitudes and inclinations most frequent in the nation as a whole.

Daninos, in *Le Secret du Major Thompson*, gives a humorous sketch of French difficulties in living in England, which he caricatures as a country with a strong, but dull, flavour. The Gascon d'Artagnan (in Dumas's *Vingt Ans Après*) had nothing good to say about it at all: 'This villainous country, where it is always cold, where the good weather is fog, the fog rain, the rain a torrent: where the sun looks like the moon, and the moon like a cream cheese.'

Shrouded in perpetual fog the English could hardly be expected to enjoy themselves, except in escapist fits of brutal pleasure. 'Les Anglais s'amusent tristement selon l'usage de leur pays.' This famous phrase, attributed to Froissart, is apparently not found in his works; but another medieval writer, the English monk Robert Mannyng, observed in the early fourteenth century:

> Frenchmen sin in Lechery
> Englishmen in Ennui.

Montesquieu wrote of the English: 'incapables de se divertir, ils aiment qu'on les divertisse.' The English eighteenth-century dramatist, S. Foote, makes his young Englishman just returned from Paris exclaim: 'But all you English are constitutionally sullen—November fogs, with salt boiled beef, are most cursed recipes for good-humour, or a quick apprehension. Paris is the place. 'Tis there men laugh, love and live!' A French opinion poll published in *L'Express* in 1972 put the English at the bottom of all the countries of the enlarged European Community for gaiety.

In the seventeenth and eighteenth centuries there was a lot of

French talk about the constitutional melancholy of the English. Misson wondered whether the wide use of tobacco could have anything to do with it:

> Ne serait-ce point cette perpetuité de Tabac qui rend le commun des hommes d'Angleterre si taciturnes, si sournois, si melancoliques? Peut-être qu'oui: mais aussi cela fait de profonds Théologiens.

Montesquieu found the English rich and free, but tormented in spirit and disgusted with, or disdainful of, everything: 'They are really quite unhappy, with so many reasons for not being so.'

The proneness of Englishmen to commit suicide was long a firmly rooted French belief. La Fontaine in the seventeenth century was already referring to English 'peu d'amour pour la vie'. Montesquieu attributed it to a physical cause—'un défaut de filtration du suc nerveux'—and said that 'les Anglais se tuent sans autre raison que celle de leur chagrin.' The English appeared to the French to combine their bulldog tenacity of purpose with a curious impatience and with an intolerance of mental and physical discomfort; they were readier to face death than to put up with inconvenience and disappointment. The Abbé le Blanc, referring to the lavish funerals in England, remarked slyly: 'Il y a une sorte de contentement à mourir en Angleterre que l'on ne connôit guère ailleurs.' A witticism in Saurin's *L'Anglomane* must have been sure of a laugh from eighteenth-century French audiences:

> Sachez, Monsieur, qu'en Angleterre
> On se pend quelquefois, mais qu'on n'y rit jamais.

If the elements of earth and water loomed on one side of the channel, those of air and fire shimmered on the other. Favourably or unfavourably the English were always struck by the rapidity, gaiety, talkativeness and sociability of the French. A late sixteenth-century traveller, the schoolmaster Robert Dallington, made out rapidity to be almost the key French characteristic; he wrote of Henri IV: 'his nature stirring and full of life, like a true Frenchman'. For Hazlitt 'mobility without *momentum* solves the whole riddle of the French character'—no indolence, but also no persevering passion. The Welshman Howell, in the early seventeenth century, described the Frenchman as 'Active and Mercuriall . . . Quick and Ayry . . . Discursive and Sociable . . . apprehends and forgets quickly. . . . It is a kind of sicknesse for a Frenchman to keep a secret long.'

The volubility of the French was as much a standing joke with the English as their own taciturnity was with the French. Addison wrote in the *Spectator* in 1714: 'I used, for some time, to walk every morning in the *Mall* and talk in Chorus with a Parcel of *Frenchmen*. I found my Modesty greatly relieved by the communicative Temper of this Nation, who are so very sociable, as to think that they are never better Company than when they are all opening at the same time.'

In another number of the *Spectator* the French appear as 'such a gay airy People' and Goldsmith wrote in *The Traveller* (1764):

> Gay, sprightly land of mirth and social ease
> Pleased with thyself, whom all the world can please.

But the sterling Englishman, Classic, in Foote's *The Englishman in Paris*, is not to be conciliated. Foppery is the French national disease: 'Their taste is trifling, their gaiety grimace, and their politeness pride.'

Sir Charles Darnley, in *London and Paris*, remarking that it was more usual in England than in France for a man to spend an evening alone with his family, admitted that French society normally meant the company of relations and long-tried friends, as opposed to the 'heartless crowds' of England. His correspondent, the Marquis de Vermont, thought that the English both paid more for their holidays than the French and got less pleasure from them; they seemed to feel that they must either live as solitaries or squander large sums on entertainment. The Abbé le Blanc was convinced that the English were rarely sociable and did not know how to enjoy life as the French did.

At the same time the English have often felt that French social responsiveness had an Achilles' heel in too much attention to outward appearances. Martin Lister emphasized the French love of 'figure' under Louis XIV. Daninos, in *Major Thompson Goes French*, suggested that the French 'could give anyone lessons in happiness' but were continually liable to make themselves out as richer or poorer than they really were.

There have always been Englishmen who sensed another, and heavier, side to the French character. Kipling, for instance, praised 'the essential humanity, honesty, goodwill, and the sane thrift of France as an agricultural nation . . .' But the discovery that Frenchmen could be serious has often come as a surprise. Chesterfield felt obliged to caution his son: 'The colder northern nations generally look upon France as a whistling, singing, dancing, frivolous nation; this notion is very far from being a true one. . . . The number of great generals and statesmen, as well as excellent authors, that France has produced is an undeniable proof that it is not that frivolous, unthinking, empty nation that northern prejudices suppose it.' The heroine of Nancy Mitford's *The Blessing* found her French husband's intellectual aunts quite unexpected: 'She had hitherto supposed that, with the exception of a few very religious people like Madame de Valhubert, all Frenchwomen, of all ages, were entirely frivolous and given over to the art of pleasing.' Maurois makes his Anglo-Scottish Colonel Bramble say during the First World War:

> Ah! messieu . . . avant la guerre on disait chez nous: la frivole France: on dira maintenant: la sévère et sage France.
>
> Oui, appuya le docteur, ce peuple de France est dur et sévère pour lui-même . . .

For Hazlitt, the surprising gravity of the French at their theatres was quite a paradox, given the ordinary prejudice in England that the French were 'little better than grown children'. For that matter, how should this prejudice be reconciled with the close attention to detail of the French and their achievements in art and science? He could see the point of Sterne's apparent jest at Versailles: 'The French, Monsieur le Count . . . are a loyal, a gallant, a generous, an ingenious, and good-tempered people as is under heaven—if they have a fault, they are too *serious*.'

The English can strike the French as being *intellectually* frivolous; but no Frenchman is likely to single out frivolity as their sole fault—even for the sake of a *bon mot*. However, just as some English have discovered weight in the French character, so have some French discovered a lighter side to the English one.

There are of course many Frenchmen who have been attracted (if others have been bored) by English civic qualities, such as fair play, liberality and the calm discipline displayed in queues and other public proceedings. The 'team spirit', contrasting with the French urge to shine individually, may have flourished most in the century 1850 to 1950; but readiness to take one's turn, and confidence that it will come, is still an English characteristic rather than a French. Misson could not understand how the belief had grown up—he had heard it all his life in France—that the English were treacherous: in fact they were so fair-minded that they could not allow a fight to take place where the parties were unequally armed. Montesquieu noted a number of attractive features in English life: an openness, a simplicity of manner, a modesty, an unenvious love of talent, a capacity for despising money as well as for valuing it.

These are all, more or less, moral attributes; but other French writers have discovered aesthetic ones. Maurois, seduced by country-house England between the two World Wars, wrote in his *Mémoires*:

> De plus en plus, la grâce de l'Angleterre m'enivrait. Ah! que ce pays était noble et charmant, et que j'aurais voulu le lier plus étroitement au mien.

He made Aurelle write to a compatriot in *Les Discours du Docteur O'Grady*: '. . . when I give you one day the letters of Charles Lister, you will see what charming grace, what culture without pedantry, what idealism without fanaticism, this race can attain.' Visiting Cambridge after the Second World War he looked through his window at the willows, the Gothic towers and the swans gliding on the water: 'A monumental fire burned in my hearth. This was England.'

Two twentieth-century French writers, Pierre Maillaud and Louis Cazamian, have both stressed the compensations of fancy and sentiment in English life. The latter noticed that, in spite of the hard practicality of the English, they preserved a certain *jeunesse d'esprit*: 'A freshness of impressions, a confidence in life, a faculty of simple gaiety, have not ceased to characterize the British, behind the cool reserve where the foreigner supposes that sadness, pessimism or spleen are always to be read.'

Both nations have accused each other of fickleness and inconstancy, though the charge has more often been levelled at the English collectively and at the French individually. Shakespeare makes Joan of Arc exclaim, when she has persuaded the Duke of Burgundy to abandon the English side for the French: 'Done like a Frenchman; turn, and turn again!' After the French had been worsted in the dispute for precedence between the French and Spanish Ambassadors,* Pepys recalled that he 'went to the French house, where I observe still that there is no men in the world of a more insolent spirit where they do well, nor before they begin a matter, and more abject if they do miscarry, than

* Cf. p. 27 above.

these people are; for they all look like dead men, and not a word among them, but shake their heads.' Dallington held that the French had been renowned since Caesar's time for 'lightnesse and inconstancy' and that they were 'sudden to begin and more sudden to ende . . . a stranger cannot so soone bee off his horse, but he (a Frenchman) will be acquainted . . . and as suddenly and without cause yee shall lose him also.' The Abbé le Blanc mentioned the French reputation in eighteenth-century England for fickleness and *légèreté*. In 1971 the *Sunday Times* recorded as one of the findings of a public opinion poll that 'nearly one Briton in three thinks the French unreliable'.

It pains the English, who feel that they are nothing if not straight-forward, to hear their country stigmatized as *Perfide Albion*. But the label seems first to have been stuck on them by Bossuet in the seventeenth century. A neutral (Dutch) historian described the English of the time of James I as 'very inconstant, rash, vainglorious, light and deceiving' and there was certainly more than a touch of perfidy about the foreign policy of Charles II. According to Ascoli, the seventeenth-century French were struck by the paradox of the calmness, reflectiveness and good sense that the English displayed personally, when contrasted with their frequent lapses into unreliability as a nation. No doubt the English did prefer a frank and straightforward approach; when they seemed guilty of perfidy or treachery it was less because of any fixed plan to deceive, than because they were restless and impatient in their search for rapid, practical, solutions.

It would be difficult to say how much this persistent English preference for cutting, rather than untying, knots should be ascribed to natural impatience; to mental laziness (the reluctance to look ahead too far); or to a realistic emphasis on practical solutions, however imperfect, and a sense of the futility of purely verbal formulae. Montesquieu would have put it down to climate: 'Une certaine impatience que le climat leur donne, et qui ne leur permet ni d'agir longtemps de la même manière, ni de souffrir longtemps les mêmes choses.'

When Bossuet exclaimed 'L'Angleterre, ah! la perfide Angleterre' in his First Sermon on the Circumcision, he was in fact referring to her conversion to Christianity and, in that context, was presumably lamenting the perfidy of the Reformation. Napoleon quoted Bossuet when he left for St Helena, though it was certainly not the Reformation that rankled in his mind.

Levelled by two such authorities, with whatever enormities in view, the charge of perfidy could not fail to stick.

In many ways the English still view the French, and the French the English, as they did 500 years ago. But there have also been important changes in attitude from century to century. The impression made by the English on the French has shifted under the impact of Puritanism, the effects of nineteenth-century power and discipline and the gradual smoothing down of insular roughness. Most people would now regard the English as quite a civil nation, relatively polite to foreigners, far from bloodthirsty in the normal course of events and correct, if not elaborate, in their manners. In the seventeenth century, however, they exhibited traces of a savage cruelty (tempered by a sense of fair play), while in the eighteenth century the lower classes could still be abominably rude to foreigners.

In the sixteenth century the English seem to have struck the French, with all their crudity, as being less inhibited and sombre than they were afterwards held to be. Perlin, who visited England at the end of the reign of Edward VI, has a lot of harsh things to say about the people; but he does not remark on their lack of sociability, their gloomy way of life or their bad cooking. On the contrary he describes the English as enjoying good cheer and being fond of feasting: 'The English are joyous with each other and are very fond of music . . . and they are great drunkards.' He was not the only foreigner in sixteenth-century England to report this.

The Restoration gave 'Merry England' a new lease of life; but Puritanism had by then deeply affected the character of the people. Yet it was probably the Puritan revival of the nineteenth century, coinciding with industrial and imperial expansion, that made the most powerful impact, both at home and abroad.

In some ways the modern Englishman—less inhibited, less formal, less concentrated—appears to be reverting from the nineteenth century to the late seventeenth-century type. Puritanism is a part of his make-up, for good or ill; but it is no longer supreme. In sexual matters, at least, this counter-revolution is already apparent to the French. In *Major Thompson Goes French* there is an admission that times have changed: 'The truth is that supposedly prudish Albion lived more than a century with a totally false reputation. The nation of Henry VIII has always been one of the bawdiest in the world.' *The Times* of 19 April 1972 reported an article in *Paris-Match* to the effect that after two centuries of 'puritanical morality and industrial assiduity' England had rediscovered its old identity, its liberal, and even licentious taste for enjoyment. Many Victorian English would have rubbed their eyes on seeing their descendants described, in the same article, as 'a people capable of such vitality in pleasure and so much apathy over their work . . . a people so warm, so spontaneous, so jovial.'

Similarly the English 'impatience' that struck French observers in the seventeenth and eighteenth centuries was less in evidence in the disciplined England of the nineteenth century. Nor would the French tributes to English practical ability, which began with the Industrial Revolution, have been so applicable to Tudor and Stuart England.

Montesquieu noted that the English had 'a great deal of imagination'. Hazlitt thought that they could rise to greater imaginative heights than the French, perhaps precisely because they were mentally more sluggish and offered more resistance to ideas. This made for force and feeling, he believed, while the quicker Frenchman was able to rest content with 'a verbal process'. During most of the nineteenth century, however, imagination would not have ranked high on the list of typically English characteristics. Writing about the same time as Hazlitt, Stendhal had asked his readers whether they really thought that the English, 'essentially calculators and men of commerce, had more imagination than us, who live in the finest climate of the universe?' When Tocqueville paid his first visit to England, in 1833, he judged the English to be 'more serious' than the French but also 'a people with less passion and imagination than ourselves'.

In the eighteenth century the Abbé le Blanc had been in no doubt of the violence of English passions—he explained them as an escape from melancholy and fogs. Even Balzac suggested that the Englishwoman was as passionate as an Italian woman when nobody saw her, though she would become 'froidement digne aussitôt que le monde intervient'. As the nineteenth century drew on, the sang-froid, impassivity and self-control of the Englishman became more and more axiomatic. In our own century the Spaniard de Madariaga thought that the French were in fact colder than the English and regarded it as 'one of the most amusing paradoxes of European life to see the English, with warm passions, calmly reproach the French—who are sometimes irritated, but always cold—with an imaginary tendency to become passionate.'

Whether or not gifted with imagination and passion the English have often suspected that the French regarded them as duller-witted than themselves. Shakespeare makes the Duke of Exeter, in *Henry V*, refer to 'the subtle-witted French' and the Duke of Orléans say of the English: 'If their heads had any intellectual armour, they could never wear such heavy head-pieces.' There was much respect for English savants in late seventeenth-century and eighteenth-century France; but there seems to be a gentle hint in La Fontaine's fable on the *Renard Anglais* that Englishmen were sometimes suspected of lacking 'esprit'. Certainly the effect of English boarding-school education in the nineteenth and twentieth centuries, in striking contrast to the best French education, was to discourage articulate speech. Maurois felt obliged to point out in *Les Silences du Colonel Bramble*:

> . . . it is a very stupid mistake to suppose them less intelligent than us. . . . The truth is that their intelligence follows different methods from ours: equally removed from our classical rationalism and from the pedantic lyricism of the Germans, it thrives on a vigorous good sense and on the absence of all system.

At least the English have acquired a reputation in France for *practical* intelligence and common sense. How otherwise could they have competed so successfully over so long a period of time? Presumably this explains why the poll in *L'Express*,* which gave the British a low rating for *joie de vivre*, ranked their intelligence remarkably high.

The Frenchman's image has also shifted with the centuries, if less noticeably than the Englishman's. The extraordinary politeness and good temper, characteristic of French society under the *ancien régime* at all levels, has gradually become less remarked on by visitors. Good temper is no more obvious in modern France than in other countries—in Paris perhaps rather less so than in some not so highly strung capitals. The Frenchman can still be exquisitely polite, but only if he makes something of an effort. Equally the imputation of smooth uniformity could hardly be brought against the French after the eighteenth century. There was as much a diversity of French types in the nineteenth century

* Cf. p. 55 above.

as there had been in England in the eighteenth century. In fact the French Revolution exerted in some ways (though not of course in regard to the pleasures of the flesh) an impact on French life comparable to the impact of Puritanism in England. The effect was to throw people on their own resources.

The French are much less of a military people than they used to be. Sir Charles Darnley, in *London and Paris*, was grieved by the continued 'dreams of warlike glory' in France and feared that nothing was 'still so dear to the heart of a Frenchman as military fame.' As late as 1859 Matthew Arnold wrote to his wife:

> The enthusiasm of the French people for the army is remarkable; almost every peasant we passed in the diligence took off his hat to this officer, though you never see them salute a gentleman as such; but they feel that the army is the proud point of the nation, and that it is made out of themselves.

One respect in which the French have certainly been more consistent than the English is their attitude to work. So ingrained is the reputation of Paris as a capital of pleasure that relatively few Englishmen realize the extent to which the average Frenchman works long and hard. The most remarkable result of the *Sunday Times* public opinion poll, which I have mentioned above,* was that only one person in eight of the thousand interviewed considered that the French were hard working. Burke knew better, when he wrote in 1791:

> In England we *cannot* work so hard as Frenchmen. Frequent relaxation is necessary to us. You are naturally more intense in your application. I did not know this part of your national character until I went to France in 1773.

Kipling, who adored France, could never have reconciled it with his Calvinist conscience to do so, if he had not seen for himself that the French were hard workers—and work was, for him, salvation. He wrote in 1913, in his poem *France*:

> Broke to every known mischance, lifted over all
> By the light sane joy of life, the buckler of the Gaul;
> Furious in luxury, merciless in toil,
> Terrible with strength that draws from her tireless soil;
> Strictest judge of her own worth, gentlest of man's mind,
> First to follow Truth and last to leave old Truths behind,
> France, beloved of every soul that loves its fellow-kind!

* Cf. p. 60.

The young La Rochefoucauld noted in East Anglia in the 1780s that the farm labourers worked from six o'clock in the morning to six in the evening, with an hour for dinner and half an hour for breakfast. In France the peasants worked longer hours and were worse paid: '. . . I can positively affirm, in spite of the feeling of some English who have travelled in France and do not agree, that their [the English] labourers work very casually, often rest and make a lot of conversation.'

The English reputation for hard work has been very uneven. At the turn of the sixteenth and seventeenth centuries the Dutchman van Meteren found the English lazier than both the Dutch and the French. Sorbière, visiting England shortly after the Restoration, professed surprise at the energy of the horses 'in a land where the men are extremely lazy . . . perhaps . . . they suppose that to know how to rest is to know how to live.' He recorded that the 'petit peuple' were much given to leaving their work and smoking and drinking in taverns; they were jealous of French artisans, who were ordinarily harder working.

The Industrial Revolution changed this image. Already, in the first half of the eighteenth century, the Abbé le Blanc wrote that the English artisans were 'aussi industrieux que laborieux' and produced neater and more solid, if less graceful, work than the French. Just before the Revolution Arthur Young found many Englishmen employed in industrial concerns in north-western France. In the sootiest days of the nineteenth century England was apt to appear to Frenchmen like a vast and gloomy factory where work proceeded at a relentless rate. Michelet referred admiringly to 'le plus industrieux des peuples' and, walking in London, felt that their prodigious activity gave the impression of 'an incalculable force'. Taine believed that the English worked more patiently than the French and could keep it up longer; but he wondered: 'Are work and power enough to make men happy?'

There have also been important changes in English and French attitudes to sex, marriage and family life. Puritanism, and the successive reactions to Puritanism, have powerfully affected English attitudes, while the gradual decline of the 'arranged' marriage has much altered the French scene. In the nineteenth century the arranged marriage, and the dowry system, were as much a part of the exoticism of the French, for the English, as wine or Catholicism. Sir Charles Darnley reflected a typical English view when he expressed distaste for the 'hymeneal jobbing' in Paris and the way in which marriages were formed without regard to the girls' inclinations. In return the French pointed out that English mothers did not scruple to keep poor and ineligible suitors away from their daughters. In any case, they were themselves shocked by the excessive freedom enjoyed by young English women and the system of 'innocent flirtation' which was unknown in France. Montesquieu noted that English girls often married 'without consulting their parents'—but he added by way of excuse that they could not take refuge in the convent as a last resort.

As Victor Hugo put it: 'La fille souveraine et la femme sujette, telles sont les vieilles coutumes anglaises.' Mrs Trollope noticed that the French regarded it as immoral to show too much gallantry to marriageable girls, while the English felt exactly the same about the young married women who took the limelight in France. Taine was struck by the submission and fidelity of English Victorian wives: 'often the husband is a despot'. But this extreme docility seems to have been another nineteenth-century phenomenon. In earlier centuries England had had something of a reputation as a paradise for married women, where the husbands compensated with tenderness for any lack of gallantry.

Whether or not wives were well treated in the home, French travellers to England were often struck—particularly in the eighteenth century—by the restricted role of women in society, as compared with France. Voltaire wrote of 'Le peu de commerce qu'on a ici avec les femmes'. The Abbé le Blanc said that the English shunned female company unless in love; those who had lived in Paris blamed their countrywomen for being less amusing than Frenchwomen—but whose fault was that?

Different attitudes towards children have provided another contrast. Daninos has pointed out how the French like to see their children precocious, while the English like to see them behave as children. As a corollary of this, French children have usually been kept on a tighter rein at home than English children have been. Misson observed in England in the seventeenth century how indulgently small children were treated. This seems to be one of the many facets of the perennial Anglo-French conflict between Art and Nature. Yet, here again, Victorian discipline for a time redressed the balance and ensured that many English children of the period were still less heard than French. Elder children, at their boarding schools, were certainly less seen.

When it comes to the various forms of love, the differences in attitude have been too numerous even to summarize. The English have always conceded a certain expertise to the French in this field. Donne described them as 'Love's fuellers'. Sterne wrote: '. . . how it has come to pass . . . I know not; but they have certainly got the credit of understanding more of love, and making it better than any other nation upon earth . . .' For the young A. D. C. Dundas (in Maurois's *Les Discours du Docteur O'Grady*) 'the idea of France was linked . . . with that of amorous adventures, and he thought it decent to have a girlfriend there, like hunting in Ireland or tobogganing in Saint-Moritz.'

Yet Dundas was not really interested in women—and indeed, both rightly and wrongly, the French have often supposed this to be the case with Englishmen. The French seem to notice pretty women in public more than the English do and certainly remark more on their clothes. Saurin's eighteenth-century Anglomane believed that the Fair Sex could have no power over an English philosopher. Balzac showed more awareness of hidden fires when he credited Lady Dudley, under her composed exterior, with strong sexual passion. Her love was a cruel love—resembling English policy—but also a thrilling one. For all her cruelty, hypocrisy and materialism, she was capable of 'tout ce que l'esprit peut ajouter de poésie aux plaisirs des sens'.

There has been a marked evolution, on both sides, in class attitudes. Daninos comments on the envious streak in the French character: the desire to remove the upper rungs of the ladder because of the impracticability of climbing them. In England, at least till recently, there has been more emphasis on climbing. Tocqueville remarked in 1835: 'The French wish not to have superiors. The English wish to have inferiors. On both sides there is pride, but it is understood in a different way . . .' He foresaw the fall of the English aristocracy, in spite of its adroitness and 'the ease with which it has opened its ranks': he thought that England would then be happier, but doubted whether it would be so great. Taine and other French observers were unpleasantly impressed by the class distinction rife in Victorian society; but they admired what the aristocratic system had done for England. The entail of estates and the sacrifice of younger children struck the nineteenth-century French as a prime example of English social ruthlessness, at once effective and inhuman. For Victor Hugo England was the aristocratic country *par excellence*; the vulture of aristocracy had nested there and hatched the eagle's egg of liberty. His novel, *L'Homme qui Rit*, was an essay in this theme. 'Everything about England is great,' he wrote, 'even what is not good, even oligarchy. The English patriciate is the patriciate in the absolute sense of the word. No feudalism more illustrious, more terrible and more full of life. Let us admit that this feudalism has been useful in its time.'

In earlier centuries things looked different. Montesquieu, at the beginning of the eighteenth century, drew quite the opposite contrast from Tocqueville's: 'The English get on well with their inferiors and cannot put up with their superiors. We adapt ourselves to our superiors and are intolerable to our inferiors.' French visitors to England, at this time and earlier, were impressed by the freedom of intercourse, in public, between men of rank and others. A nobleman would put away his sword and offer to fight a cabman with his fists: this would have been unthinkable in France.

Dallington found the sixteenth-century French nobility numerous, of honourable pedigree and 'valorous and courteous'; but he reproached them with being unlettered. As a good schoolmaster he regretted 'this French humour, so much to esteeme Armes, and nothing at all to regard learning'.* Burke formed rather the same impression when he visited France in 1773. By that time the English nobility had become more reserved. It seemed to Burke that French noblemen comported themselves towards inferior classes 'with good nature, and with something more nearly approaching to familiarity, than is generally practised with us in the intercourse between the higher and lower ranks of life'. Nineteenth-century travellers to France found that the French treated their servants less stiffiy than the English—or at least that there was less stiffness in the way in which their servants treated them.

Already in the time of Elizabeth, Dallington noticed that the English distinction between nobility and gentry did not obtain in France. The resulting contrast between the 'gentleman' and

* In the eighteenth century, too, both Chesterfield and the Abbé le Blanc found more learning in England than France. Voltaire regarded Bolingbroke as combining 'all the erudition of his country and all the politeness of ours'. But Chesterfield noted of the French aristocracy: 'However classically ignorant they may be, they think it a shame to be ignorant of the history of their own country . . .'

the 'gentilhomme' was to provide another major theme in Anglo-French comparisons. In the nineteenth century the ideal of the 'gentleman' began to acquire an enormous prestige in France and, although it had points in common with the French concept of the 'honnête homme', the word has, more or less, passed into the French language. Maurois embalmed the type of the English (actually Scottish) gentleman in his portrait of Colonel Bramble: 'Un gentleman, un vrai, c'est bien près d'être, voyez-vous, le type le plus sympathique qu'ait encore produit l'évolution du pitoyable groupe de mammifères qui fait en ce moment quelque bruit sur la terre. Dans l'effroyable méchanceté de l'espèce, les Anglais établissent une oasis de courtoisie et d'indifference. Les hommes se détestent; les Anglais s'ignorent. Je les aime beaucoup.'

Frenchmen have not always been able, or willing, to emulate the sobriety of manner which has been part of the gentleman's image. Perhaps it becomes easier with advancing years. Hazlitt wrote: 'I can hardly conceive of a young French *gentleman*, nor of an old one who is otherwise.' Harold Nicolson used to compare the Frenchman to a peach, that ripens slowly towards its autumnal best.

At times it seems that the French and English national characters could be expressed in a series of antitheses: wit/humour; logic/ tradition; gallantry/courage; thrift/expenditure; taste/comfort; town/country; vanity/pride.

The wit/humour antithesis has been readily enough accepted on both sides of the Channel. Even in the eighteenth century, according to the Abbé le Blanc, the English regarded humour 'as a thing which has only been given to their Nation'. French appreciation of English humour, as of Shakespeare, has developed slowly, but more or less surely. The English have always given the French good marks for wit. Taine found that they freely acknowledged French taste and wit; they themselves, he thought, did not really know how to enjoy conversation, but he conceded that their humour was tonic, if somewhat savage. In *England and the English* (1833) Lytton accepted French superiority in conversation, English conversation being in his view 'for the most part carried on in a series of the most extraordinary and rugged abbreviations—a species of talking shorthand. Hesitating, Humming and Drawling, are the three Graces of our Conversation.'

The French are just as conservative as the English, except in their political institutions. A truer antithesis than logic/tradition might be logic/empiricism or logic/compromise. But at least political and legal problems are more often settled in England in accordance with the precedents than they are in France. In any case we must bow to the authority of the Frenchman in Anthony Powell's *A Question of Upbringing*, who tells the narrator:

> 'Our countries have even, as you would say, agreed to differ. You lean on tradition: we on logic.'
>
> 'I was not then aware how many times I was to be informed of this contrast in national character on future occasions by Frenchmen whose paths I might happen to cross . . .'

Gallantry and courage are not very different things; but the words have a different colour and the frequency with which English writers have described the French as 'gallant' is striking. Smollett, trying to make amends for his surly account of his travels in France, wrote to a correspondent that he respected the French nation for the number of great men it had produced in all arts and sciences:

> I respect the French officers, in particular, for their gallantry and valour; and especially for that generous humanity that they exercise towards their enemies, even amidst the horror of war.

Although the French can certainly be thrifty, the English have not always been spenders. However, this fourth antithesis reflects the greater prosperity and carelessness of the English working class in comparison with the French, in the earlier centuries. Between the wars André Siegfried could still write that 'the taste and sense of economy' were not exhibited by the English working man and his wife, in the way that they were in France. But the superior comfort of the Englishman's home has always been acknowledged—together with the generally inferior taste of his food and of his daughter's clothes.

The town/country, or art/nature, antithesis could be lavishly illustrated. One of the charms of the English for the eighteenth-century French Anglomane was their close communion with nature. This has on the whole remained an English tendency, in spite of urbanization. A modern French writer, Jean Queval, refers to their 'esprit rural'. In *The Blessing* Grace loves the country and nature, while her French husband cannot bear them and adores art. Hazlitt is severe: 'A Frenchman's eye for nature is merely *nominal.*'

It was Montesquieu who first established the vanity/pride antithesis when he wrote of the English:

> Ils ont plus d'orgueil que de vanité; une nation voisine a plus de vanité que d'orgueil.

The English have often tended to regard the French as a vain people—perhaps more particularly in the eighteenth century, when it was a virtually universal commonplace that they were so. But allusions to French boastfulness go back to the sixteenth century; thus Shakespeare's Henry V exclaims before the French Herald:

> Yet, forgive me, God,
> That I do brag thus!—this your air of France
> Hath blown that vice in me . . .

In return the French, though (like the Abbé le Blanc) they might find that the English were comparatively modest as individuals, were frequently appalled by their collective pride. Tocqueville wrote:

> In past times what most distinguished the English people from any other was its satisfaction with itself. . . . This proud disposition was even further increased by the French writers of the eighteenth century, who all took the English at their word and carried their praises even further than they.

In fact a contest of arrogance between the two peoples would be a very near-run thing, ending (if it could ever end) in a draw. But the arrogance has taken different forms. The Frenchman has shown his arrogance by inviting foreigners to model themselves on him; the Englishman has shown his by taking his own inimitability for granted.

The French view of the English has been affected by their own novelists. The reverse is less true. There are of course a number of French characters in English fiction; but they make a less representative impact. I have never met an Englishman who admitted to taking his ideas of the French from a character in an English novel; but I have met a highly educated Frenchman who told me that his first ideas of an Englishman were based on Colonel Bramble. Perhaps there has been less scope for interpreting the

French to educated Englishmen, since they have traditionally travelled rather more in France, and tended to read more French literature, than vice versa.

At a less sophisticated level Englishmen have been only too ready to suppose that the small, hirsute, gesticulating Frenchman, who used to be presented as a figure of fun in farces and the music-halls, was an average, or even universal, type. 'Have you ever seen in our country before the war, messieu,' said the Padre in Flanders in *Les Silences du Colonel Bramble*, 'the Frenchman of the music-hall, the little man with a black imperial who gesticulates and perorates? . . . I believed in him, messieu, and I hardly imagined, I assure you, these devout and hard-working villagers.'

The French have been given some more serious portraits to study. Paul Morand defined the typical Englishman of eighteenth-century French fiction as commending himself 'through his sombre and solid qualities, his love of nature, his simple tastes, his middling condition, the refinement of his sensibility, and the elevation of his sentiments . . .' This is now an old portrait and its colours have faded; but it still occupies a dim corner of the gallery.

There is no really sympathetic English character in Balzac's work.* Lady Dudley, in *Le Lys dans la Vallée*, is presented as the personification of English nineteenth-century materialism. She is by no means stupid, or lacking in inner fire, or physically unattractive. But she is accused of having no soul or sentiment, of being intensely egoistical and arrogant, of switching passion on and off and of paying too much attention to outward propriety. She is in many ways quite the reverse of the 'philosophic' English character presented in the eighteenth century. Ironically enough, she is contrasted with Mme de Mortsauf, who might be thought the more traditionally English of the two in her attachment to her valley and her home, her avoidance of parties and her sexual repression. There is a brilliance of colouring in Balzac's treatment of Lady Dudley which recalls a portrait by Lawrence: less faded, but also less representative than the picture of the eighteenth-century 'philosopher', it hangs on a better-lit wall.

Many French children, in the late nineteenth century, must have regarded Jules Verne's Phileas Fogg (*Le tour du Monde en 80 Jours*) as a typical, if eccentric, English gentleman. He is the personification of sang-froid, impassivity and exactitude. Although a figure

* Cf. Félicien Marceau, *Balzac et son Monde* (pp. 365–70).

of fun in his manias and his lack of curiosity ('étant de cette race d'Anglais qui font visiter par leur domestique les pays qu'ils traversent') he has sterling qualities: his courage, determination and good heart are heroic. His French servant, Passepartout, indiscreet, excitable, high-spirited, inventive, expansive, is a perfect foil. Together with Mrs Aouda they make a monumental group—each striking suitable attitudes—over the fireplace.

Maurois's Colonel Bramble is a more realistic character, thoroughly representative of the honourable, rather inarticulate, type of English/Scottish gentleman. General Byng organized a dinner for Maurois after the First World War at which he said: 'We are all Brambles here.' But of course not all Englishmen—not even all English gentlemen—were, still less are, Brambles. However sympathetic the portrait, it encouraged the French to form a stylized, and rather old-fashioned, conception of the English. It was easier for them to admire the type than to regard it as part of their own world.

Daninos's Major Thompson is a modern variety of Bramble, rather more extrovert and (since he has to describe the French) a good deal more articulate. The Major Thompson series are really about the French rather than the English. But the autopsy of an Englishman in *Les Carnets du Major Thompson* reveals a collection of stage properties symbolic of the conventional Englishman as he was often presented, or presented himself, in France: a battleship, a raincoat, a royal crown, a cup of tea, a dominion, a policeman, the rules of the Royal and Ancient Golf Club of St Andrews, a Coldstream Guard, a bottle of whisky, the Bible, the timetable of the Calais-Mediterranean express, a Westminster Hospital nurse, a cricket ball, fog, a bit of land on which the sun never set, and, at the bottom of the subconscious, a cat-of-nine-tails and a schoolgirl in black stockings.

There are elements of most of these portraits in a twentieth-century summing-up by Pierre Maillaud: 'The picture conjured up by the fairly well educated Continental would present the English as sporting, practical, sparing of words, businesslike, conservative, disciplined, either puritanical or oddly eccentric and melancholy.' But a new generation is already waiting for a painter.

Matthew Arnold wrote to his mother in 1865: 'It is good for us to attend to the French, they are so unlike us . . .' This chapter has been full of contrasts and antitheses. But differences tend to be more obtrusive than resemblances and both the French and the English are highly self-conscious peoples. When all is said, they belong to the same species and do not react so very differently to the many experiences that they have in common. The 'typical' Frenchman and the 'typical' Englishman (in so far as they exist) have been brought up differently and are guided by different conventions. But they are less dissimilar in natural tastes and temperament than some French, and some English, are from others.

THREE

Travellers

TRAVEL DOES NOT always make the mind much broader. But it does bring home, even to the most shielded and inoculated traveller, that foreign countries really exist. In place of a myth, or an abstraction, he comes across living people, houses, clothes and manners. He may find it difficult to carry on a conversation; but he cannot avoid hearing and seeing—and, what he does hear and see, he will judge.

A man who visits a foreign country for a short space of time, particularly if he is not used to living abroad, is likely to regard everything that happens as being typically local and to judge the country accordingly. If the sun shines, he will suppose that it usually does so. If he is cheated, he will suspect that the people as a whole are dishonest. If he is tired, he will find everything disagreeable. Some people draw sweeping conclusions from the behaviour of a porter or customs official, or from the look of an airport—especially if it confirms them in an existing prejudice.

There is nothing new about this. Before the nineteenth century foreign travel, even between France and England, was a considerable undertaking and the shortest excursion was likely to be a matter of weeks and not days. There was no way of being whisked from capital to capital; the journey took longer; the approach was gradual; and impressions had more time to form. But those who were not good linguists could stick to their own countrymen (the French patronized certain hotels in London and the English certain hotels in Paris) and they could leave after several weeks with notions not much less superficial than those of a weekend tourist today.

There have been so many contacts between England and France, at least since the eighteenth century, that travellers' accounts of what they have suffered and enjoyed have probably done less to shape the two national images than one might suppose. Some of the strongest feelings that the two peoples have had about each other have been the result, not of personal contacts, but of political or religious sympathies and antipathies. Saurin's Anglomane had never visited England, though he burned to do so; he was attracted by England's reputation for political and intellectual freedom. Yet this reputation would not have been what it was if it had not been for French travellers like Montesquieu, Voltaire and the Abbé Prévost d'Exiles.

Tourism is only one of the bridges between England and France and it does not carry the heaviest traffic. But the experiences of the tourist are at least vivid and important to himself; while they can confirm his prejudices, they can also completely change his attitude towards a foreign country. In any case, without travel of one kind or another, there could never have been any political or intellectual contacts at all. If it had not been for travellers, no Frenchman could ever have met an Englishman; nor could any books, fashions and ideas have crossed the Channel.

The stream of travel has traditionally flowed stronger from north to south and from the outer to the inner parts of Europe. The English have had to pass through France to get to Italy or Switzerland; they have yearned for sun, wine and culture; they have coveted prestige, amusement or instruction; sometimes they have simply wanted to 'go abroad', to vary their insular routine. In the seventeenth and eighteenth centuries it was part of the usual education of a young Englishman of means and family to spend several months touring France and other European countries. James Howell, who first went abroad in 1618, wrote his *Instructions for Forreine Travell*, in 1642, as a cautionary guide to young travellers of this sort. He advised them to spend the winter in Paris and then to visit Spain, passing through Gascony and Languedoc. 'The first Countrey that is most requisite to the English to know', he wrote, 'is France, in regard of neighboured, of conformity in Government in divers things and necessary intelligence of state, and of the use one shall have of that language wheresoever he passe further: and the younger one goeth to France the better, because of the hardnesse of the accent and pronunciation . . .' He rubbed this last point in: 'The French

Tongue . . . will put one often into fits of despaire and passion . . . but the Learner must not bee daunted . . .'

Howell allowed his charges to borrow good qualities from other countries: there could be 'some choyce and change of habit', though the heart must remain English. The great advantage of French travel was that it helped to rub off English shyness: 'France useth to work one good effect upon the English, she useth to take away the mothers milk (as they say) that blush and bashful tincture, which useth to rise up in the face upon sudden salutes. . . . For the Gentry of France have a kind of loose becomming boldnes, and forward vivacity in their carriage . . .' It was important to learn their exasperating language in some place unfrequented by other English, since '. . . the greatest bane of English Gentelmen abroad is too much frequency and communication with their own Countrey-men . . .'

This was still the cry a century later. Chesterfield warned his son in 1750 against frequenting the English coffee-house in Paris, 'the resort of all the scrub English, and also of the fugitive and attainted Scotch and Irish: party quarrels are very frequent there; and I do not know a more degrading place in all Paris.' He described the life of 'les Milords Anglais' as being 'regularly, or if you will, irregularly' as follows: rise late, breakfast together, go by coachfuls to the Palais, the Invalides and Notre-Dame, thence to the English coffee-house, then to a tavern for dinner, then to the play (in fine clothes 'very ill made by a Scotch or Irish tailor'), then to the tavern again to get drunk and quarrel. 'Their tender vows are addressed to their Irish laundress . . . they return home, more petulant but not more informed, than when they left it; and show, as they think, their improvement, by affectedly both speaking and dressing in broken French.' As a rule, wrote Chesterfield, they had too little French to frequent the best French company. A proof of this was that 'there is no one instance of an Englishman's having ever been suspected of a gallantry with a French woman of condition, though every French woman of condition is more than suspected of having a gallantry.' It is only fair to add that, if the English often spoke bad French, French travellers before the eighteenth century hardly spoke English at all.

Some English, of course, have always preferred to avoid their own countrymen abroad. Sensitive travellers, of all nationalities, tend to feel a peculiar horror when they see their compatriots looking hot, uneasy and badly dressed and hear them talk their own language loudly or the local one badly. The future Bishop Douglas was irritated when he found Paris and its theatres full of the English in 1748. He, too, formed the impression that they were 'seldom or never in company with the natives of the country' either because of shyness or because of inadequate French. There is a dreadful authenticity in Hazlitt's account of his travelling alone in a French diligence with another Englishman. Not a word was exchanged except that at one stage his companion asked in 'thick broken French' how far it was to Evreux and Hazlitt replied, in English, that he did not know.

One object of travelling abroad was to prove that it was better to stay at home. Classic, in Samuel Foote's play, *The Englishman in Paris*, held that a short residence in Paris was a necessary stage in the education of all men of fashion by giving them 'a true relish for their own domestic happiness; a proper veneration for their national liberties; a contempt for adulation; and an honour for the extended generous commerce of their country'. In *The Englishman Returned from Paris*, Lord John, young but wise, is only a shade less inflexible. Forms and customs should not be transplanted, however right in their place; but there might be something to be said for 'the shaking-off some native qualities, and the being made more sensible, from comparison, of certain national and constitutional advantages'.

Whatever their motives and reserves the English have never ceased, in peacetime, to flock to Paris. Walpole wrote in 1789 how English money used to be lavished in France: 'When I was there in 1765, their late king said that by the returns from Calais, 40,000 English had passed through there, but two years after the peace: if half were tradesmen, cooks and barbers *pour s'instruire*, not one went and returned for so little as five pounds.' During the Peace of Amiens there was a similar rush. At the beginning of the summer of 1802 something like five thousand British subjects were in France and, by September, the total had risen to ten to twelve thousand. About a thousand of them, who were still in France when the Peace broke down, were arrested and imprisoned until Napoleon's fall. Thackeray, in *The Book of Snobs*, was pleased to think 'how many gallant British Snobs there are, at this minute of writing, pushing their heads out of every window in the courtyard of "Meurice's" in the Rue de Rivoli; or roaring out "Garsong, du pang", "Garsong, du vang" . . .' They were not of course only to be found in the Rue de Rivoli: 'That brutal, ignorant, peevish bully of an Englishman is showing himself in every city of Europe. One of the dullest creatures under heaven, he goes trampling Europe under foot. . . . A thousand delightful sights pass before his bloodshot eyes, and don't affect him.'

French tourists in England were less numerous and it was only towards the end of the seventeenth century that private travel from France to England became at all frequent. Those Frenchmen who did cross the Channel usually did so for a specific reason—official, commercial or scientific. The Abbé le Blanc wrote: 'Those who only leave home to amuse themselves, hardly ever come to England. The prejudice is against the climate, and London does not promise them enough pleasure to tempt them.' It was because there were fewer tourists in England, he thought, that the respectable classes could claim that they showed them more active hospitality. Some houses in Paris were open to foreigners; but it had to be admitted that there were many more 'où l'on craint leur présence'. In the Abbé's view the French did not travel enough, while the English, living in an island, travelled more than any other people in Europe. But they often travelled too young and with too much national prejudice. They had 'je ne sais quoi de brusque dans le caractère' and, when they came to Paris fresh from the University or the cafés of London, they were apt to sport 'un air embarrassé'.

However, in the two decades before the French Revolution, there was a good deal of social traffic in both directions. Walpole wrote in 1776: 'We have coveys of foreigners, particularly French.' As for intellectual traffic, the French have often sent distinguished explorers to England. Voltaire and Montesquieu were among the earliest and most famous; in the nineteenth century they were followed by writers like Stendhal and Prosper Mérimée. The new industrial England called for serious study. Tocqueville was one such observer; another, Michelet, noted in his diary, on arriving at Dover in August 1834: 'Bentham, Malthus, Martin, sont l'expression de l'Angleterre . . . l'intérêt, la foule, l'étouffement de la population . . .'* *Sur les Chemins de l'Europe* records a dinner at the French Embassy where Talleyrand, ostentatiously Anglophile, seemed to think that France should remain a purely agricultural country. Michelet maintained that it could not be

* Quoted by Jean Seznec in *John Martin en France* (1964).

right for England to become more and more industrial while other countries became more and more agricultural.

Travellers have not always been loved. Howell observed that the Englishman was too much given to 'the excessive commendation and magnifying of his own Countrey'. Sorbière thought that the rude reception that French seventeenth-century travellers were liable to get at Dover (cries of 'Mounseer' quickly turning to 'French Dog') was partly to be explained by the noisy ostentation with which they stepped ashore.

Dr Martin Lister records a flattering conversation with French officers at Marly in 1698:

> They willingly allowed the English to be truly brave; and now in peace they found also, that they were as civil, and well bred as brave . . . they did see a great difference between them and other nations; they did not stare, and carelessly run about, or hold up their heads, and despise what they saw; but had a true relish of every good thing . . . and therefore the king took pleasure to have them showed every thing.

Dr Lister was in the suite of an English Ambassador and there is a diplomatic ring to this conversation. Samuel Foote's Buck returns from Paris as an exaggerated Gallomane, full of fatuity and French expressions (though still with a faulty accent). But, when he first goes there, he is anything but appreciative. He exclaims: 'The men are all puppies, mincing and dancing, and chattering, and grinning; the women a parcel of painted dolls; their food is fit only for hogs; and as for their language, let them learn it that like it.'

The most xenophobe Frenchman could hardly judge the English tourist more severely than some Englishmen did. Hazlitt wrote that his countrymen had to think themselves ill-used to be happy abroad: 'It is the incapacity of enjoyment that makes them sullen and ridiculous.' They 'carry their own defects as a standard for general imitation; and think the virtues of others (that are not *their* vices) good for nothing. Thus they find fault with the gaiety of the French as impertinence, with their politeness as grimace.' Again: 'We despise others for their inferiority, we hate them for their superiority; and I see no likelihood of an accommodation at this rate. The English go abroad; and when they come back, they brood over the civilities or the insults they have received with equal discontent. The gaiety of the Continent has thrown an additional damp upon their native air . . .'

Thackeray was still more biting:

> We are accustomed to laugh at the French for their braggadocio propensities, and intolerable vanity about la France, la gloire, l'Empereur and the like; and yet I think in my heart that the British Snob, for conceit and self-sufficiency and braggartism in his way, is without a parallel. There is always something uneasy in a Frenchmen's conceit. . . . About the British Snob, on the contrary, there is commonly no noise, no bluster, but the calmness of profound conviction. . . . And I am inclined to think it is this conviction, and the consequent bearing of the Englishman towards the foreigner whom he condescends to visit . . . that makes us so magnificently hated throughout Europe as we are. . .

No doubt Thackeray was acutely sensitive; but a French contemporary, Théophile Gautier, gave in *Jettatura* the following description of the English passengers on a steamboat from Marseilles to Naples:

> On the deck, in the space reserved for first-class passengers, stood the English trying to keep as separate as possible from each other and to mark out an inviolable demarcation circle around themselves; their splenetic faces were carefully shaved, there was not a wrong fold in their neck-ties . . . One would have said that they were fresh from one of the compartments of their dressing cases; their correct dress showed none of the little disorders of toilette which are the ordinary results of travelling.

The party included Lords, MPs, merchants and tailors. All were 'respectable, all solemn, all impassive, all bored'.

Hated or not, eighteenth- and nineteenth-century English travellers were rich and their money was welcome. As a merchant said to R. L. Stevenson in the Cévennes: 'The English have always long purses . . .' Cazamian wrote of the many English visitors to France between the two wars: 'Nous les regardons passer. On les reconnait presque toujours au premier coup d'œil: corps maigres et osseux, têtes longues, aux énergiques mâchoires; un air de froideur, où nous lisons comme un orgueil engourdi.' Most of these visitors were ordinary people; but 'nous gardons la vieille idée de nos pères: l'Anglais est plus or moins un milord.'

Certainly French innkeepers were delighted when English clients reappeared after the Napoleonic Wars: there was something reassuring, as well as lucrative, about them. Besides, it is difficult to hate what one does not take quite seriously—and Frenchmen have not always taken the English tourist very seriously. Daninos describes him as traversing the planet 'like a little Great Britain in movement, at once close and inaccessible, like his island'. The Englishman observes with detachment; he does not usually look for converts; he seldom expects to be converted. By contrast, according to Daninos, the French tourist (a comparatively recent phenomenon) wants to love and be loved, to dispense the lustre of France; nothing abroad seems very real to him: 'at bottom, he is always asking himself the question: "How can one be Persian?"' For the Englishman it comes as less of a surprise that other people should be different; he tends to be more surprised when he discovers points in common with himself.

The actual crossing of the Channel was enough to deter idle curiosity in the seventeenth century. The Frenchman would embark for Dover at Calais or Dieppe, having already travelled five days from Paris. Sailings were twice a week, but irregular; with a favourable wind the crossing might take three hours, but more often it lasted twelve or fourteen hours. In England the road to London went through Gravesend and the last stage of the journey might be by river. A traveller in 1659 had to spend twenty-three hours at sea, which seemed to him longer than twenty-three years. Sorbière, in the 1660s, spent twelve hours, crossing in a calm sea. Louis XIII's Ambassador, Bassompierre, receiving VIP treatment in 1626, took three days to get to Dover on his return journey, with overnight stops at Gravesend, Sittingbourne and Canterbury. Then he had to wait for nearly two weeks until the weather was good enough for the crossing.

By the middle of the eighteenth century the journey was normally accomplished more rapidly. Sterne claimed to have 'left London with so much precipitation that it never enter'd my mind that we were at war with France . . .' He took a place in the Dover stage; the packet sailed at nine the next morning and by three o'clock that afternoon he was dining in France. The Rev. William Cole had a still quicker passage in October 1765. He set out in the Dover coach from London at 4 a.m., breakfasted at Rochester, dined at Canterbury and arrived at Dover at about 7 p.m. He went aboard the boat at 10 a.m. next day and arrived at Calais just over three hours later ('every Passenger was sick except myself'). Twenty years later, however, François de la Rochefoucauld had to wait two days at Calais because of bad weather. Finally he left at 2 p.m. but, because of the wind, could not get into Dover until 3.30 a.m., by which time he and his companions were all ill. He spent a night at Canterbury before going on to London.

At the beginning of the nineteenth century there were sailings from Brighton to Dieppe. Hazlitt took this route in 1824. At Brighton in the evening a Frenchman was singing to a guitar: 'As we heard the lively musician warble, we forgot the land of Sunday-schools and spinning-jennies. The genius of the South had come out to meet us.' Some years later Surtees makes Mr Jorrocks catch 'the nine o'clock Dover heavy' in London on Saturday morning. At Gravesend 'the first foreign symptom appears, in the words "Poste aux Chevaux" '; but lunch is at Rochester. 'Towards the decline of the day, Dover heights appeared in view . . .' Next day there was strenuous competition for Mr Jorrocks's custom between French and British sailors. The Frenchmen, unsuccessful, 'shrugged up their shoulders and burst out a laughing, one calling him "my Lor Rosbif" and the other "Monsieur God-dem".' The crossing was to Boulogne; there were three hours on board and everybody was sick.

There was always the risk of difficulties with the Customs. Smollett's books were seized at Boulogne in 1765 and sent to Amiens at his expense, so that they could be examined to ensure that they had nothing prejudicial to State or Religion: 'a species of oppression which one would not expect to meet with in France, which piques itself on its politeness and hospitality.'

Those travellers who were not too sick to notice, were immediately struck by the contrast between the two countries. Young La Rochefoucauld, at Dover, thought himself 'transported into another world'. At the beginning of the nineteenth century Sir Charles Darnley found everything different on landing at Dieppe: darker complexions, more marked features, different sounds, the fierce looks of the military. As Arthur Young had it: 'The strait that separates England, so fortunately for her, from all the rest of the world must be crossed many times before a traveller ceases to be surprised at the sudden and universal change that surrounds him on landing at Calais.' Young was struck by the admirable roads in France, though also by the smaller traffic on them than in England. Bad in the seventeenth century, the French roads, due to the corvée system, became the best in Europe in the eighteenth century. But they were neglected during the Revolution and did not recover their excellence until well into the nineteenth century. Another feature of eighteenth-century France to make an early impression on English travellers was the efficiency of the police. Cole noted: 'The police is so good thro'out all the King of France's Dominions, as never to hear of any Robbery on the High Way.'

By the early nineteenth century English roads had improved. The Marquis de Vermont, Sir Charles Darnley's correspondent, was impressed on arrival in England by the rapid posting, beautiful horses, civil drivers, excellent roads, handsome grounds and houses and general appearance of comfort. The roads had become safer, too. Chateaubriand, arriving at Dover as Ambassador in 1822, was greeted with enormous respect at the Shipwright Inn, where he was provided with a dinner 'of enormous fishes and monstrous quarters of beef'. Next day he travelled to London in a light carriage with four fine horses and two elegant postilions: 'At Blackheath, formerly a heath haunted by robbers, I found a completely new village. Soon I discerned the immense cap of smoke that covers the city of London.'

Like everything else, French and English inns offered a contrast to each other; where the English inns were bad, the French tended to be good, and vice versa. In the seventeenth century it was not the badness but the lack of English inns that attracted comment. Misson noted that, because of this, travellers were obliged to take lodgings; on the other hand, he wrote, it was respectable in England (which it was not then in France) to take simple meals—meat, bread and beer—in public *rôtisseries*. Some sixty years later Smollett described his experiences on both sides of the Channel with an almost impartial peevishness. The road to Dover, he discovered, was 'the worst road in England, with respect to the conveniences of travelling and must certainly impress foreigners with an unfavourable opinion of the nation in general. The chambers are in general cold and comfortless, the beds paultry, the cookery execrable, the wine poison, and the bills extortion; there is not a drop of tolerable malt liquor to be had from London to Dover.' He told the story of a Canterbury publican 'who had charged the French Ambassador forty pounds for a supper that was not worth forty shillings'.

Surtees's Mr Jorrocks did not fare very much better in the nineteenth century. At Rochester the neat landlady was smirking and smiling to inveigle the stagecoach passengers into her house. But they found a dark dingy room, with a rain-bespattered window, where the table was covered with a thrice-used cloth and set out with lumps of bread, knives and two- and three-pronged forks laid alternately. The menu consisted of 'two dishes of pork, a couple of ducks, and a lump of half-raw, sadly mangled cold roast beef, with waxy potatoes and overgrown cabbages'. This was washed down with beer, brandy-and-water and Devonshire cider. It was followed by cheese—'we have no tarts we can recommend.'

But perhaps the most authoritative judgement on English inns just before the railway era was that of the Marquis de Vermont in *London and Paris*. He (or rather his English creator) found the inns comfortable and well furnished, with blazing fires and good carpets; and he was well and civilly served. But his miseries began with the bill of fare: it was very long, but nothing was ready. In the end he would be obliged to eat boiled cod, with a very insipid sauce of oysters, followed by a plate of hard and raw mutton chops, accompanied by uninviting potatoes and underboiled greens. An ill-made apple-tart and some tasteless jelly would follow. The claret would be adulterated and the coffee watery. It was the same everywhere: 'The only real choice . . . between a tough mutton chop and a hard beefsteak, between an ill-cooked veal cutlet and a half-roasted leg of mutton, and between stale pastry and insipid jelly.' The traveller who survived this ordeal had to face the intolerable heat of the feather-bed and the excessive charges of the next morning's bill.

The preparations for English tourists in France were on a more extensive and accommodating scale. Dessein's Inn at Calais had 130 beds and a large staff. At Boulogne Mr Jorrocks found an English waiter, beef, boiled potatoes and stout. Hazlitt, who lacked the gastronomic curiosity of some later English tourists ('. . . real French dishes are an abomination to the English palate') was delighted to dine at Rouen off 'a roast fowl, greens, and bacon, as plain, as sweet, and wholesome, as we could get at an English farmhouse'.

Arthur Young's considered view, based on a good deal of

experience, was that French inns were 'on an average better in two respects, and worse in all the rest than those in England'. Their two superiorities, he thought, were eating/drinking and beds; for general comfort and service English inns were better. One of the things that struck him most was the taciturnity of French travellers at the tables d'hôte, in comparison with the volubility and spirits he had expected. He could never speak too highly of the 'cheerful and facile pliancy of disposition' in which the French far excelled the English; but, to his surprise, he did *not* find them superior in formal politeness, loquacity or good spirits.

The beds of French inns had been long renowned for luxury and fine linen. John Evelyn spent a blissful night at a famous inn in Rouen in 1646: '. . . we indulged ourselves with the best that all France affords . . . the supper we had might have satisfied a Prince: we lay that night in Damask bedds and were treated like Emperours.' Sir Charles Darnley also approved of the beds; but he thought that, otherwise, French innkeepers sacrificed comfort to grandeur. One would find arabesque figures, marble chimneys and magnificent glasses; but the floors would be dirty, the carpets rare and the window-panes broken. A boy of fourteen who waited on him—voluble, lively and gracefully officious—said he was very partial to the English and was going to Brighton to learn the language. But Sir Charles was shocked to the core when the boy emptied the glass in the fireplace and shook the cloth full of crumbs under the table.

Smollett and other travellers were surprised that the French landlords did not come to the door as their English colleagues did: 'It is a very odd contrast between France and England: in the former all the people are complaisant but the publicans; in the latter there is hardly any complaisance but among the publicans.'

There was certainly grandeur in the *Fidèle Berger* at Abbeville: a long brick-floored room with 'the walls plentifully decorated with a panoramic view of the *Grande Nation* walloping the Spaniards at the siege of Saragossa.' But there were culinary compensations, too. Mr Jorrocks was at first disappointed by the watery soup and the 'beef boiled to rags'; but he cheered up with the appearance of fowls and turkeys, stewed eels, wild duck and fricandeau de veau, mutton and beef, larks and snipes, custards and a *soufflé*, coffee, dessert, etc. 'Faith, but this is not a bad dinner after all's said and done, when one gets fairly into it.' It cost him exactly the same as the much less plentiful meal he had eaten at Rochester.

John Sican, a graduate of Trinity College, Dublin, wrote to Swift from Paris in October 1735:

> The roads are excellent, the postchaises very commodious, and the beds the best in the world; but the face of the country in general is very wretched, of which I cannot mention a more lively instance than that you meet with wooden shoes and cottages like those in Ireland before you lose sight of Versailles.

The comparative prosperity of the English peasantry was a frequent theme of French and English travellers in the seventeenth and eighteenth centuries. Sorbière said that poverty existed in seventeenth-century England, as it did elsewhere; but it was not so great; there were no signs of extreme misery. Voltaire wrote:

> The [English] peasant's feet are never bruised by wooden shoes, he eats white bread, he is well clothed, he has no worries about increasing the number of his beasts or covering his roof with tiles out of fear that his taxes may be raised the following year.

According to Adam Smith:

> The wages of labour are lower in France than in England. When you go from Scotland to England, the difference which you may remark between the dress and countenance of the common people in the one country and in the other sufficiently indicates the difference in their condition. The contrast is still greater when you return from France. France, though no doubt a richer country than Scotland, seems not to be going forward so fast.

The standard defence of pre-Revolutionary France was that the people might be poor, but they were happy. The Abbé le Blanc wrote that English writers represented France 'comme un Royaume riche en apparence, mais pauvre en effet, où le faste règne parmi les Grands, mais où tout le reste vit dans la misère.' He conceded that the English peasant was better-off and better-clothed; but the Englishman was not so gay, even when drunk. 'The People in France is good-tempered and content with little' —'parmi nous tout le monde chante'. Some English travellers got the same impression. Cole noted that 'the People, amidst all their Beggary, Poverty and Misery, seem to be happy and contented.' Sterne exclaimed: 'Happy people! that once a week at least are sure to lay down all your cares together, and dance and sing, and sport away the weights of grievance, which bow down the spirit of other nations to the earth.'

During the Revolution French buildings fell into decay, but the peasantry began to look better-fed and better-clothed. Of course the degree of poverty had always varied from region to region. Dr Rigby, a Norwich doctor, found in French Flanders in 1789 that the people seemed happier and more prosperous than he had expected—as well as more industrious.* Later on, in the nineteenth century, it was the turn of the French to be shocked by the contrasts between English wealth and poverty. The English countryman might still live more cleanly and comfortably than his French counterpart, though according to Taine he was less economical and lacked 'l'art de faire beaucoup avec peu de chose'. But it was another matter in the poor districts of London and the industrial towns. Taine was by no means the only French writer to stress the misery, dirt and drunkenness that prevailed there, while Théophile Gautier found the extremes of wealth and poverty more marked than in France. 'Et leurs pauvres!', exclaimed Jules Vallès, 'Spectacle dont le brouillard de Londres et sa boue, si epais qu'ils soient, ne parviennent pas à voiler et à noyer l'horreur!'

Travellers from both countries agreed that the average Englishman was better educated and informed. In the late eighteenth century Arthur Young boasted that the French 'were, I apprehend, in the reign of Henri IV far beyond us in towns, houses, streets, roads, and in short, in everything. We have since, thanks to liberty, contrived to turn the tables on them.' People, wealth and ideas circulated less freely in France: 'It is impossible to describe, in words adequate to one's feelings, the dullness and stupidity in France.' Newspapers in the provinces were scarce and the level of general instruction was so low that a Frenchman had asked him whether there were trees and rivers in England. Both La Rochefoucauld and Taine commented favourably on the general level of education in England, while Taine was particularly impressed by the cultivation of the Victorian educated classes and their knowledge of languages. In *London and Paris* the Marquis de Vermont admired the general appearance of cleanli-

* According to François de la Rochefaucauld, however, Flanders appeared to the traveller to be the richest province of France; but it was nothing in comparison with England.

ness and respectability in England, the public spirit and liberality of individuals and the general mania for reading newspapers—though the press was unfortunately vitiated by too much abuse of 'everything which is great or venerable'.

The material finish of English civilization—the good quality of clothes, furniture and other manufactured articles—began to attract notice in the eighteenth century. By contrast English travellers to France (for instance, Mrs Gaskell in 1862) often admired the superior taste and elegance of the materials they could buy there.

The natural advantages and disadvantages of the two countries could usually be compared without too much *amour propre* on either side. Dallington, in the sixteenth century, wrote of the 'happie fruitfulnesse' of the French soil, combined with its 'very temperate and wholesome climate'. 'Doe but conceyt in your imagination,' he implored, 'the faire Townes of Italy heere seated, and in them, the English Nation planted; and in my opinion ye have the right idea of Platoe's happy state: o utinam! o si!' Dr Martin Lister enthused on the dryness of French air and confessed that it was 'the chiefest reason of my leaving London at that time of the year'. England was a green and pleasant land: 'but we pay dearly for it in agues and coughs, and rheumatic distempers'. Deeply fond of nature and the sun, he had a passion for Languedoc and a bee in his bonnet that Louis XIV ought to settle there.

Dr Lister put his finger on two of England's most salient features: its humidity and its greenness. Travellers from France had already found these out. The English climate might be healthy and temperate, in principle; but in practice it was depressingly damp and cloudy, inducing melancholy, scurvy, rickets and consumption. French writers have almost always reacted to it as if they lived in the south of their country. According to Saint-Amant in 1643 it was 'the worst of climates'. The English reputation for fog—the effect of coal fires as well as humidity—was already well-established in the seventeenth century. In the nineteenth century Mrs Trollope relished the clear view from Notre-Dame, while Taine was obsessed by the moral and physical effects of English dampness. It gave the English their need for air and exercise; it 'prescribes action, forbids indolence, developes energy, teaches patience'; 'La tristesse et la sévérité de la nature coupent net toute conception voluptueuse de la vie.'

Voltaire gives a charming picture of his visit to Greenwich on a fine day in May 1726. He was enchanted both with the weather and with the plebeian holiday crowds in the Park. He found himself next to a Danish courier who 'seemed to me in the throes of joy and surprise. He thought that the whole nation was always gay, that all the women were beautiful and lively, and that the sky of England was always pure and clear; that nobody thought of anything but pleasure . . .' But alas, next day, the east wind began to blow . . .

The greenness of the English landscape was some compensation for the humidity, if scarcely an adequate one, and so was the absence of wolves. Perlin admired the rich and thickly wooded English countryside. Sorbière found Kent beautiful and fertile; it could have done with more architectural ornament, but the bowling lawns were like billiard cloths. Because of its greenness the countryside always seemed smiling to the Abbé le Blanc. La Rochefoucauld praised the English trees and the parks of the country houses; he was also impressed, towards the end of the eighteenth century, by the elegant houses on the way to London. Sir Charles Darnley found the scenery of Normandy delightful, but lacking 'those elegant villas, thatched cottages and romantic villages' so common on the English side.

Whatever the charms of the two countrysides the chief poles of attraction for travellers were, of course, London and Paris. It was a perpetual subject for debate as to which was the larger and more impressive city. In the sixteenth and early seventeenth centuries honours were not too uneven; but Paris seems to have won by a head. Perlin found London 'fort belle ville, et excellente, et après Paris l'une des plus belle, grande et riche de tout le monde.' By the end of Elizabeth's reign Paris struck Dallington as being greater, fairer built and better situated than London, with 'very fayre, high, and uniforme' stone buildings. But he thought London was richer, more ancient and more populous. Thomas Coryat commented on Paris in 1608: 'This Citie is exceeding great, being no lesse than ten miles in circuit, very populous, and full of very goodly buildings, both publique and private, whereof the greatest part are of faire white freestone.' For Howell Paris was 'that hudge though durty theater of all nations.'

As the seventeenth century wore on, Paris increased its advantage. London still held its own in wealth and size, while the re-building after the Great Fire gave the City a more open and monumental appearance; but most travellers agreed that Paris had more distinguished buildings. Sorbière was surprised by the vast extent of London and wrote scornfully of the young French who only knew the district around Covent Garden. The city as a whole seemed to him bigger in circumference, if not in population, than Paris, though in many respects it was not to be compared with it. Perhaps no town had so many and such fine shops; but the public buildings were unremarkable. At the end of the century Misson estimated that London, including Westminster, was probably the biggest city in Europe and 'an extraordinarily rich city, as everyone knows'. His contemporary, Dr Lister, was awed by the magnificence of Paris, both within doors and without. But he found its streets very narrow; there were many English conveniences lacking; and the place swarmed with importunate beggars. When asked by a French lady what had pleased him most, he gave her a typical, and charmingly precise, reply: 'The middle walk of the Tuileries in June, betwixt eight and nine at night'.

Early in the eighteenth century Montesquieu thought that Paris was 'a fine city where there are uglier things, London a mean city, where there are very fine things.' For the Abbé le Blanc there was no doubt which was the more beautiful city: 'The French capital sees in London a worthy rival, whose jealousy makes continual efforts to dispute her precedence . . . a very big, rich and gloomy city, where coal smoke tends to poison the air that one breathes.' He thought little of the architecture of London, including St Paul's, and was not surprised that the great and rich should be eager to leave it for the country. Bishop Douglas noted that the Parisian streets of the 1740s were narrow, but cleaner and better paved than the London ones ('the dirtiness of London is a proverb among foreigners'); the squares of London were better, but there were fewer fine houses there. By the 1780s, however, the cleanliness of the London streets had improved. François de la Rochefoucauld found London full of magnificent shops and by no means the ugly place that it must have been before the Great Fire. An admirer of St Paul's, he regretted that the Palace (St James's) was not more palatial.

As soon as the London streets got cleaner, the Paris streets seem to have got dirtier. Arthur Young thought that no city could be a better place of residence than Paris for men of literary or scientific tastes. But he did not care for the 'horrid fatigue' of the streets: '. . . it is almost incredible to a person used to London how dirty the streets of Paris are and how horribly inconvenient and dangerous walking is without a foot pavement.' William Cole admired the 'most elegant, beautiful, grand and stately Gothic Pile' of Notre-Dame. But he too inveighed against the narrow streets and their lack of cleanliness, as well as the gloomy shops, the poor trees and the mean appearance of the lower floors of most of the houses: 'Upon the whole, it is one of the most dreary and gloomy cities I have been in . . . some few artificial Perfections . . . a dirty nasty Ditch of a River . . . a very indifferent Situation. . . . Others may see it in a different Point of View. I went prejudiced in its Favour . . .'

William Cole's reactions were far from typical of English visitors to Paris in the following century, though Hazlitt still noted that the absence of footpaths made for 'continual panic'. It was more usual to be 'enchanted with the variety of lively amusement' (Sir Charles Darnley); to savour the charm of the autumnal weather (Surtees); to succumb to the magical effect of light-hearted gaiety exhibited in public (Mrs Trollope); to divide one's time conscientiously between the Louvre, the Tuileries, the Garden of Plants, Père la Chaise and Notre-Dame; to contract 'the fatal habit of high play' or to submit to 'the equally dangerous and equally irresistible dominion of a "*belle Françoise*"' (Sir Charles Darnley's phrases).

Matthew Arnold, visiting Paris under the Second Empire, only half liked the new buildings: 'They make Paris, which used to be the most historical place in the world, one monotonous handsomer Belgravia . . .' Mrs Gaskell, too, had mixed feelings about the broad new boulevards: '. . . a great gain in all material points; a great loss to memory and to that kind of imagination which loves to repeople places.' But Paris was never more glittering, externally, than at that time. Swinburne fell in love with it in 1861, on his first visit at the age of twenty-four. Matthew Arnold's visit in 1865 was not his first; but he prophesied: '. . . the shops are splendid, and for show, pleasure, and luxury this place is, and every day more and more, the capital of Europe; and as Europe gets richer and richer, and show, pleasure and luxury are more valued, Paris will be more and more important, and more and more the capital of Europe.'

Nineteenth-century French travellers to London were struck by its wealth, power and comfort; but they were less attracted by its pleasure and show. The Marquis de Vermont was disappointed by London's failure to impress at first sight, though he was dazzled by its richness and by the variety of well-lit shops. Taine was depressed by the fog and blackened buildings: after an hour's walk in the City on a Sunday 'on a le spleen, on conçoit le suicide.'

Few travellers confined their comments to inns, streets and public buildings. To acquire an intimate knowledge of French or English life it was not enough to stay in hotels or go to theatres; there was really nothing for it but to board with a family. At least in the towns, not many foreign visitors had the wish or opportunity to do this. But some mixed more in society than others and even those who frequented no *salons* could of course learn quite a lot by keeping their eyes and ears open.

Some English travellers in France used to regret that they could not keep their noses shut. For Hazlitt the prevalence of unpleasant smells contrasted curiously with French refinement in other respects. Cole was shocked by French spitting and by the indelicacy of their sanitary arrangements: 'We carry to an excess our Delicacy in these Matters, while our Neighbours exceed in the other offensive Extreme. A proper Medium would certainly be the Best.' Arthur Young also reported uninhibited spitting and found the French dirtier in their houses than the English; but he was impressed by the bidet and thought that the French were cleaner in their persons.

French travellers to England commented on the spit and polish in household management. François de la Rochefoucauld observed that there was everywhere a great *surface* cleanliness, though he would not have recommended too close an inspection of kitchens. Far from being struck by the excessive delicacy of the English, La Rochefoucauld was surprised to see the men making free use of chamber pots, placed on the sideboard, after dinner. However, he took it all in his stride. Although he disliked coal fires at first—particularly the smell—he got used to them in time and, when he had done so, found them warmer than wood fires and needing less attention.

Wood and coal offered one of the earliest and most obvious contrasts between England and France. The English were very proud of their coal fires, in spite of the way in which they polluted the environment, and pitied the French for their more primitive form of heating. Misson, at the end of the seventeenth century, conceded that the smell of coal fires was more of a nuisance in the streets than in the houses themselves; but he would observe slyly to his English friends that it was a strange thing that the King, and all the great personages of England, should want to cast themselves voluntarily into the misery of the poor French, by only burning wood in their chambers! A couple of centuries later the standard French complaint in the larger English houses was not the type of heating, but the virtual absence of any heating at all.

One of the most persistent criticisms of the French tourist in England has been the dreariness of the English Sunday. Voltaire attributed it to the influence of the Presbyterians, who had secured that there should be no work or amusement on the Sabbath, no opera, no theatre, no concerts. Could there be anything more boring in the world, La Rochefoucauld wondered, than a strictly observed English Sunday? Stendhal in 1826 was depressed by the use which the English made of their one day of rest—and indeed, though 'heaped with kindness' in England, he was saddened by the general unhappiness of its population. Prosper Mérimée contrasted the freedom of English society in Pepys's time with its nineteenth-century stiffness and formality: 'On comprend qu'on ait donné à l'Angleterre d'alors l'épithète de joyeuse, *merry*, England, qui ètonne un peu l'étranger d'aujourd'hui, surtout le dimanche.' Taine wrote that London on a Sunday presented 'the aspect of an immense and decent cemetery'.

The French Sunday made a cheerful contrast. According to Surtees:

> Sunday is a gay day in France and Boulogne equals the best town in smartness. The shops are better set out, the women are better dressed, and there is a holiday brightness and air of pleasure on every countenance. Then instead of seeing a sulky husband trudging behind a pouting wife with a child in her arms, an infallible sign of a Sunday evening in England, they trip away to the rural *fête champêtre*, where with dancing, lemonade, and love, they pass away the night in temperate if not innocent hilarity.

French aptitude for dancing has often charmed, or irritated, the English. Even in the sixteenth century, when the English had quite a reputation for dancing themselves, Dallington noted its excellence and universality in France:

> . . . rather than faile, the old women themselves, both Gentle and base, who have more toes than teeth, and those that are left, leaping in their heads, like Jacks in Virginals, will beare their part. This argueth (I will not say a lightnes and immodesty in behaviour) but a stirring spirit, and livelynesse in the French nature.

Sir John Carr observed in 1802: 'A stranger is always surprised at beholding the grace and activity which even the lower orders of people in France display in dancing.' Sir Charles Darnley, who was everywhere astonished 'at the prevalence of gravity and silence where I expected nothing but gaiety and noise', noticed the serious attention which Frenchmen devoted to dancing, as well as to their meals and theatres. The 'Countess Benvolio', who helped Mr Jorrocks spend his money in Paris, was 'as all French women are' an admirable dancer. The ball in which she danced with Mr Stubbs 'proceeded with the utmost decorum, for though composed of shopkeepers and such like, there was nothing in their dress or manner to indicate anything but the best possible breeding.'

If Englishmen had been sprightly dancers in the sixteenth century most of them had lost the knack by the time of Victoria. At Mrs Perkins's ball Thackeray condemns M. Canaillard to watch Bob Hely dancing 'like a true Briton, and with all the charming gaiety and abandon of our race, *cavalier seul* in a quadrille.' Turning to his German companion M. Canaillard gives vent to his feelings: 'Oh, ces Anglais! quels hommes, mon Dieu! Comme ils sont habillés, comme ils dansent!'

The English might be inhibited on the dance floor, but they were already famous in the seventeenth century for energetic walking. There are frequent references in all periods to their love of different forms of sport, their preoccupation with horses and their addiction to violent exercise. In particular their fondness for armed and unarmed 'gladiatorial combats' intrigued or shocked seventeenth- and eighteenth-century travellers, who were inclined to see in these crude spectacles a Roman survival in an abandoned outpost of Empire. Yet, in the sixteenth century, it was an Englishman, Dallington, who reproached the French with their immoderate love of exercise and wrote that tennis was played avidly by all classes there: 'Ye would think they were borne with Rackets in their hands.'

In the seventeenth century French travellers to England

recorded heavy smoking, drinking and eating. François de la Rochefoucauld, in the 1780s, was struck by the enormous consumption of meat, tea, beer and port; even the peasants drank quantities of tea. For Louis Blanc, in 1861: 'Tea, in this classic land of inequality, is perhaps the only thing, with death, that tends to equalize conditions a little.' La Rochefoucauld wrote also of the large numbers of servants in well-to-do English houses, many of them idle. The women servants did most of the work; the menservants were largely for show. The Abbé le Blanc had little good to say of English servants: they insisted on tips and gave their masters worse service than the French. Their only virtue was the national one of cleanliness. But then, to the English, 'every form of dependence is unsupportable'.

All in all La Rochefoucauld was rather attracted by English countryhouse life. It was very quiet and retired, but the English themselves did not seem to be bored by it. In the morning everything was free and easy: breakfast at nine o'clock, followed by shooting, fishing or walking. The evenings were more formal. Dinner would begin at four o'clock and drag on for two hours. Then wines and fruit were placed on the brilliantly polished table and, after half an hour, the women would retire. 'C'est alors le plaisir: il n'y a pas un Anglais qui ne soit bien content a ce moment-là.' (The English preference for male society, in clubs and coffee-houses, was a continual surprise to the French.) The young Frenchman enjoyed the political conversation, though found some of the talk rather indecent. Afterwards there would be tea and whist.

Mrs Gaskell in 1862 was more struck by the *breakfasting* arrangements in the Parisian household where she stayed. The first breakfast was extremely simple, though she was given butter 'in deference to our English luxury', and eaten *en déshabillé*. It was followed at eleven by the *grand déjeuner*, by which time Madame would be fully dressed. Mrs Gaskell found it strange living in a flat, but thought the system had distinct advantages: 'I do not dislike this plan of living in a flat especially as it is managed in Paris . . . it seems to me to save one's servant's work, at the least: and besides this, there is the moral advantage of uniting mistresses and maids in a more complete family bond.'

Travellers can be abnormally sensitive to slights and pathetically grateful for attentions. Until the late eighteenth century a Frenchman did not have to be abnormally sensitive to find the rudeness of the English populace distressing. All foreigners in England in the sixteenth century tended to suffer from this, though they have left tributes to the courtesy of the upper classes. But perhaps the French were particularly badly treated. Perlin in 1558 wrote: 'The people of this nation have a mortal hatred of the French as their ancient enemies, and commonly call us French knave, French dog; also whoreson . . .' He was offended by the contrast between this rudeness and the reception of the English in France 'where they are honoured and revered like little gods'. Misson was inclined to regard the incivility of the vulgar in England as more apparent than real. But, just after the Seven Years' War, Cole was told by a Frenchman as a fact that a Frenchman 'known to be such, in London, could not with safety . . . go about his Business' and he could not deny 'but that there is too much Truth in it.' *London and Paris* records an improvement by the time of the early nineteenth century.

Montesquieu's impression of educated English society was that: 'Les Anglais vous font peu de politesses, mais jamais d'impolitesses.' He was ready to dismiss the complaints of French residents at the lack of English hospitality: 'How should the English like foreigners? They do not like themselves. How should they invite us to dinner? They don't invite themselves.' In most capitals, at most periods, resident foreigners have tended to feel neglected—except for the few who have been lionized. The Abbé le Blanc's comments suggest that, in this respect, things were no better in Paris.

When La Rochefoucauld and his party arrived at Bury in the 1780s, there were no other Frenchmen living there. At first people would point them out in the street and say 'Frenchmen, Frenchmen.' ('. . . les Anglais, en général, ne nous aiment pas (surtout le peuple) . . .'); but at the end of four months they came to be regarded as inhabitants. They made quite a lot of acquaintances and the educated citizens showed them much kindness and hospitality, taking the trouble to speak English slowly to them. La Rochefoucauld concluded that one should not be put off by apparent coldness in England: 'The intention is good, it is only the forms that are lacking.'

In pre-Revolutionary France the forms were not lacking and English travellers seldom had to complain of incivility. According to Lister, who visited Paris in 1698: 'The French nation value themselves upon civility, and build and dress mostly for figure:

this humour makes the curiosity of strangers very easy and welcome to them. . . . It is certain the French are the most polite nation in the world, and can praise and court with a better air than the rest of mankind.' Chesterfield advised his son that the Parisians were 'particularly kind to all strangers, who will be civil to them, and show a desire of pleasing. But they must be flattered a little, not only by words, but by a seeming preference given to their country, their manners, and their customs. . . .'

Even the dyspeptic Smollett admitted that the French were generally civil, though he went on to complain that they had 'no sentiment' and that 'their ignorance and superstition put me out of all patience.' Sterne was much less grudging. The French were, for him, 'a people so civilized and courteous and so renowned for sentiment and fine feelings . . .' On being told by a Paris barber that his wig would stand if immersed in the ocean, he detected in this instance of 'the French sublime' a national tendency to profess more than could be performed; but it did not disconcert him.

Of course the French tourist industry had an interest in civility towards foreigners. Cole noted an alertness 'to take all Opportunities to cheat, and make the most of the English . . . who come to make but a short stay among them.' It was different the other way round, he thought, because the French never visited London to spend money, but only to make it. However, let the last word rest with a very typical Englishman: Cobbett, who went to France in 1792, newly married, for the purpose of learning French and studying fortified towns. The six months he spent there were the happiest in his life: 'I went to that country full of all those prejudices that Englishmen suck in with their mother's milk, against the French and against their religion: a few weeks convinced me that I had been deceived with respect to both. I met everywhere with civility, and even hospitality, in a degree that I had never been accustomed to.'

Eighteenth- and nineteenth-century English travellers found much to admire in French social life. Many English had no halfway house between family life and formal entertaining; French society was more relaxed. Arthur Young wrote: 'The French are quiet in their houses and do things without effort.' He found this an agreeable contrast to English love of display. Philip Thicknesse, in the 1760s, formed a high opinion of French society after a stay at St Germain en Laye; he thought that too many of his compatriots had been misled by an acquaintance with 'low-bred' people. 'I am sure that we do not make so much of society as the French do,' wrote Dr Rigby two decades later, 'and I am also sure we are great losers by it'. After visiting Italy, Switzerland, Germany and Holland, he exclaimed: 'How every country and every people we have seen since we left France sink in comparison with that animated country!'

Mrs Trollope, in the 1830s, also welcomed the spontaneity and lack of ceremony in ordinary, educated, Parisian intercourse. The French were less reserved with chance acquaintances than the English and there were more leisured people in Paris, often living in quite a small way, who had time to cultivate the graces of life. Generally speaking she regarded French society as being the most delightful, the liveliest and the gayest in the world. There was only one shadow: ladies of doubtful reputation could still—if of birth and talents—enjoy social standing. Indulgently, Mrs Trollope attributed this fault to a kind of 'sans souci', rather than to absolute immorality.

Mrs Gaskell's French hostess received once a week. There was not much 'preparation of entertainment' and the results could sometimes be dull and sometimes delightful; equally the room would sometimes be full and sometimes empty. But there was always strict punctuality and Madame would accompany 'every departing guest to the room-door, and they part with pretty speeches of affection and good will, sincere enough I do not doubt, but expressive of just those feelings which the English usually keep in the background.'

After staying with a French family Mrs Gaskell realized the falsity of the standard English notion that French society 'is very brilliant, thoughtless, and dissipated: that family life and domestic affections are almost unknown, and that the sense of religion is confined to mere formalities.' She had also had to hear some criticism of English customs. One objection made to her was that the daughters of wealthy houses in England were brought up in luxurious habits, but given too little money when they married: this made 'both children and parents anxious and worldly in the matter of wedlock.' Another was against the English insistence that each married couple must have its own home:

> Somehow tonight we began to talk upon the custom of different families of relations living together. I said it would never do in

> England. They asked me, why not? And, after some reflection, I was obliged to confess we all liked our ways too much to be willing to give them up at the will of others—were too independent, too great lovers of our domestic privacy; I am afraid I gave the impression that we English were too ill-tempered and unaccommodating, for I drew down upon myself a vehement attack upon the difficulties thrown in the way of young people's marrying in England.

Englishmen sometimes found French evening parties less amusing than they had hoped. Mrs Gaskell clearly wilted occasionally while, earlier in the century, Sir Charles Darnley contrasted the 'gloom and formality' in private circles with the liveliness of the streets and promenades. The soirées seemed to him frankly boring, with their lack of noise and locomotion.

From the other side of the Channel the Marquis de Vermont could only describe English society as a series of contradictions:

> The English, supposed to be fond of retirement, were constantly to be found in public.
>
> Simple in their personal habits, they were ostentatious in their establishments and hierarchical in their social life. Their great object was to invite titled people to dinner.
>
> Although devotees of law and liberty, they sided with the oppressors everywhere.
>
> They were well informed and cultivated literature; but they seldom talked about science and letters.
>
> Patrons of music, they never listened to it in silence.
>
> The young ladies were supposed to be domestic, but often behaved with impropriety.
>
> Morality was strict, but prostitutes thronged the streets.

Every country has its paradoxes and there are exceptions to every rule of national behaviour. Voltaire had seen how the English could be gay, when the weather was good enough, and Louis Blanc, watching the mid-Victorian crowds return from Epsom, was enthusiastic: 'Let those who believe the English a grave, cold, phlegmatic people come just now to see what happens on the road. . . . What exuberance of life! What thundering peals of gaiety!' Louis Blanc's contemporary, Taine, was one of those who regarded the English as a phlegmatic people, yet perhaps he would have seen nothing very paradoxical in this momentary exuberance. It would have struck him as the degraded nourishment of violent appetites, originally inherited from gross Germanic tribes and repressed by Puritanism and mechanical labour. In effect, he regarded the Englishman as a highly disciplined savage:

> If the man is Germanic in race, temperament and mind, he was gradually compelled to strengthen, change and entirely turn over his original nature; he is no longer a primitive animal, but a trained animal . . . he has become of all mankind the most capable of acting usefully and powerfully, in all directions. . . .

But Taine, acute observer as he was, was the prisoner of his own racial theory and could, in any case, only observe his own epoch. The impressions of a twentieth-century traveller were very different. When Pierre Maillaud came to England in the 1930s, he found the people 'more easy-going, more casual in business, less tense in their work and more detached in most pursuits than was commonly imagined abroad.' He went on to point out that English individualism was often obscured by English understatement and 'reluctance to display intellectual and moral features'. 'English life does not stimulate nor do English people captivate. . . . The charm, to which one may or may not respond, lies precisely in that which at first is most disconcerting: an extreme freedom of movement and thought, unimpaired by the weight of the community . . .'

This, too, was acutely observed of its epoch. A traveller to England today could still find traces of Taine's 'disciplined animal' and of Maillaud's 'understated individualist'; but he might be more struck by older, or newer, characteristics.

The accounts of French travellers in England have perhaps dwelt more on the perplexities of the English character than has been the case in reverse. If this is so, one part of the reason may be the classical quality of traditional French civilization, with its emphasis on form rather than on individual character. Another may be the French flair for criticism and analysis, as opposed to the English skill at empirical observation.

Except when it comes to things that can be weighed and measured, travellers' accounts are unavoidably subjective, coloured by personal aptitudes and prejudices and shaded by states of digestion and fatigue. A traveller who feels unwanted, who cannot cope with the language, who fails to make friends, or believes that he has been offended, is likely to take a jaundiced view of everything. Older travellers may be put off their stride by unfamiliar food. Younger travellers can fall in and out of love with a people when they fall in or out of love with a person. Intellectuals need fuel for their principles and patriots for their national pride.

One of the earliest French travellers to England, Etienne Perlin, had a few kind things to say about the country; but he was too much of a patriot, or too offended by the patriotism of his English hosts, to give a basically sympathetic account. The English were, for him, foes to good morals and good letters; arrogant, false and seditious; neither strong in war, nor faithful in peace. Justifiably irritated by the English kings' pretensions to the throne of France, he consoled himself with the reflection that, though the English might claim to have beaten the French, they had been chased out of the French kingdom 'like mad dogs' at a time when it was at least seven times smaller than in his own day.

A seventeenth-century French guidebook to England, written by a Jesuit during the time of the Commonwealth, was no more flattering. It described the English people as combining mad violence with northern stupidity: a country 'formerly the home of angels and saints' was become 'a place of demons and parricides.'* (In earlier times the Nordic mists that shrouded the British Isles had displayed, at a distance, tints of sanctity and Arthurian romance.)

After the Restoration, however, Samuel Sorbière was able to record his impressions of a short visit without political prejudice. He found points to criticize: presumption, a certain '*rudesse*', a natural tendency towards idleness and a kind of extravagance of thought. But he also found patriotism and intrepidity: 'Il se trouve en eux je ne scay quoy de grand, qui paroist tenir de l'ancienne Rome.' He respected the English, too, for wanting to be told the truth—though it made them difficult to handle, because they could be as suspicious of politeness as of hostility. Sorbière could speak no English and saw nothing of the country but Kent, London and Oxford; his relatively favourable im-

* Quoted by Jean Jacqart, *L'Angleterre jugée par les Français du XVIIe siècle.*

pressions suggest that he had been well received by educated people. In all his travels, he recorded, he had encountered no greater civility than that shown to him by two merchants at Dover. On his return journey to Dover, the people seemed to him less rude, and the country more beautiful, than when he arrived.

Maximilien Misson's picture of England, at the end of the seventeenth century, was still more sympathetic. It was coloured by gratitude for the generosity shown towards the Huguenot refugees. He conceded that there were faults in the English; but, on the whole, the more one knew them, the more they were to be liked and esteemed. 'What moderation, what generosity, what integrity of heart, what piety and charity . . .' He invoked an eternal blessing of peace and prosperity on the country.

Half a century later the Abbé le Blanc was too orthodox a Frenchman to lose his guard, too much of a chauvinist not to find English chauvinism disgraceful. Nevertheless he had discovered things in England to like and admire; he seldom lost his sense of proportion; he struck a fair balance of compliments and insults. If the insults sometimes predominate, a gift for acid expression may be partly to blame; he was an effective writer, rather than a deep or original observer. He was also writing at a time of acute Anglo-French rivalry. The fifth edition of his work, which appeared two years after the beginning of the Seven Years' War, had to be introduced by a patriotic apology for what he had found to praise.

The young La Rochefoucauld, who was a friend of Arthur Young and spent two years in Suffolk in 1784–5, was a representative of the liberal French aristocracy at a time when it was at its most Anglophile. It was almost inevitable that he should have been enthusiastic about English justice, administration and public spirit. Some aspects of English life made him less enthusiastic and he evidently had moments of (scarcely astonishing) boredom at Bury; but he wrote a decidedly friendly account of his visit as a whole. One of the things he liked was the way in which Englishmen tended to marry later than in France and to choose their partners because they were fond of each other; his present feeling was that an English wife would suit him. Perhaps he had particular, as well as general, grounds for feeling this. At any rate he admitted frankly one subjective factor that recommended English life to him: the dancing was so bad that, although accounted a bad dancer in France, he had a great success at English balls.

A more erudite observer, Hippolyte Taine, visited England in 1861 and 1862 and again in 1871. He saw a great deal and analysed it with scholarly skill and objectivity. So much of what he wrote is brilliant and penetrating that it seems presumptuous to criticize him for drawing too sharp a contrast between humid, 'Germanic' England and sunny, 'Latin' France, between the northern races—inclined to melancholy, violence and drunkenness—and the 'sobres et vives population du midi'. In a closing comparison between Victorian England and France he found advantages on both sides. Three things were better in England:

(a) The political constitution—stable, public-spirited, aristocratic, liberal;

(b) Religion—the subordination of rites and dogmas to morality;

(c) Acquired wealth, productive capacity and the general level of education.

Three things were better in France:

(a) The climate ('On ne peut imaginer combien six ou huit degrés de latitude en moins épargnent de misères au corps et de tristesses à l'âme');

(b) The more equitable distribution of wealth and the relative absence of extreme poverty;

(c) Family life and society—gayer, more agreeable, less inhibited, less hierarchical.

These were not necessarily eternal verities; but it was a balanced comparison—and a largely justified one in the third quarter of the nineteenth century.

English travellers have certainly been no more successful than their French colleagues in attaining complete objectivity. Smollett's disgruntled account of his travels, which had a wide sale in 1766, was heavily influenced by asthma. Sterne, who spent some time in France between 1762 and 1766, looked through rosier spectacles. In his *Sentimental Journey* he described Smollett as the 'learned SMELFUNGUS' who 'travelled from Boulogne to Paris—from Paris to Rome—and so on—but he set out with the spleen and jaundice, and every object he passed by was discoloured or distorted—he wrote an account of them, but 'twas nothing but the account of his miserable feelings.'

Horace Walpole admitted in a letter from France in 1765: 'For so reasonable a person as I am, I have changed my mind very often about this country.' (Hazlitt confessed, during his own stay in France, to changing his opinion about it 'fifty times a day'.) When he visited Paris towards the end of 1765 Walpole wrote that he had been well treated and was on the whole well amused, but the city appeared much worse to him than he recollected: 'The French music is shocking as I knew it was. The French stage is fallen off. . . .' Although the women were good humoured and easy, 'most of the men are disagreeable enough. However as everything English is in fashion, our bad French is accepted into the bargain. Many of us are received everywhere. Mr Hume is fashion itself, although his French is almost as unintelligible as his English.' Walpole developed gout and found that the French had become less gay and cheerful than formerly, too much addicted (alas for Anglomania!) to whist and philosophy. He even decided that the fogs and damps were greater and more frequent than in England. However, everybody was so nice to him in his invalid state 'that I grow to like them exceedingly, and to be pleased with living here, which was far from the case at first.' On leaving Calais in April 1766 he wrote to Sir H. Mann that he had received 'uncommon civilities and real marks of friendship' and certainly meant to return. 'I wish the two nations to live eternally at peace, and shall be glad to pass my time between them. My principles can never grow monarchic, but I never entered in the least into their politics.' He did return to France—in 1769, 1771 and 1775.

Horace Walpole's friend, the Rev. William Cole, had a sadder experience, in that he returned disillusioned after setting out with high hopes. He left for France in October 1765, as a bachelor in his fifties, with the thought that the French climate, food, wine and 'boasted Cheapness' would 'wonderfully accommodate both my Constitution and Fortune'. He also had a great desire to see Paris, because of its reputation as 'the Centre of Taste, Magnificence, Beauty and every Thing that is polite'. Unhappily, whether because of his character as a Protestant clergyman or because of the resentment engendered by the Seven Years' War (in spite of the fashionable Anglomania in Paris), he 'never could see the least Advance . . . but rather the Reverse, in a stiff and reserved distance of any civil Communication.' Cole was only in Paris for a month; he saw something of Walpole, who had not yet warmed to the country, but otherwise does not seem to have gone into society. He did once go to the Comedy and saw a farce called *Le François à Londres*:

> . . . where the English were well ridiculed in the Character of Jack Roast-Beef, a Gentleman of Fortune, but . . . dressed more like a Quaker than any one else: indeed the Character was *outré* overdone: however to do them Justice, the French Marquis was as extravagant a Character; and the winding up of the Scene acknowledged that if the French had more Politeness, the English had more Reason. . . .

In spite of this soothing acknowledgement the sensitive Cole evidently got the feeling that the French looked down on the English. He burst out, apropos of sedan chairs: 'I make the longer Stay upon these Trifles, to shew that these great Regulators of Europe in Point of Trifles, are even outdone by those they affect to treat with Contempt, and call Savages.' Perhaps there was a still more intimate trouble. When, on 6 November, he was 'indisposed with wind in my Stomach', he attributed it to the change in his diet. Abstemious at home because he cared neither for beer nor for Portuguese and Spanish wines, he was now drinking near a bottle a day of Beaune.

Cobbett's happiness in France in 1792 was no doubt heightened by his recent marriage. Arthur Young, who travelled extensively in France just before and just after the Revolution, was conducting a factual inquiry into the state of French agriculture and was less obviously affected, one way or the other, by personal feelings. Yet he too, like Taine, had a subjective bias of a kind, since—apart from his rooted objection to small farm holdings—he was convinced that government could make or mar society and that the faults and iniquities of the French Government were responsible for the lower standard of prosperity and activity in France than in England. Gratified by his criticism of the *ancien régime* the Convention ordered 20,000 copies of his work to be printed in 1793 and distributed gratuitously. But Young, already regretting that he had supplied fuel for revolutionary flames, published *The Example of France a Warning to Britain* in the same year. In spite of his criticisms of the *ancien régime* Young always regarded the French nation as a great one, distinguished by great talents; at one time he was tempted by the idea of acquiring a property and settling in France. True to his principles, he wrote:

> We are too apt to hate the French; for myself I see many reasons to be pleased with them; attributing faults very much to their government; perhaps in our own, our roughness and want of good temper are to be traced to the same origin.

Kipling, who became a great traveller in France and regarded the French and English civilizations as the only ones that really mattered since the fall of Rome, fell in love with France in 1878 at the age of twelve. It was his first visit to France and he paid it with his father, who was in charge of the Indian Arts and Industries section of the Paris Exhibition of that year. He went back to school with the knowledge of a strange, totally different country where everything was charming and the food exquisite. A country of exquisite food and, as he later discovered, 'incredible beauty', hard work and thrift: an irresistible combination for an aesthete/moralist.

I have written of subjective bias as if it was to be taken less seriously than objective appraisement. But of course, when it comes to relations between people and between peoples, it is the subjective element—however capricious and irrational—that matters. Even subjective impressions usually take some account of fact; yet it is sobering, from what small cuttings of hearsay or experience vast creepers of liking or dislike can grow.

FOUR

Exiles

⚜ ❁

TRAVELLERS CAN GET to know everything about a foreign country except what it is like to live there with no prospect of an early return home. That knowledge, which the exile cannot help having, gives him a different outlook. He tends either to identify himself with his new surroundings or to keep himself, nostalgically, as distinct from them as possible. In either case, though his experience of the country may be more intimate than the traveller's, his impressions of it are likely to be less vivid.

There have of course been willing exiles, as well as reluctant ones; but the greater number have settled abroad, and remained there, under compulsion of one kind or another. If this is particularly the case with the French exiles in England, it is not because they have been less adaptable, or the English less welcoming, but because the majority have been political and religious refugees. There were similar English refugees in France, at any rate in the earlier centuries; but they were later outnumbered by people in search of a warmer climate or cheaper living conditions. That, too, could be a form of compulsion—but at least there was an element of choice. The grey skies of England have been less seductive to more or less voluntary exiles of this kind.

Naturally there have been degrees of reluctance, even among the compulsory exiles. The Huguenot refugees of the sixteenth and seventeenth centuries must have been deeply distressed to leave their native land; but they knew that they had to adapt themselves to their new country and they already felt a religious sympathy with it. It was different with the other great wave of French refugees, the *émigrés* who came to England after the French Revolution. Some of them liked or admired England; but they did not look on it as their country; they were marking time there until they could return.

At one extreme of compulsion the English have counted, among their French exiles, a few illustrious captives. King John of France, captured at the Battle of Poitiers in 1356, was imprisoned in England until the sale of a French princess to the Duke of Milan procured his ransom. Charles d'Orléans, father of Louis XII, was taken prisoner after Agincourt and spent twenty-five years in England, mainly at Dover Castle, writing poetry, gazing across the Channel and longing for peace. The most celebrated French exile of all, Napoleon, ended his life, a British captive, in St Helena.

Other royal and imperial French exiles, if reluctant, were at least not under duress. The future Louis XVIII left the Continent to settle in England after Napoleon's victories at Austerlitz, Jena, Eylau and Friedland. His brother, the future Charles X, lodged in Holyroodhouse, Edinburgh, from 1796 to 1799 and returned there for two years after the 1830 Revolution. When Charles's successor, Louis Philippe, lost his throne in 1848, he was smuggled across the Channel by the British Consul at Le Havre, disguised as 'Mr Smith'. Twenty-two years later it was the turn of the Imperial family to fly to England.

Louis XVIII, the only one of these monarchs to die in office, perhaps had the qualities to enjoy exile most. Byron pictured him, in 1823, regretting the quiet comforts of his English country retreat:

> Good classic Louis! is it, canst thou say,
> Desirable to be the 'Desiré'?
> Why wouldst thou leave calm Hartwell's green abode,
> Apician table, and Horatian ode,
> To rule a people who will not be ruled,
> And love much rather to be scourged than school'd?

Crowned heads apart, the revolutions in nineteenth-century France produced a number of political exiles in England—Victor Hugo and Louis Blanc among them—though on a much smaller scale than the 1789 Revolution. It was not until the arrival of the Free French during the Second World War that there was to be another big exodus. But few of these exiles were as long, or as consciously impressive, as Victor Hugo's. He spent eighteen years in the Channel Islands, first in Jersey and then in Guernsey, before returning to Paris in 1870. In his historical novel about seventeenth- and early eighteenth-century England, *L'Homme qui Rit*, he painted his own self-portrait in the person of Lord Clancharlie, republican, stoically virtuous, incorruptible and exiled in Switzerland. Describing the admiration felt for Louis XIV in the England of Queen Anne, Hugo allowed himself an urbane thrust at English acquiescence in the regime of Napoleon III: 'L'amour des Anglais pour leur liberté se complique d'une certaine acceptation de la servitude d'autrui.' A political exile of the 1870s, Jules Vallès, was less urbane. His articles in *La Rue à Londres* contained much to offend—and did offend—English readers. Vallès found London heavy and depressing, tumultuous yet lifeless. But at least he appreciated English liberty and the facilities of the British Museum. Magnanimously he concluded: 'J'ai passé neuf années douloureuses et fécondes entre les murs de la Ville noire, n'ayant véritablement de haine et de mépris que contre le Soho.'

Other French exiles in England had nothing to do with politics. There were always adventurers who wanted to avoid prosecution or embarrassment at home, as well as professional men, artisans and servants in search of money and employment. The Abbé Prévost, one of the first writers to publicize England in France, fled across the Channel in 1733 because he was wanted for debt. Verlaine stayed in England on and off in the 1870s, studying and teaching English, writing or conceiving poetry, and living first with Rimbaud and later with Lucien Létinois. Though some of these exiles returned to France as soon as they could, others stayed on; some became acclimatized, others never.

There were frequent openings in England for French cooks, ladies' maids and hairdressers; but they were seldom in such vogue as after the Restoration of Charles II. Dryden concludes his *Essay of Dramatick Poesie* by making his company of wits separate at the foot of Somerset Stairs. They 'were all sorry to separate so soon, though a great part of the evening was already spent; and stood a while looking back upon the water, which the moonbeams played upon, and made it appear like floating quicksilver: at last they went up through a crowd of French people who were merrily dancing in the open air, and nothing concerned for the noise of Guns which had allarmed the Town that afternoon.' These merry French dancers, oblivious to the sounds of Anglo-Dutch conflict, were no tourists, but servants and artisans. There were other French residents in seventeenth-century London of higher social status. The Duchess of Mazarin installed herself there in 1675, formed a lively Anglo-French circle and, together with her sister, nearly persuaded La Fontaine to come over and join them. Saint-Evremond, whose critical writings had a great vogue in England in the three decades from 1684, was a member of this circle and, although speaking no English, obtained a place at Court as Keeper of the King's ducks.

France's exports of unfortunate rulers in the nineteenth century had already been earned by similar imports in the seventeenth century. Henrietta Maria had to return to her native France in 1644; at first lodged in the Louvre, she was moved to the Palais Royal after Charles I's death. Charles II was also in Paris for a time, but was obliged to move to Brussels when Mazarin concluded his treaty with Cromwell. Louis XIV's hospitality to the fallen James II was more open-handed. La Bruyère witnessed the moving scene when Louis welcomed him at St Germain en Laye in 1688; beef and mutton had been ordered for the English King 'afin de ne rien changer aux habitudes de son pays.' The palace of St Germain en Laye was put at James's disposition and remained the Court of the Stuarts for nearly forty years; the local church is still full of their monuments.

English Roman Catholics had taken refuge in France since the sixteenth century. In the 1600s a number of religious establishments were set up in Paris to minister to their needs. Some of these had long lives. The *Couvent des Filles Anglaises*, founded in 1634, was suppressed in 1796, but restored to its owners by Napoleon. French girls of good family were educated there, partly in English; George Sand was a boarding pupil from 1817 to 1820.

The Jacobite refugees were a familiar sight in the Paris streets of the early eighteenth century. Many of them were from Scotland and Ireland, rather than England: these were 'the fugitive and attainted Scotch and Irish', who frequented the English coffee-house in Paris and against whom Chesterfield warned his son. Bolingbroke wrote scornfully of the 'busy' Irish faces expressing hope and care at the court of the Pretender.

Other English exiles went to France to practise their trades. There were several opportunities for skilled men in factories in the earlier years of the Industrial Revolution. There was also scope in private service, just as there was for French servants in England—though for grooms and nannies, rather than for cooks and ladies' maids. Fugitives from justice, or from morality, were numerous in both directions. Oscar Wilde died in Paris, as Verlaine had lived in England. Englishmen sometimes fought duels on French soil, while Boulogne was famous as a haven for English debtors. Mr Jorrocks, on landing at Boulogne, was indignant to see an Englishman who owed his firm £100 and whom he could not touch. Thackeray paints a lurid picture of the 'English Raff Snob that frequents *estaminets* and *cabarets*; who is heard yelling, "We won't go home till morning!" and startling the midnight echoes of quiet Continental towns with shrieks of English slang. . . . He talks French with slang familiarity; he and his like quite people the debt-prisons on the Continent.'

Even relatively respectable people might have financial reasons for settling in France. Arthur Young wrote of Boulogne:

> It is well known that this place has long been the resort of great numbers of persons from England, whose misfortunes in trade, or extravagance in life, have made a residence abroad more agreeable than at home.

Thackeray's Mr and Mrs Pendennis selected 'the romantic seaport town of Boulogne for their holiday residence' one autumn; their 'main amusement in this delightful place was to look at the sea-sick landing from the steamers.' General and Mrs Baynes were not primarily in search of amusement when they moved, first to Boulogne and later to Paris and Tours. The General's financial conscience was not completely clear: 'To live abroad was cheaper and safer than to live at home. Accordingly Baynes, his wife, family and money, all went into exile and remained there.'

In the nineteenth and early twentieth centuries a sub-species of the impoverished English exile was the young writer or artist, tempted not only by cheap, but also by uninhibited, living. It was usually easier and more enjoyable to be Bohemian in Paris than at home. Thackeray's Philip Firmin, though perhaps not a desperate Bohemian, had 'a crib' on the Left Bank recommended to him by artist friends when he was reduced to writing for an English weekly. 'In former days my gentleman had lived in state and bounty in the English hotels and quarter. Now he found himself very handsomely lodged for thirty francs per month, and with five or six pounds, he has repeatedly said since, he could carry through the month very comfortably.' It was the happiest period of his life: 'Absinthe used to be my drink, sir . . . It makes the ink run, and imparts a fine eloquence to the style.'

Even back in the eighteenth century Horace Walpole had noticed how considerable numbers of English settled in France from motives of economy, though he found it difficult to believe that they could save as much as they had hoped. In a letter of November 1789 he told the Countess of Ossory:

> Two years ago there were above sixty English families at Nice; and a year ago there were said to be 40,000 English in France and Lorraine—numbers indeed from economy; but thrift itself does not live in France on French money nor on what it proposes to save: nor is it easy to save, where everything is charged so high to a Milor Anglais.

Horace Walpole moved in circles where expense was difficult to avoid. Less distinguished and fastidious Englishmen found that they did not have to make the effort of social display in France that would have been expected from them at home. In any case English settlers on the Continent had health and climate, as well as economy, in mind. This must certainly have been the case with the 'sixty English families at Nice'—even Smollett had found the weather there tolerably agreeable. Hazlitt had his own, typically pungent, explanation of why the southward emigration was not still more massive:

> A French gentleman, a man of sense and wit, expressed his wonder that all the English did not go and live in the south of France, where they would have a beautiful country, a fine climate, and every comfort almost for nothing. He did not perceive that they would go back in shoals from this scene of fancied contentment to their fogs and sea-coal fires, and that no Englishman can live without something to complain of.

It was not only the Mediterranean coast that attracted English residents, though no part of France could offer a greater contrast with conditions at home. The invasion of the Dordogne is a recent one; but Pau, in south-western France, became popular with the English upper classes in the years after Waterloo and at one time an English hunt was organized in the neighbourhood. Alfred de Vigny met and married his English wife there. Chantilly had a horse-racing community and an English chaplain. Other Channel resorts, besides Boulogne, had substantial English colonies; Dinard, for instance, was partly 'opened up' by American and English settlers in the nineteenth century and boasted an Anglican church.

Some of the English exiles were absorbed, more or less rapidly, into French society. But many remained partly, or almost wholly, aloof. One of the reasons why the Bayneses moved to Paris was that they had heard that 'the English were invited and respected everywhere.' Once installed in Paris 'Mrs General Baynes' did begin to go out a good deal to evening parties; but they were 'the parties of us Trojans—parties where there are forty English people, three Frenchmen, and a German who plays the piano'. Philip Firmin really lived not in Paris, but in a 'little English village' in the centre of it. Naturally he had occasion to speak French from time to time; 'but it never came very trippingly from his stout English tongue'. When he finally returned to England he was 'glad to be back in the midst of the London smoke, and wealth, and bustle. The fog agreed with his lungs, he said.'

George Moore had a different experience later in the century:

> The years that are most impressionable, from twenty to thirty, when the senses and the mind are the widest awake, I . . . had spent in France, not among English residents . . . but an enthusiast, striving heart and soul to identify himself with his environment. . . . When I returned home England was a new country to me . . . an Englishman was at that time as much out of my mental reach as an Esquimaux would be now.

George Moore was an imaginative and susceptible Irishman; but there were always a number of English exiles who felt the same enthusiasm and were delighted to be taken, however fleetingly, for French.

Bolingbroke, who had done so much to establish peace between England and France, was a striking example of the assimilated English exile. The Abbé le Blanc complained that, whereas the English tended to judge the French after adventurers, some Anglophile Frenchmen tended to judge the English after exceptionally polished specimens, like Bolingbroke and Chesterfield. Bolingbroke had had plenty of time to acquire this polish. He was first attracted to France when he visited it, on his continental tour, as a young man. Having wintered in Paris he wrote from Geneva to Sir William Trumbull, in May 1698:

> France has all the melancholy marks of war and absolute government, which are two of God's sharpest judgements . . . but in spite of all this misery, the luxury and extravagance of Paris is rather increased than diminished; and that is the only place

where effeminacy and courage are friends, and where the pursuit of pleasure does not divert their diligence or lessen their bravery, but the King of France may say this of his soldiers, as Caesar did of his, *Milites suos etiam unguentatos bene pugnare posse.*

Seventeen years later, deprived of office and favour after the return of the Whigs to power, Bolingbroke fled from England disguised as a valet to one of the French King's messengers. An initial period in the Pretender's service did not last long; but, even after he had quitted St Germain en Laye in disgust, he was obliged to spend many years in exile in France. He made the best of them, mixing widely in Paris society and cultivating the company of French scholars. A Frenchwoman, the Marquise de Villette, became his mistress and, later, his second wife. In 1720 he moved to the Chateau de la Source, near Orléans, 'the most beautiful place that Nature ever adorned', where he covered the grounds with inscriptions testifying to his unstained patriotism and stoical tranquillity of mind. Voltaire visited him here and was struck by his command of French. Subsequently, in the 1730s, he lived at Chanteloup in Touraine and Argeville near Fontainebleau.

However much at home in French society, and familiar with French culture, Bolingbroke remained an Englishman, with a full sense of his country's interests. His ambitions were centred in England and, although they were never satisfied, he returned to work and die there. For all his vanity, he managed to bridge the two civilizations with poise and grace. Through his eloquence, learning and fine manners, he contributed a great deal, both in France and in England, to the admiration for England which became good form in the last decades of the *ancien régime*.

The contribution of the Jacobite exiles to French life was in no way comparable with the impact of the Huguenots on England. For one thing, the Huguenot immigration was spread over a longer period. It began early in the sixteenth century, though the refugees were not numerous enough to establish churches and communities in English towns before the Massacre of St Bartholomew. However, the flow did not become a really massive one until after the Revocation of the Edict of Nantes, in 1685. It has been calculated that, after this year, some 70–80,000 refugees were established in England—almost one-fiftieth of the combined population of England and Wales at the time. In the centres where they were chiefly concentrated their proportion to the native population must have been much higher.

The Huguenots were of all ages and classes—gentry, intellectuals, bankers, goldsmiths, weavers. They and their descendants obtained an important position in English commerce: 99 out of 542 London merchants who presented an address to the King in 1745 were of Huguenot stock. Frugal and hard-working they enriched the trades and crafts of the country in all kinds of ways, and played a notable part in preparing England for the Industrial Revolution. A number became wealthy and founded prominent English families.

On the whole the English rallied manfully in the face of this invasion. Writing in his Diary in November 1685 John Evelyn lamented: 'The French persecution of the Protestants raging with the utmost barbarity, exceeded even what the very heathens used . . .' He regretted the 'uncharitable indifference' with which the refugees were received in England. But sooner or later sympathies were aroused and the reception improved. In spite of his own Catholicism James II was obliged to authorize public collections, while Parliament voted funds. Public appeals were periodically made up till 1699; the proceeds were supplemented by payments from the Privy Purse and an annual grant of £15,000 was made by Parliament from 1690 to 1702. A French contemporary, Misson, could not speak too highly of the generosity of the English towards the Huguenots.

There were of course flies in the ointment. Nobody presumably complained (except her husband) when an Englishwoman kept 'four *French* Protestants continually employ'd in making diverse Pieces of superfluous Furniture, as Quilts, Toilets, Hangings for Closets, Beds, Window-Curtains, easy Chairs and Tabourets. . . .'* But the refugee artisans were sometimes blamed for taking the bread out of English working men's mouths. As late as 1711 a petition submitted to the Court of the Goldsmiths' Company by fifty-three working goldsmiths complained 'that by the admittance of necessitous strangers, whose desperate fortunes obliged them to work at miserable rates, the representing members have been forced to bestow much more time and labour in working up their plate than hath been the practice of former times, when prices of workmanship were greater.' Misson observed: 'Since the normal thing is to run down everything which does not con-

* *Spectator*, 17 March 1712.

form to one's own customs, it is not surprising if the English and French who live together criticize each other continually.' But his own view was that, when in Rome, sensible people should behave like the Romans. The Huguenots, generally, must have followed this advice, or they would not have been assimilated so quickly. In the course of a generation or so, they no longer needed to follow it, since they had become Roman themselves.

Countless modern English families must include a French Protestant among their ancestors. The connection has been a source of pride to most Englishmen who have been conscious of it. But the effect on Anglo-French relations has been twofold, since the sense of cousinship with the French has been balanced by an inherited resentment of the persecutions to which the Huguenots were subject before they came to England.*

The emigration after the 1789 Revolution made a considerable psychological impact on the English; but the *émigrés* had a much less direct effect on English life than the Huguenots had done. Equally English life, in general, had a less direct effect on them. The total number of *émigrés*, though considerable, was only a third of that of the late seventeenth-century Huguenot refugees. At one time there were some 25,000 *émigrés*, including a substantial quota of clergy; but these numbers gradually shrank. The clergy began to go back to France in 1801 and by 1802 under two thousand exiles were in receipt of aid.

As a rule the *émigrés* were treated with courtesy and respect. Chateaubriand records how, returning to London as Ambassador, he 'no longer saw my compatriots strolling around, recognizable by their gestures, their way of walking, by the cut and oldness of their clothes, I no longer perceived those martyr priests, wearing the little cape, the three-cornered hat, the long black threadbare frock coat, whom the English would salute in passing.' As in the previous century funds were raised to help. A Committee was set up 'for the Relief of the suffering Clergy of France in the British Dominions'; when a collection was taken for them in the churches, a sum of over £40,000 was raised. Parliament made substantial grants between 1794 and 1810 and those *émigrés* who were not too

* In my own family a Huguenot refugee bequeathed his Bible to his English descendants, together with a dramatic account of the way in which, surviving imprisonment and torture 'by Popish Philanthropy', he returned to his estate in the Ile de France to retrieve the Bible before leaving for England.

proud to apply for it were entitled to a daily shilling. Burke founded a school for children of the poorer *émigrés*. Oxford University had special New Testaments printed and distributed to the priests. In an epistle to the French clergy in 1793 the Bishop of St Pol de Léon wrote:

> The generosity of the English nation surpasses all the instances of benevolence recorded in the history of nations.
>
> May the God of mercies shower down his chosen blessings on a people who seem chosen by heaven to vindicate the violated laws of nature and humanity. May heaven, attentive to our prayers, grant peace and plenty to a country where we are so hospitably entertained. . . .

Naturally enough the *émigrés* were sometimes irritated, as well as grateful, and few of them could ever feel gratitude for the English climate. Those without special English connections tended to live a good deal in each other's company. The more well-to-do settled north of Oxford Street, in a rough square between Portman and Harley Streets. The poorer *émigrés* were more widely scattered, working in the coal trade, making straw hats together with their wives or giving French lessons.* However poor, they kept their social gaiety. The English noted with surprise—with admiration but also with a touch of disapproval—how light-hearted they seemed to be in adversity. According to Chateaubriand: 'They were all very gay. The fault of our nation, lightness (*légèreté*) had at this moment of time changed into a virtue.'

Many years later Mrs Gaskell drew a quiet, sympathetic, idealized portrait of an *émigré* nobleman in *My French Master*. Perhaps she based it on what she had heard in her childhood, or perhaps she was expressing what had become a standard English conception. M. de Chalabre, patient, gentle and neat in appearance, habitually courteous to women of any class or age, was reduced to giving French lessons in an English country neighbourhood. Before 1793 he took the line that 'his assumption of his new occupation could only be for a short time; that the good cause would—*must* triumph.' Then came the terrible news of the execution of Louis XVI. When it was followed by that of Marie Antoinette the English girls in the story cried at night:

* Mrs John Dashwood, in *Sense and Sensibility*, gave each of the Miss Steeles 'a needle book, made by some emigrant'.

> Sitting up in bed, with our arms round each other's necks and vowing, in our weak, passionate childish way, that if we lived long enough, that lady's death avenged should be. No one who cannot remember that time can tell the shudder of horror that thrilled through the country at hearing of this last execution. At the moment there was no time for any consideration of the silent horrors endured for centuries by the people, who at length rose in their madness against their rulers. This last blow changed our dear M. de Chalabre. I never saw him again in quite the same gaiety of heart as before this time.

After the Restoration M. de Chalabre was unable to get back his estate in Normandy. So he returned to England, dropped his 'de' and married a countrywoman 'who did not know a word of French; who regarded the nation (always excepting the gentleman before me) as frog-eating Mounseers, the national enemies of England'.

The *émigrés* who returned to France for good must have done so with mixed feelings about their exile—some gratitude, some respect, some memories of happiness, but also some sense of having lived in a strange land under inevitably humiliating conditions. Except for the grander and wealthier among them they had not been able to mix in England with their social equals, at least not on an equal footing. Perhaps the rather complex way in which the French upper classes seem sometimes to have reacted to the English—a tendency to cultivate English manners and to respect English institutions, while remaining patriotically Anglophobe—dates back to, or was confirmed during, this period. Nevertheless, few of the *émigrés* can have gone home with the feeling that the only relationship possible between France and England was one of hostility.

Napoleon's exile left a bitterer taste. The dreary captivity in St Helena, the petty persecutions of Sir Hudson Lowe, became a part of French folklore. Chateaubriand, always struggling between his admiration and disapproval of Napoleon, thought that the English failed to rise to the occasion when, rejecting the defeated Emperor's appeal to 'the most powerful, the most constant and the most generous' of his enemies, they denied him asylum in England itself. Stendhal sketched the outline of a prose tragedy, entitled 'The Return from the Island of Elba':

> The fifth act is about Waterloo, and the last scene of the fifth act shows the arrival on the rock of St Helena, with the prophetic

> *vision* of six years of torments, base vexations, and pin-prick assassinations, executed by Sir Hudson Lowe.

For Byron the captive was 'the fetter'd eagle'. For Victor Hugo the captor was 'the vulture England':

> Il est, au fond des mers que la brume enveloppe,
> Un roc hideux, débris des antiques volcans,
> Le Destin prit des clous, un marteau, des carcans,
> Saisit, pâle et vivant, ce voleur du tonnerre,
> Et, joyeux, s'en alla sur le pic centenaire
> Le clouer, excitant par son rire moqueur
> Le vautour Angleterre à lui ronger le cœur.

Wellington, as usual, delivered an unruffled verdict. Earl Stanhope records that, late in life, the Duke 'said that he thought the treatment of Napoleon at St Helena gave no substantial ground of complaint, but that Sir Hudson Lowe was a very bad choice. He was a man wanting education and judgement.' At another time Wellington said that he knew Sir Hudson Lowe very well: 'He was not an ill-natured man. But he knew nothing at all of the world and, like all men who know nothing of the world he was suspicious and jealous.'

Chateaubriand himself had a more varied, and on the whole a happier, experience of exile. He successively endured the reluctant exile of the *émigré*, the more or less willing exile of the assimilated and the professional semi-exile of the diplomatist. He first arrived in London in May 1793, and was lodged by a cousin in a Holborn attic. After experiencing the privations and consolations of London *émigré* life, he moved to Beccles in Suffolk where a local antiquarian society wanted a Frenchman capable of deciphering French twelfth-century manuscripts. It was here that he almost became reconciled to his separation from France. He was hospitably entertained in the neighbourhood and struck up a particular friendship with a clergyman's family living four miles from Beccles.

The Rev. Mr Ives had a young wife and a daughter of fifteen. Mr Ives, a Hellenist and a mathematician, had travelled in America and was glad of an audience. 'We drank in the manner of the ancient English and we stayed two hours at table, after the ladies.' It was then the turn of the rest of the family. The daughter, Charlotte, played the piano, while the susceptible Chateaubriand gazed and listened.

But this innocent happiness could not last for ever. Charlotte was susceptible, too, and both she and her mother hoped for a match. Finally the dreadful moment came when Chateaubriand confessed that he was already married and, in deep distress, fled back to London. Later in life he wondered what it would have been like if he had been able to marry Charlotte: 'buried in a county of Great Britain, I would have become a sporting gentleman: not one line would have issued from my pen; I would even have forgotten my language, for I was writing in English and my ideas were beginning to form themselves in English in my head. . . . I would by now count many days of calm, instead of the days of trouble which have fallen to my lot.'

It is intriguing to think of Chateaubriand as an English country gentleman; but it is difficult to imagine him not writing in one language or another, however deeply and permanently buried in Suffolk. Even as it was, he became remarkably well versed in English history and literature. Back in London he made the most of the adjoining countryside: 'We often used to dine in some solitary tavern at Chelsea, on the Thames, while speaking of Milton and Shakespeare. . . . We returned at night to London, by the failing beams of the stars, submerged one after the other in the fog of the city.'

Chateaubriand's picture of late eighteenth-century England has the charm of a romantic watercolour, subdued, vaporously misty, but with touches of luminous colour. Looking back from the 1820s he recalls the countryside sprinkled with small churches, each with its tower and Gray-type churchyard: 'everywhere narrow and sandy paths, valleys filled with cows, heaths mottled with sheep, parks, countryhouses, towns: few forests, few birds, the wind of the sea.' Not to be compared with the fields of Andalusia or the Roman *campagna* it was none the less quietly beautiful: '. . . such as she was, this England, surrounded by her ships, covered with her flocks and professing the cult of her great men, was charming and redoubtable.'

What Chateaubriand most admired were the great Englishmen of this period: the enlightened aristocracy which had produced 'one of the finest and greatest societies to have done honour to the human species since the Roman patriciate'. Separated from the Continent by the long war, the English had kept their national character and unity; there were basically only two classes: patrons and clients; the conservative country gentry were still what they had been; the clergy were 'learned, hospitable and generous'; the great ladies, in their sedan chairs, 'étaient les filles dont le duc de Guiche et le duc de Lauzun avaient adoré les mères'. Chateaubriand used to see Pitt walking through St James's Park to visit the King, dressed in black, sword at side, hat under arm, climbing up two or three steps at a time: 'Il ne trouvait sur son passage que trois ou quatre émigrés désoeuvrés: laissant tomber sur nous un regard dédaigneux, il passait, le nez au vent, la figure pâle.' Later Chateaubriand had a sight of the old, mad King at Windsor, wandering like Lear:

> Il s'assit devant un piano dont il connaissait la place, et joua quelques morceaux d'une sonate de Händel: c'était une belle fin de la vieille Angleterre. Old England!

La vieille Angleterre! Many French patriots have had a weakness for it, who have had misgivings about the England of their own times. Chateaubriand's memories of eighteenth-century England are brilliant and perceptive; but they are tinged with nostalgia for his own youth and softened by the lack of current conflict. When he turns to Waterloo and St Helena the English become 'the implacable enemies of France' and the 'seducers of the waves'. For all his opposition to Napoleon, he could never completely forgive—or even really admit—the Emperor's defeat at English hands.

Chateaubriand was made much of when he returned briefly to London, as Ambassador, in 1822. He found things and persons to respect or admire, including Castlereagh and the former Charlotte Ives, now Lady Sutton. But he looked at the present with less sympathy than the past. The fashionable ladies failed to attract him (one was singled out for praise because of her French manner); he found that English society had become more frivolous than French society ('Tous les Anglais sont fous par nature ou par ton'); he was oppressed by the pomp of his Embassy; and he regretted the disappearance of Old England. With interest, but without enthusiasm, he observed the effects of the Industrial Revolution, the advent of *general* ideas and the way in which society had lost its *private* character. 'Summoning before me the centuries of Albion, passing in review reputation after reputation, seeing them collapse in turn, I feel a sort of painful dizziness.'

Things change; societies dissolve and re-form; people outgrow our conception of them. A man living in one country has time to adjust himself to successive developments. But few experiences can be more disturbing than change in a foreign country, known and perhaps loved in youth and re-visited in old or middle age.

The Norman French may be the last people to have conquered England; but, in the nineteenth century, the English retaliated by colonizing parts of France. It was not of course quite the same thing as in more remote parts of the world. The natives were not so 'native'; the local authorities had to be taken more seriously; mixed marriages were not unthinkable; and tame Frenchmen might turn up at English parties. Free from imperial responsibilities the colonizers could allow themselves, more or less, to relax. But the framework of clubs, croquet parties, charades, Anglican churches and enterprising horticulture was as inevitable in the French resorts most frequented by the English as in any tropical outpost.

Perhaps the supreme example was Cannes. Lord Brougham first planted the flag there, in 1834, after being prevented by a cholera epidemic from getting to Nice. Struck by the climate, rather than by the beauty of the site, he decided to build a house there for his invalid daughter. He paid three times the market value of a piece of land and got a French architect to put up a villa, which was completed in 1838 and which he called, after his daughter, the Chateau Eléonore-Louise. He was never tired of vaunting his perspicacity in selecting exactly the right climatic spot—infinitely healthier, he was convinced, than the other side of Cannes. He returned to it every winter until his death in 1868.

Brougham took a great interest in the English colony and had some distinguished French friends. One of these, Prosper Mérimée, reported him in 1859 as 'dissatisfied with everybody and uttering Jeremiads on everything'. But his only lasting link with a local personality seems to have been with M. Borniol, a notary and former Mayor, with whom he corresponded ceaselessly about personal and local business. Brougham was excessively authoritarian and often difficult to manage; but he had, after all, something to contribute to the neighbourhood. Perhaps spurred on by Borniol, he applied to Louis Philippe for a grant of money for making a harbour. When this was inaugurated in 1838, a local versifier paid him a handsome tribute:

Honneur à Brougham l'orateur
D'Albion la plus belle gloire!
Du Port il fut l'instigateur;
N'en perdons jamais la mémoire.

Cannes has indeed been faithful to Brougham's memory; three years after his death J. R. Green visited the place and wrote:

> . . . this Cannes is not so much Provincia Romana as Provincia Britannica or Broughmannica; its centre being 'Le Squar de Lordbrougham' and its shrine his tomb whereon is written a verse of 'His Lordship's favourite hymn'. Tait, whom I caught up here, tells me that hymns were Brougham's last mania. . . .

A statue, erected in 1878, still stands near the Old Port, which Brougham helped to promote. It shows him standing, deep in thought but rejuvenated by the climate, with his left hand resting on a palm tree and clutching a rose. ('Il enlace au palmier la rose d'Angleterre . . .') Somewhere at the foot of the monument reposes a benevolent lion.

Stéphen Liégeard composed sixteen eloquent strophes to celebrate the erection of this monument. Here, particularly eloquent, are the two last:

Brougham est parmi nous . . . Regardez! sa grande ombre
Pour le marbre éclatant délaisse l'urne sombre,
Westminster et ses nefs le réclamaient en vain;
A tous ces froids honneurs, fils de la brume grise,
Il préfère un ciel bleu, l'onde immense, ou la brise
Dans les bruyères du ravin;

Et premier citoyen de la ville bénie
Que tira du néant l'éclair de son génie,
Il offre, en joyeux don, son âme par moitié
Aux deux nations soeurs dont la main détrompée
Signa, sous la mitraille, et du bout de l'épée
Le pacte saint de l'amitié.

Another creator of modern Cannes, T. R. Woolfield, bought some property there in 1846. Later he settled in the Villa Victoria, where he laid out a croquet lawn, planted gooseberry bushes and sowed eucalyptus trees with seed obtained from the Royal Botanic Gardens in Sydney. He secured permission from the French Government, in 1855, to build an English church at his own expense; the work began the same year and the completed building was consecrated, rather appropriately, by the Bishop of Madras. Although the population of Cannes were eager to have a wealthy English colony (they could see the prosperity that foreign residents had brought to Nice), their clergy were not so eager to allow the Protestant cult this foothold. But these suspicions were in time overcome; the Protestant clergymen were so evidently not there to proselytize, but to make their English parishioners feel at home. In the palmiest days of the colony there were as many as four Anglican churches and one Presbyterian.

Woolfield's gardener, John Taylor, became estate agent, banker and general purveyor to the English colony and was appointed British Vice-Consul in 1884. His business was continued by his son, who could speak Provençal, and grandson. There was no lack of clients; for most of the nineteenth century the English had a clear lead over other visitors to Cannes. About half of those who stayed at the Hôtel de la Poste, between 1836 and 1846, had been English. A list of visitors kept by John Taylor and son in 1876 showed 750 English, 490 French, 90 Germans, 52 Americans and 24 Russians. Later, the French began to go to Cannes in increasing numbers themselves and by 1901 less than a third of the winter visitors were English. But the connection was still strong enough to ensure the success of celebrations held in 1929 to mark the twenty-fifth anniversary of the *Entente cordiale*. In the presence of the Lord Mayors of York, Manchester, Cardiff and Norwich, as well as of visiting French and British cruisers, four official banquets were held, together with a battle of flowers and a Venetian fête terminating in an 'Anglo-French apotheosis'.

The social life of the English colony seems to have been curiously reminiscent of Simla, except that it was naturally more fashionable and cosmopolitan. There were many grand visitors. A bust of Edward VII, on the Croisette, recalls that he was a faithful guest. Prince Leopold died at the Villa Nevada in 1884 and Queen Victoria, herself a winter visitor to Grasse, had a monument put up to him in the English Cemetery. In 1869 the Crown Princess of Prussia and Princess Alice spent two months at the Grand Hôtel. When a local band came to play beneath their windows, the musicians were gently told that it was against English principles to hear secular strains on a Sunday, but were asked to return at eight o'clock the following morning.

The colonizers left their mark in stone. A French nineteenth-century guidebook to Cannes, referring to the numerous English villas at one end of the Rue d'Antibes, was discreetly tactful:

> All these villas are more elegant, more grandiose, the one than the other. Their graceful architecture would suggest that, in the town of Cannes, British stiffness (*la morgue britannique*) is no longer any more than an empty word.

Not all reactions were so kind. One visitor was bewildered by the style of the more imposing mansions: should he be admiring a Venetian palace, a Hindu temple or a Gothic fortress? Prosper Mérimée wrote to the eminent architect, Viollet-le-Duc, in 1856:

> The English have settled here as in conquered territory. They have built fifty villas or chateaux each more extraordinary than the other. . . . It is impossible to pass in front of these abominations without longing to set fire to them.

But no part of Cannes recalls its Victorian English residents more poignantly than the Cemetery which the Empress of India herself visited in 1887 and declared 'well and prettily kept'. In peaceful and fragrant surroundings rows of tombstones, set up between the 1850s and 1920s, record the names of men and women born in Grimsby, Liverpool, Bristol, Ipswich, Edinburgh and London. Colonels of Engineers lie here with their wives, Comptrollers of Customs, Vicars, First Baronets, Physicians, Children of Scottish Peers. One or two memorials show that, after their husbands' deaths, widows returned to live in England, pending reunion in the grave. The familiar quotations ('God is Love' or 'Is it well with the Child? It is well') are mostly in English; but here and there are French phrases and some families were clearly Anglo-French.

It is difficult to know what is so moving about the sight of these graves, unless it is that the contrast between English conventions and Mediterranean sights and scents evokes the fragility of exile and so deepens the usual graveyard sense of the fragility of life. When Matilda Hankey, the eldest daughter of a Sussex gentleman, died in Cannes in 1872, at the age of forty-six, somebody chose an austerely suitable inscription for her tomb:

> We have not here an abiding city.
> But we seek that which is to come.

Perhaps the English had no 'abiding city' in Cannes and perhaps, however delightful they found it, they were aware of this at the bottom of their hearts. But, after years of foreign sunshine, they would have been exiles in their own land, too. Protected by familiar objects and routines they may have felt themselves as much at home as they could expect, in any country, to be.

FIVE

The Glass of Fashion

It would be difficult to say which of the two peoples, the French or the English, is the more conservative in its personal habits. In some ways the French have been even more firmly attached than the English to their way of life, less ready to change their eating habits and their furniture, more reluctant to experiment with new modes of behaviour. Yet, at the same time, fashion has traditionally been taken more seriously in France than in England.

Perhaps this paradox is more apparent than real. The mass production of modern times has tended to make all classes fashion-conscious; but until quite recently it was only a small class in any country that had the means and the leisure to compete. If French society as a whole used to be still more conservative than English society it was not that the French were more reactionary by temperament and perhaps not even that their civilization was more perfect. It was rather because France had remained primarily Catholic and rural; because there was less diffusion of wealth in the earlier centuries; and because, after the Revolution, the old establishment tended to cherish tradition in self-defence.

However conservative the masses, the French classes have as a rule been keener and more sure-footed in their pursuit of fashion than their English counterparts. This is partly explained by the greater importance, the more central position, and the more polished civilization, of France in the earlier centuries. But it also seems to reflect something in the French character: a quickness, a love of elegance, a definiteness of taste and a reluctance to be bored. Back in the sixteenth century Dallington observed the swift changes of fashion in France, much more frequent than in other lands. In the eighteenth century Chesterfield wrote:

Fashion is more tyrannical at Paris than in any other place in the world; it governs even more absolutely than their King, which is saying a great deal.

There have been few times when French styles have not been noted, and imitated, in England. For a long time the balance of fashion was entirely in France's favour. The influence of English styles on the French was slight before the eighteenth century and, since then, has been spasmodic rather than regular. Sometimes English fashions have attracted the French by suggesting superior moral force or discipline; sometimes through a vigorous extravagance which has shocked, but temporarily silenced, French good taste. French Anglomania in the eighteenth century could be violent, though it was far from universal: beginning with admiration for English philosophy and the free English constitution it spread to novels, horses, gardens, even hats and tea. Similarly, in the nineteenth century, the disciplined type of the English gentleman—his clothes, pursuits and deportment—gained ground in France as the symbol of a sort of English superiority. The type seemed so immutable, almost so definitive, as to discourage the whole notion of fashion. But, for all its sobriety, it had a moral, as well as sartorial, elegance which appealed.

Quite different was the appeal of Byronism and of the English dandies of the early nineteenth century. This was pure fashion, unalloyed by virtue; its success was that of exotic energy and abandon. (There was something a little mad, even in Brummell's austerity.) The same seems true of the success of English pop fashions, in clothes and music, in the 1960s.

It follows that English fashion in France tends to veer between the conventional and the extreme. Alternately bored/edified and shocked/excited by the English taste, the French take to it—or rather to their own version of it—when they feel the need of moral fibre or fresh blood. The influence of French fashion in England has been more pervasive but, at least latterly, more discreet. It has tended to refine, rather than to fortify; it has shone less fitfully; perhaps it has been more genuinely, because less consciously, absorbed.

The most substantial and lasting achievements of English fashion in France have been masculine: sport, particularly anything to be with horses; well-cut men's clothes; dignified study and dining-room furniture. French fashion in England has had a more feminine target: cookery; clothes for smart women; elegant furniture for the bedroom and the boudoir. This is not surprising given the traditional importance of women in French 'society'. England still strikes the French as a man's world, where the club is mightier than the *salon*.

Lamenting the decline of chivalry, Burke wrote in his *Reflections on the Revolution in France*:

> It is not clear, whether in England we learned those grand and decorous principles and manners, of which considerable traces yet remain, from you, or whether you took them from us. But to you, I think, we trace them best. You seem to me to be—*gentis incunabula nostrae*. France has always more or less influenced manners in England; and when your fountain is choked up and polluted, the stream will not run long, or not run clear, with us, or perhaps with any nation.

When Burke wrote this passage, the claim that France had 'always more or less influenced manners in England' was more self-evident than it would be today. Since the Norman invasion, if not before, good manners in England had been (Anglicized) French ones. Nicander Nucius, a native of Corfu who visited England in 1545–6, found little goodwill towards the French, but noted the extent of French influence:

> As regards their manners and mode of living, ornaments and vestments, they [the English] resemble the French more than others, and for the most part they use their language. And in feasts and drinkings, and in pledgings of health and carousels, they differ in nothing from the French.

Burke's contemporary, Arthur Young, found at the Duc de Liancourt's country seat 'the mode of living, and the pursuits, approach much nearer to the habits of a great nobleman's house in England than would commonly be conceived. . . .' No doubt this was partly because the Anglophile Duke had adopted some English customs; but it was basically because the French aristocracy had set standards which became the civilized norm in England and elsewhere.

Elizabeth's Court was both strict and splendid. In his tragedy, *Bussy d'Ambois*, George Chapman makes Henri III exclaim:

> . . . Our French Court
> Is a mere mirror of confusion to it:

The king and subject, lord and every slave
Dance a continual hay; our rooms of state
Kept like our stables; no place more observ'd
Than a rude market-place: and though our custom
Keep this assur'd confusion from our eyes,
'Tis ne'er the less essentially unsightly . . .

But this did not stop the young courtiers of Tudor and Stuart times from following, at a distance and with a provincial difference, the fashions set by French courtiers. According to Bastide '. . . vers 1632 et vers 1670 tout ce que le pays comptait de gens frivoles, désœuvrés et irréfléchis souhaitait paraître français.' In *Henry VIII* Shakespeare makes the older men at Henry's Court react as they must have done in his own experience. The Lord Chamberlain asks indignantly:

Is't possible the spells of France should juggle
Men into such strange mysteries?

'New customs', replies Lord Sands,

Though they be never so ridiculous,
Nay, let 'em be unmanly, yet are followed.

Sir Thomas Lovell reports to willing ears a new proclamation for the reformation of 'our travell'd gallants, that fill the court with quarrels, talk and tailors':

. . . They must either—
For so run the conditions—leave those remnants
Of fool and feather, that they got in France,
With all their honourable points of ignorance
Pertaining thereunto—as fights and fireworks;
Abusing better men than they can be,
Out of a foreign wisdom—renouncing clean
The faith they have in tennis, and tall stockings,
Short blister'd breeches, and those types of travel,
And understand again like honest men;
Or pack to their old playfellows: there, I take it,
They may, cum privilegio, wear away
The lag end of their lewdness, and be laugh'd at.

The company feels that this would be good riddance, but a loss to the ladies, since 'the sly whoresons/Have got a speeding trick to lay down ladies:/ A French song and a fiddle has no fellow.'

French fashions, as adopted in England, often had the spice of the immoral. The *Spectator*, striking a bluff English note at a time of war with France (1711), wished there was an Act of Parliament for prohibiting the import of 'French fopperies':

> The Female Inhabitants of our Island have already received very strong Impressions from this ludicrous Nation . . . the whole Discourse and Behaviour of the *French* is to make the sex more Fantastical, or (as they are pleased to term it) more awaken'd, than is consistent either with Virtue or Discretion.

A year later the *Spectator* castigated the immodesty of 'Female Cavaliers' who imitated the dress of the opposite sex by wearing riding habits:

> I must observe that this Fashion was first of all brought to us from France, a Country which has infected all the Nations of Europe with its Levity. I speak not this in derogation of a whole People, having more than once found fault with those general Reflections which strike at Kingdoms or Commonwealths in the Gross. . . . I shall therefore only Remark, that as Liveliness and Assurance are in a peculiar manner the Qualifications of the *French* Nation, the same Habits and Customs will not give the same offence to that People, which they produce among those of our own Country. Modesty is our distinguishing Character, as Vivacity is theirs. . . .

Misson had frankly to admit that there was less gaiety at English balls than in the French Court, though he added sagely that 'the sweetest pleasures are not the most turbulent and tumultuous ones.' The English have often been uneasily conscious that their neighbours' manners were fitter than their own for getting the best out of social occasions. Chesterfield wrote of 'the cheerful, easy good-breeding of the French'. He found the English more awkward in their civilities and duller at conversation in mixed companies, probably because Englishwomen, besides being 'naturally more serious and silent', were 'not near so well informed and cultivated as the French'. Again: 'It must be owned that the Graces do not seem to be natives of Great Britain. . . . Since barbarism drove them out of Greece and Rome, they seem to have taken refuge in France. . . .' However fatuous, Buck, the anti-hero of Foote's *The Englishman Returned from Paris*, draws an effective contrast between the ease, the wit, the wine, the *badinage* of a French table and the dull formality of many English eighteenth-century entertainments:

> Then, in solemn silence, they proceed to demolish the substantials, with perhaps, an occasional interruption, of, 'Here's to you, friends', 'Hob or Nob', 'Your Love and mine'. Pork succeeds to beef, pies to puddings. The cloth is removed: madam, drenched with a bumper, drops a courtesy, and departs: leaving the jovial host, with his sprightly companions, to tobacco, port and politics.

French influences no doubt helped gradually to refine the English social scene; but it was uphill work. Disraeli, in *Coningsby*, described Rome as the type of conquest; Jerusalem, of faith; Athens, of art: 'In modern ages, Commerce has created London; while Manners, in the most comprehensive sense of the word, have long found a supreme capital in the airy and brightminded city of the Seine.' He agreed with Arthur Young* in praising the elegant informality of French receptions, as compared with the pompous and unhomely English 'at homes':

> The art of society is, without doubt, perfectly comprehended and completely practised in the bright metropolis of France. An Englishman cannot enter a saloon without instantly feeling he is among a race more social than his compatriots . . . There is, indeed, throughout every circle of Parisian society, from the chateau to the cabaret, a sincere homage to intellect. . . . In England, we too often alternate between a supercilious neglect of genius and a rhapsodical pursuit of quacks. In England when a new character appears in our circles, the first question always is, 'Who is he?' In France it is, 'What is he?' In England, 'How much a year?' In France, 'What has he done?'

The French were even more convinced of their superior social talent than the English were. For that matter, still fewer French could understand good English conversation than vice versa. But, in spite of this, the prestige of Victorian England ensured that English manners made penetrating raids into France throughout the nineteenth century. Proust records some of the snobbish Anglicisms that came into vogue. Odette has visiting cards made for her husband, with 'Mr Charles Swann' inscribed on them. Octave at Balbec is sporting, unintellectual, good at clothes,

* Cf. p. 98 above.

cigars, horses and 'English drinks'. 'The lady in pink', whom the narrator meets when he calls on his Uncle Adolphe, is delighted with the boy:

> 'He will be a perfect gentleman' she added, closing her teeth to give the phrase a light British accent. 'Couldn't he come some time to take a *cup of tea*, as our neighbours the English say?'

Bloch reappears at the end of *Le Temps Retrouvé*, transfigured by a monocle and an English *chic*:

> The mere presence of this monocle in Bloch's face was enough to dispense with the question whether it looked well or not, as with those English objects of which a shop assistant says 'c'est le grand chic', after which one no longer dares to wonder whether one likes them.

Somebody wears a *smoking*, or dinner jacket, and Proust rightly comments that in France every more or less British article is given the name that it does *not* have in England. M. de Charlus, determined to kiss Charlie Morel on both cheeks, insisted that good manners were 'les vieilles manières françaises sans ombre de raideur britannique.'

All this was, more or less, the *chic* of disciplined convention, not of vigorous excess. The latter was more in vogue earlier in the nineteenth century. In 1822, as Ambassador in London, Chateaubriand noticed the rapid changes in modish English slang. The 'Fashionable' of the time, he later wrote, was required to look ill and unhappy:

> . . . il devait avoir quelque chose de négligé dans sa personne, les ongles longs, la barbe non pas entière, non pas rasée, mais grandie un moment par surprise, par oubli, pendant les préoccupations du désespoir; mèche de cheveux au vent, regard profond, sublime, égaré et fatal; lèvres contractées en dédain de l'espèce humaine; cœur ennuyé, byronien, noyé dans le dégoût et le mystère de l'être.

By 1839 it had become the turn of the well-groomed dandy, who was expected to cultivate a light, conquering, insolent air:

> . . . il décèle la fière indépendance de son caractère en gardant son chapeau sur la tête, en se roulant sur les sofas, en allongeant ses bottes au nez des ladies assises en admiration sur des chaises

devant lui . . . Il faut que sa santé soit parfaite, et son âme toujours au comble de cinq ou six félicités.

During the heyday of the 'Fashionable', when a second wave of Anglomania was just beginning to break down the post-Waterloo resentment of French youth, a treatise on cravats, 'freely translated from the English', was published in Paris. There is still (in 1823) a strong dash of bitters in this work. The foreword laments that the French public should seek 'new emotions in the romantic productions of Walter Scott, and nervous contractions in the phantasmagorical conceits of Lord Byron'. A letter from London to the translator, enclosing the treatise, refers to the respect mistakenly felt on the Continent for English gravity and claims that, contrary to the general belief, fashion has quite as great a power in England: 'If its courtiers here have less elegance and less grace, perhaps they make up for it by a blinder devotion and a more absurd servility.' The French *élégant* is the equivalent of the English 'fashionable'; the French *petit-maître* is the English 'exquisite'; the 'dandy' is a bit of both; the 'Corinthian' is *un jeune homme du suprême bon ton*; as to the 'ruffian', he is 'an essentially English character'.

In this letter there is a portrait of the young Sir G., who at first appears as an 'exquisite', surrounded by bric-à-brac and cosmetics. So tightly laced in his corset that he is unable to dine very actively, he whistles throughout the opera and then goes to an evening reception where he lies down on a sofa in front of a glass. Six months later he has turned himself into a 'ruffian', this time surrounded by saddles, bridles and whips. No more corset, so he has a very intemperate dinner, animated by bets rather than conversation, and followed by street exploits which end in a night in gaol. In his third metamorphosis Sir G. gets himself elected to Parliament.

It was a sign of the times that the French should take any interest, however jaundiced, in English methods of tying cravats. Until towards the end of the *ancien régime* fashions in dress, male as well as female, moved almost exclusively westwards. Sir Fopling Flutter, in Etherege's *The Man of Mode*, brings back a French *valet de chambre* with him from his travels and extols his genius with cravats: 'By heavens! An Englishman cannot tie a ribbon.' There was a brief attempt at rebellion in 1666, when Charles II and the men of his Court abandoned French fashions for a time; but they soon came back to them. Earlier in the seventeenth century the French Count of Montsurry is made to say of the English, in Chapman's *Bussy d'Ambois*:

> No question we shall see them imitate
> (Though afar off) the fashions of our Courts,
> As they have ever ap'd us in attire;
> Never were men so weary of their skins,
> And apt to leap out of themselves as they,
> Who, when they travel to bring forth rare men,
> Come home delivered of a fine French suit;
> Their brains lie with their tailors and get babies
> For their most complete issue; he's sole heir
> To all the moral virtues that first greets
> The light with a new fashion, which becomes them
> Like apes, disfigur'd with the attires of men.

Arthur Young wrote on the eve of the Revolution that the French had given the *ton* in dress to all Europe for more than a century, though he added that clothes had by his time become an object of greater expense in England. The Duke of Wellington, when Ambassador at Paris, was not too patriotic to adopt contemporary French fashions, notably trousers instead of breeches.

However, by Wellington's time the tide had turned. Even in the eighteenth century English male fashions had begun to advance in France. The *redingote* (riding coat), a big coat buttoned up in front with slits for riding and a high collar, crossed the channel in about 1725. Damis appears in Saurin's *L'Anglomane* 'en habit à l'Anglaise, avec une petite perruque ronde', while the maid Finette is obliged to wear 'un petit chapeau à l'Anglaise'. In the 1780s a fashion of dressing more simply, in the English—or rather American—way, became widespread in France. Men's clothes got darker and plainer; they began leaving powder out of their hair and would sometimes even dine in boots. The Comte de Ségur recorded in his Memoirs:*

> Our imitation of their dress was not a triumph accorded to their taste, industry and superiority in the arts. . . . It was the desire to naturalize among ourselves their institutions and their liberty.

After the Revolution had broken out, Arthur Young was struck by the dishevelled appearance of the *enragés*—so different from the

* Quoted by Lockitt, op. cit.

frivolous elegance cultivated by the French before more serious things came to occupy their minds.

What the French were beginning to imitate was not the formal dress of upper-class Englishmen, which was still more or less imitated from the French, but the simpler dress worn by men who lived in the country and avoided ceremony. Yet the Abbé le Blanc had already noted in England, some decades before, an excessive 'affectation of simplicity' even among the clothes-conscious. In contrast to the foppish and bejewelled French *petit-maître*, he wrote, the young English blood affected 'a short periwig without powder, a handkerchief round the neck instead of a cravat, a sailor's jacket, a tough knotted stick, vulgarity of speech and manner, the affectation of the airs and imitation of the morals of the vilest part of the population.'

As early as 1785 Pinkerton, in *Letters of Literature*, felt able to sound a note of patriotic triumph: 'As we now lead the French in fashions in dress, let us attempt to lead them in literature.' The Vicomte de Noailles admitted to Horace Walpole, at the Duke of Queensbury's in 1792, that the English had made big advances both in their clothes and in their food. 'What a nation they are!' was Walpole's comment: 'Even their vanity amidst all their miseries and disgraces is not to be allayed, is unalterable. . . . I believe he thought he remembered that we used twenty years ago to wear goatskins and live upon haws and acorns.' During the long war, the emancipation of English male fashions became complete. By the end of it (according to *London and Paris*) no sartorial indulgence was accorded to foreigners in London: a hat too wide, a waistcoat too short, or a coat too long, were enough to banish them from 'the elegant circles of this gay metropolis'. The unfortunate visitor must be fitted out by an English tailor before he could 'pass unquizzed through a crowd of dandies'. In another few years the Frenchman was hardly safe from English quizzing even in his own capital. The severe restraint imposed by Brummell set the standard for the correct Englishman for well over a century. Impregnable in his own correctness he could seldom regard any foreigner as a serious competitor: there was always something not quite right about the fellow. Mrs Trollope, watching the crowds in the Tuileries in the 1830s, was pained by the whimsy—bordering, she felt, on ridicule—of some of the male clothes she saw.

Supreme self-confidence is difficult to resist. The French almost ended by conceding English superiority in male fashions, though they preferred to wear them with their own kind of dash. English tailors and English cloth still have a reputation in France. There was a time when perfectionists had their laundering and starching done in England.

If Mrs Trollope disapproved of the men's clothes she saw, she had nothing but praise for the neatness and good taste of the women's dresses. Everywhere in the world, she said, you could see French fashions, but you had to go to Paris to see how cleverly Frenchwomen wore them. It was all the more admirable, because they changed their dresses less frequently during the day than some Englishwomen did, and usually dressed less formally.

When it comes to women's fashions, it is only recently that the English have been able to compete at all—except perhaps in country clothes. Misson was told by Englishwomen at the end of the seventeenth century that 'we [the French] do the inventing, and they refine our inventions.' But he does not seem to have been interested enough in dress to judge how far the refinements were improvements. Taine was not impressed by the Hyde Park review of toilettes between 5 and 7 p.m.; the colours were crude, he thought, and the taste exaggerated: 'Beauty and finery abound; but taste is lacking.' Treminta wrote to the *Spectator* in 1712 bewailing how, during the war, her sex had had to labour 'under the insupportable Inventions of *English* Tire-women, who tho' they sometimes copy indifferently well, can never compose with that *Goût* they do in *France*.' She declared herself 'so great a lover of whatever is *French*, that I lately discarded an humble Admirer, because he neither spoke that Tongue, nor drank Claret.'

Miss Nancy Mitford makes Charles Edouard say to his future wife, in *The Blessing*:

> . . . Frenchwomen always give one to understand that arranging themselves is full-time work. Now you English, like flowers in a basket, are not arranged, which is quite all right when the flowers are spring flowers.

If most Englishwomen have traditionally spent less time in arranging themselves than Frenchwomen, they have also tended to give less time and thought to preparing food. English cooking is, for most Frenchmen, a rich joke but a poor experience. This has been so for centuries. It was a late eighteenth-century Italian who said that, while there were sixty religious sects in England, there was only one sauce; but the reaction was typically French. Sorbière wrote in the middle of the seventeenth century:

> The English are not great epicures, and the table of the greatest Lords, when they have not got French cooks, is only covered with large pieces of meat. . . . The pastry is coarse and badly cooked. The stews and preserves are uneatable. The use of forks is almost non-existent . . .

Over a century later La Rochefoucauld condemned English food as being badly prepared, even in the best houses; the great luxury was to have a French cook, but it cost a lot of money. Taine thought that the English cuisine was tasteless: 'One is amply and wholesomely nourished, but one has no pleasure in eating.' Hence the widespread use of spices and condiments. Jules Verne painted a gruesome picture of the meal which, in all essentials, the eccentric Phileas Fogg ate twice every day. It:

> consisted of an hors d'œuvre, a boiled fish set off by a 'Reading sauce' of first quality, some scarlet roast beef flavoured by mushroom ketchup, a pudding filled with rhubarb stalks and green gooseberries, a morsel of Cheddar—the whole washed down by some cups of that excellent tea, specially selected for the pantry of the Reform Club.

Of course there were some compensations. English meat was always famous; in the earlier centuries it was a commonplace that the English ate more meat and the French more bread. The Duke of Alençon in Shakespeare's *Henry VI* taunted the famished English army with wanting 'their porridge and their fat bull-beeves'. It took a Swiss (Muralt at the end of the seventeenth century) to be really enthusiastic; he found that people of all classes ate well in England and he particularly relished the roast beef, the delicious oysters, the puddings and the golden pippins. But a contemporary Frenchman, Misson, had some qualified praise. Though the mutton and poultry were probably less good than in France, the beef was generally held to be better and the roast beef and pudding of the English Sabbath were renowned. There might not be much refinement in the cuisine as a whole; but (words to warm an Englishman's heart!): 'Ah! l'excellente chose qu'un *English Pudding*.' Even some of the many varieties of beer were good, though 'quoi qu'il en soit, la Bière est Art, et le Vin est Nature; Et vive la Nature.'

Tea and whisky have spread to France from England and Scotland. 'Rosbif' and 'biftek' have become French words. English biscuits and preserves are admired while, when they get the chance, French schoolchildren relish the sort of breakfasts that the English used to eat. But one never hears of a Frenchman making a gastronomic pilgrimage to Britain. Although there is a lot to be said for good materials simply cooked, the French are usually happier when Art has improved Nature. It is at least partly a love of paradox that makes the elderly Alexandre, in Roger Vailland's *La Fête* (1960), sympathize with young Lucie in her dislike of 'les plats cuisinés':

> The height of art is the steamed potato (la *pomme de terre à l'anglaise*), piping hot, which sets off the coolness of the butter just beginning to melt on top of it. Lucie is right to prefer the English *cuisine*, as she seems to do. If we insist we can get the chef to renounce his creams, his sauces, his chickens, his gorged birds, and to prepare for Lucie a slice of grilled fillet.

For their part the English have shown their appreciation of French food by frequently importing French cooks. Pepys, whose wife had been brought up in a French convent, wrote of having had a fine French dinner in London and of his patron's thoughts of getting a French cook. The Marquis de Vermont, in *London and Paris*, reported the early nineteenth-century English as adopting not only French dishes but the French names for them. It did indeed become almost obligatory for menus to be written in French, both in hotels and at private dinners. Of course French titles did not always mean French cooking—and even French cooking tasted rather different in France. Thackeray contributed to *Punch* in 1849 reflections 'on some dinners at Paris': 'A man who comes to Paris without directing his mind to dinners, is like a fellow who travels to Athens without caring to inspect ruins . . .'

English epicures had been equally respectful in the eighteenth century. Chesterfield held that the French kitchen was as delicious as the German was execrable. Lady Eleanor Butler asked a correspondent for a recipe: '. . . something *Very Good* out of *Nothing*, the cheaper the more convenient. The French understand those things better than any people upon earth . . .'* Arthur Young made no bones about it:

* Quoted by Elizabeth Mavor, *The Ladies of Llangollen*.

> In the art of living, the French have generally been esteemed by the rest of Europe to have made the greatest proficiency. . . . Of their cookery there is but one opinion . . . that it is far beyond our own, I have no doubt in asserting.

He referred contemptuously to English 'greens boiled in water' and to the standard English 'pot luck'—or 'pot ill luck'—of a joint of meat and a pudding. Even the beef at Paris was, in his view, unrivalled. The English dishes that could compare with the French were few indeed: a turbot and lobster sauce, ham and chicken, turtle, a haunch of venison, a turkey and oysters; that was about all.

Of course the chorus of praise was not universal. Much to Misson's indignation the common people of the seventeenth century chose to believe that the French lived exclusively on herbs and roots. At all periods there were Englishmen, especially the less travelled or the more dyspeptic, who disliked 'made-up dishes' and preferred the wholesome simplicity of their own fare:

> Dear Lucy, you know what my wish is,
> I hate all your Frenchified fuss:
> Your silly entrées and made dishes
> Were never intended for us.

This was Thackeray, in consciously insular vein. Scott, in the introduction to *Quentin Durward*, professed a longing for 'genuine steak', beer and Port. Constable wrote of his son John, in 1834, as being 'returned from France, much pleased and wonderfully strong and well, ready and willing for a winter fog in London. . . He was amused with France, but with the food he was annoyed, as he says they put vinegar into everything they eat and drink.'

French wines and brandy were always in favour with the English upper class; but taxation made them prohibitively expensive throughout the eighteenth century and for many decades Claret had to yield to Port. Claret had been the most fashionable wine of Stuart England. It was only natural that, in the earlier centuries, the wines of Bordeaux should be better known in England than those of distant Burgundy, though at that time the latter were more prized in France.

The English used to have a great reputation as trenchermen in France; but in turn they have noticed that the French sometimes care for quantity as well as quality. The Elizabethan Dallington wrote that, although French tables were ordinarily furnished less plentifully with meat than in England and the poor peasants ate worse—if better than in Italy—the French were both *gourmets* and *gourmands* and 'in banquets they far exceed us'. The English might be reputed heavy drinkers; but 'a Frenchman of all other (except the Dutch) hath least cause to taxe us of drinking: for we may see by many of their noses, what pottage they love'.

In the nineteenth century, at least, the English out-rivalled the French with the luxury of their table appointments and with their frequent changes of plates and cutlery. Their food might be less good, but they were determined to eat it more grandly. Even in the sixteenth century a foreign visitor (Hentzner) observed that the English were 'more polite in eating than the French . . .' But one of their chief boasts was, and still is, the heating of plates. Disraeli ascribed the success of Lord Monmouth's dinners in Paris (in *Coningsby*) to this simple superiority:

> . . . at Paris, in the best appointed houses, and at dinners which, for costly materials and admirable art in their preparation, cannot be surpassed, the effect is always considerably lessened, and by a mode the most mortifying: by the mere circumstance that every one at a French dinner is served on a cold plate. The reason of a custom, or rather a necessity, which one would think a nation so celebrated for their gastronomical taste would recoil from, is really, it is believed, that the ordinary French porcelain is so very inferior that it cannot endure the preparatory heat for dinner. . . . Now, if we only had that treaty of commerce with France which has so often been on the point of completion, the fabrics of our unrivalled potteries, in exchange for their capital wines, would be found throughout France. The dinners of both nations would be improved . . .

Plus ça change. . . . Quite recently a correspondent in *The Times* made, more or less, the same point.

Taine had a fixed idea that only the Gothic style of architecture suited the English climate. The classical style, he thought, belonged properly to the elegant, rational and sunny south. Fortunately not all Englishmen (certainly not Lord Palmerston, who was determined against a Gothic design for the Foreign Office) have agreed with him. Reluctant to accept that their culture must be totally Cimmerian, they have insisted on applying Greek, Italian, even French, notions. Wren visited France for about nine months in 1665, at the age of thirty-three, and was greatly influenced by the new buildings in Paris. He was less impressed by Versailles:

> . . . the Mixtures of Brick, Stone, blue Tile and Gold make it look like a rich livery: not an Inch within but is crowded with little Curiosities of Ornaments: the women as they make here the language and Fashions, and meddle with Politicks and Philosophy, so they sway also in Architecture.

Some traditional differences between French and English domestic architecture—for instance, the prevalence of French windows and outdoor shutters in France—were presumably due to the overall climatic difference between the two countries. Another important contrast came from the Parisian habit of living in flats, under the conciérge system, at a time when well-to-do English families always lived in houses. Mrs Trollope, while admiring the taste and style shown in French dwellings, reacted typically of her countrymen when she found the approaches and staircases poor. However, like Mrs Gaskell, she accepted that the French system had advantages and was more economical. She reported in 1835 that a trial had recently been made in Paris with small houses designed for one-family use; but they had been made too small, she said, and the experiment had not been a success. Yet a few years later the Rue de l'Elysée was constructed in imitation of a London street, with basement kitchens and steps up to the front doors of the houses. Another English innovation, according to Mrs Trollope, was the introduction of pedestrian pavements in Paris.

Throughout the nineteenth century the French insisted, and the English often agreed, that their industrial design was in better taste. Prosper Mérimée accused English industry of a lack of artistic sense, though he advised his countrymen not to rest on their laurels:

> England, which surpasses almost all the countries of Europe in the quality of her industrial products, has for long lagged behind in the manufacture of objects where art and taste should direct industry; the manufacturers of Manchester and other big commercial centres feel their inferiority, and for quite a long time have been seeking to recruit artists and designers, mostly French. Today they want to train them from among their compatriots.

Whatever their artistic deficiencies, the nineteenth-century English were acknowledged arbiters of comfort. Balzac, attacking their materialism ('la divinisation de la matière'), wrote that England

> possessed in the highest degree that science of existence which improves the smallest units of materiality, which sees to it that your slipper is the most exquisite slipper in the world, which gives your linen an ineffable savour, which lines drawers with cedar and scent . . . which turns matter into something soft and sustaining, brilliant and clean, in the midst of which the soul expires in enjoyment. . . .

Taine found England pervaded with comfort; sometimes it was embarrassingly obtrusive. The Comtesse Jean de Pange recalled that, when she was a child at the end of the nineteenth century:

> My mother used to say that only the English understood comfort and she would often talk of the times that she had stayed, so 'comfortably', with the Wallaces in the English countryside, so much so that I imagined England as a country where there was nothing but sofas, little pillows and hot water-bottles.

Perhaps one of the more useful products of English materialism (at any rate it was given an English name) was in Proust's words: 'Ce qu'on appelle en Angleterre un lavabo et en France, par une anglomanie mal informée, des water-closets.'

During the great age of French and English furniture, the eighteenth and early nineteenth centuries, there were influences in both directions, but on the whole the French gave more than they took. Arthur Young might claim that English craftsmen were more advanced, notably in the use of mahogany; but, in 1738, the *London Magazine* had cited furniture, as well as clothes and food, as an instance of the ridiculous English disposition to imitate the French. It was Robert Adam himself who wrote: 'The French style . . . is best calculated for the convenience and elegance of life.' The Prince Regent's architect, Henry Holland, was an admirer of French styles and the Prince became an ardent collector of French furniture at the sales of aristocratic property after the Revolution. Not only did the Louis Seize manner affect the Regency style in England, but there was a fresh wave of French influence after the fall of Napoleon. According to Ackermann's *Repository* in February 1815:

> The interchange of feeling between this country and France, as it relates to matters of taste, has not been wholly suspended during

> the long and awful conflicts which have so greatly abridged the intercourse of the two nations, and as usual the taste of both has been improved.

Seven years later the *Repository* noted:

> The Taste for French furniture is carried to such an extent that most elegantly furnished mansions, particularly in the sleeping rooms, are fitted up in French style.

Nevertheless the Regency style in English furniture, perhaps because it combined French elegance with English discretion, won a considerable vogue in France and is still widely reproduced there.

When French interiors appealed to the Victorian English, perhaps this was as much because of the way in which objects were arranged, as because of the objects themselves. There is a pleasant tribute in Dickens's *A Tale of Two Cities*, which both Mrs Trollope and Mrs Gaskell would have endorsed:

> Although the Doctor's daughter [Lucie Manette] had known nothing of the country of her birth, she appeared to have innately derived from it that ability to make much of little means, which is one of its most useful and most agreeable characteristics. Simple as the furniture was, it was set off by so many little adornments, of no value but for their taste and fancy, that its effect was delightful. The disposition of everything in the rooms, from the largest object to the least; the arrangement of colours, the elegant variety and contrast obtained by thrift in trifles, by delicate hands, clear eyes and good sense; were at once so pleasant in themselves, and so expressive of their originator, that, as Mr Lorry stood looking about him, the very chairs and tables seemed to ask him, with something of that peculiar expression which he knew so well by this time, whether he approved.

Helped by their humid climate the English asserted their independence of French influence sooner, and more completely, in their exteriors than in their interiors. Maurois makes Colonel Parker remark 'that France and England were the only two countries where one could find beautiful gardens'; but one suspects that, in his heart, Colonel Parker would not have put French gardens first. Few Englishmen have preferred the classical style of French gardening to their own green lawns, fine trees and massed flowers. Charles II had Le Notre over to improve St James's Park, but it was not improved too drastically and he developed Windsor Park in the English style. Taine wrote that the English park or garden displayed, better than anything else, 'le rêve poétique d'une âme anglaise'. The English garden was, for him, made for solitude: 'les yeux et l'âme font la conversation avec les choses naturelles.' The traditional French garden, on the other hand, was 'an open-air *salon* or gallery for walking and talking in company.'

In the 1750s a vogue for planting English gardens began to spread in France. Eraste, the Anglomane of Saurin's play, is found busy creating a '*Boulingrin*' (bowling green) out of a *parterre*. Bored with a classical French garden, laid out by Le Nôtre, he indulges in a riot of picturesque fancy:

> . . . des vallons, des collines,
> Des prés, une plaine, des bois,
> Une mosquée, un pont Chinois,
> Une rivière, des ruines . . .

At about the same time Horace Walpole, during one of his visits to Paris, reported to an English correspondent that 'English gardening gains ground here prodigiously'.

Was it really 'English gardening', though? Arthur Young had his doubts. He wrote of one such garden, Mortefontaine, that it

> has been mentioned as decorated in the English style . . . a garden of winding walks, and ornamented with a profusion of temples, benches, grottos, columns, ruins and I know not what. I hope the French who have not been in England do not consider this as the English taste.

Few things now seem more typically French than the eighteenth- or early nineteenth-century 'jardin anglais' as it can still be seen in France. The lines are not straight, but curved; the general effect is sombre rather than brilliant. But there is not much question of nature triumphing over art.

The prestige of their gardening was only a part of the general reputation of the English for living in the open air, communing with nature, taking exercise, loving sport and excelling at country life. Just before the Revolution Arthur Young noted that Rousseau's influence had encouraged a new fashion among the French upper class of spending some time in the country in the autumn: 'This remarkable revolution in the French manners is certainly one of the best customs they have taken from England.'

Ever since the eighteenth century the horse, with all his appurtenances, has been a powerful symbol of English fashion in France. Eraste orders—and is of course thrown by—an English horse; Astley's *manège* was opened in 1781; in 1833 the expatriate Lord Henry Seymour founded the society which gave rise to the French Jockey Club. More recently the French have adopted the English word 'weekend' and have increasingly come to accept that team games, apart from cricket, can be watched and even played.

The English have taught the French some indoor games, too. Horace Walpole wrote in 1765 that the French were imitating the English in their two most depressing products: Whist and Richardson. But on the whole the French have shone brighter by candlelight. Dances, in particular, have preferred to travel west. In the years after Waterloo, according to *London and Paris*, London society was seized with 'a dansomania Gallica' and persisted, disastrously, in attempting the quadrille.

Perhaps it is a pity that in music and the fine arts, where there is no need for translation, the two countries have usually had less to offer each other than in literature. In spite of Claude's popularity in eighteenth-century England the influence of French on English painting, before the great French masters of the later nineteenth century, was much less than that of the Italians and the Dutch. In 1712 Steele referred rather disparagingly, in the *Spectator*, to the French talent for 'Gay, Janty, Fluttering Pictures'. In another number Addison dreamed of visiting an art gallery:

> The first I observed at work in this Part of the Gallery was VANITY, with his Hair tied behind him in a Ribbon, and dressed like a *Frenchman*. All the faces he drew, were very remarkable for their Smiles, and a certain smirking Air which he bestowed indifferently on every Age and Degree of either Sex. The *Toujours Gai* appeared even in his Judges, Bishops, and Privy-Counsellors: In a Word, all his Men were *Petits Maitres*, and all his Women Coquets. The Drapery of his Figures was extremely well suited to his Faces, and was made up of all the glaring Colours that could be mixt together; every Part of the Dress was in a Flutter, and endeavoured to distinguish itself above the rest.

Constable admired Claude, Poussin and Watteau, but rejected Boucher and David. Hazlitt, while conceding that the French excelled 'in pieces of light gallantry and domestic humour', did not admire 'the grand style of French art'. In an imaginary dialogue in a gallery he makes an Englishman say to his French companion:

> . . . I cannot think our faults any justification of yours, or yours of ours. For instance, here is a landscape by a countryman of mine, Mr Constable. Why then all this affectation of dashing lights and broken tints and straggling lumps of paint, which I dare say give the horrors to a consummate French artist? On the other hand, why do not your artists try to give something of the same green, fresh, and healthy look of living nature, without smearing coats of varnish over raw *dabs* of colour (as we do), till the composition resembles the ice breaking up in marshy ground after a frosty morning? Depend upon it, in disputes about taste, as in other quarrels, there are faults on both sides.

The tone is not arrogantly chauvinist; but neither is it deferential.

In music, too, French influence in England was less than Italian and German, particularly in the eighteenth century. The English of that time had a decided preference for the Italian opera, though Montesquieu, who thought that the cold climate blunted the sense of pleasure, was struck by the undemonstrative way in which they listened to it:

> I have seen the operas of England and Italy; these are the same pieces and the same performers: but the same music produces such different effects on the two nations, the one is so calm, and the other so transported, as to seem inconceivable.

Arthur Young, typically English in this as in other respects, did not care for the classical French music of Lully and Rameau and was glad to find Italian opera gaining ground in France.

The influence of English music and painting in France was, as a rule, still weaker. Saurin's Anglomane, convinced that English superiority extended to the fine arts, produced the names of Handel and Hogarth—only to be reminded that the former was really German. It was more usual in eighteenth-century France to take the view of the Abbé le Blanc that 'Painting is an Art in which, despite all their efforts, our neighbours have only made feeble progress.' In the next century Prosper Mérimée wrote that England had lagged a long while, artistically, behind other European countries; the masses cared nothing for such 'useless frivolities', while the aristocracy collected foreign pictures. Only the portraitists had been really successful, he thought, particularly Reynolds and Lawrence. At the beginning of the century there had been a period marked by too much love of colour; now, with the Pre-Raphaelites, there was more preoccupation with form. But another French visitor, Taine, did not take to the Pre-Raphaelites: 'Entre l'ouvrier et le poête l'artiste a manqué'; he held that, generally speaking, the English were as mediocre in the fine arts as they were great in poetry. This was decidedly the view of Théophile Gautier, who believed that the northern races had been denied 'le don de la plastique'.

Perhaps there was only one period when English painting made a real impact in France—and that was at the beginning of the nineteenth century, in spite of Prosper Mérimée's strictures. Whatever the French borrowed from Constable, Turner and Bonington was to be repaid with interest by the Impressionist and Post-Impressionist painters. But they had borrowed something. Constable wrote in 1824, in a detached vein, of the interest which the French were taking in his paintings. He said that the artists were 'struck with their vivacity and freshness, things unknown to their own pictures', while 'the French critics by profession are very angry with the artists for admiring them. All this is amusing enough, but they cannot get at me on this side of the water, and I shall not go there.' In spite of the attacks of the professional critics, which Constable found 'amusing and acute, but shallow', the King of France awarded him a gold medal in 1825.

In the theatre both countries developed flourishing, but opposed, traditions before either stage could come under the influence of the other. The great period of English drama, in the sixteenth and early seventeenth centuries, owed little or nothing, and for a long time meant less, to the French. There were occasional visits to France by English actors and acrobats in the sixteenth century; but, if they pleased, it must have been through action not words, since in most parts of France at that time there was nobody who could understand the English language.

The seventeenth-century French theatre, like everything else belonging to the *grand siècle*, was bound to have an influence on Restoration England. Voltaire wrote that the 'custom of bringing love irrelevantly into dramatic works passed from Paris to London, in about the year 1660, together with our ribbons and our wigs.' There are frequent French expressions and motifs in

Restoration and early eighteenth-century English plays: quick-witted French servants, gallant French officers, Frenchified fops. Mrs Sullen, the Squire's wife in Farquhar's *The Beaux' Stratagem* (1707) says of Count Bellair, after rejecting his advances: 'There goes the true humour of his nation—resentment with good manners, and the height of anger in a song!' Sir Fopling Flutter, in Etherege's *The Man of Mode* (1676) arrives 'piping hot' from Paris, with a train of French servants and 'a pretty lisp' in imitation of French people of quality. He is delighted to find an attractive coquette 'more *èveillée* than our English women commonly are . . .' Dorimant comments: 'He went to Paris a plain bashful English blockhead, and is returned a fine undertaking French fop.'

For all this, the seventeenth-century English stage did not lose its native vitality. According to Ascoli, English actors were already noted for their realism. Sorbière found the Comedy in Restoration London entertaining and the acting admirable; although no respect was shown for the unities, this did not prevent the passions, vices and virtues being convincingly portrayed.

In so far as the French were aware of the English stage, they levelled two main reproaches at it: first, its barbarous contempt for the unities of time, place and action; second, its still more barbarous delight in bloodshed. René Rapin (*Réflexions sur la Poétique d'Aristote*, 1674) conceded the English a gift for tragedy; he attributed this to their taste for horrors as well as to the aptness of their language for 'grandes expressions'. He wrote:

> Les Anglais nos voisins aiment le sang, dans leurs jeux, par la qualité de leur tempérament; ce sont des insulaires, separés du reste des hommes, nous sommes plus humains. . .

In the eighteenth century the English themselves became more squeamish. The *Spectator* regretted the 'dreadful butchering of one another' on the English stage: 'Several French Criticks, who think these are grateful Spectacles to us, take Occasion from them to represent us as a People that delight in Blood.' Samuel Foote's Buck is completely won over by the French theatre:

> Oh, how I detest blood and blank verse!
> There is something so soft, so musical, and so natural, in the rich rhymes of the *Théâtre français*!

Chesterfield, a great admirer of Corneille, Racine and Molière, proposed diplomatically:

> I could wish there were a treaty made between the French and the English theatres, in which both parties should make considerable concessions.
>
> The English ought to give up their notorious violations of all the unities, and all their massacres, racks, dead bodies and mangled carcasses . . .
>
> The French should engage to have more action and less declamation . . .
>
> The English should restrain the licentiousness of their poets, and the French enlarge the liberty of theirs . . .

Dryden had taken a more robust attitude in his *Essay of Dramatick Poesie*. He makes Neander say that the French might be right about the bloodshed: 'But, whether custom has so insinuated itself into our Countreymen, or nature has so form'd them to fierceness, I know not; but they will scarcely suffer combats and other objects of horrour to be taken from them.' In Neander's view the English dramatists, though less great than previously, excelled in 'the lively imitation of Nature'; the French, though they had done much to reform their stage, displayed on it the beauties 'of a Statue, but not of a Man':

> I acknowledge the French contrive their Plots more regularly and observe the Laws of Comedy, and decorum of the Stage (to speak generally) with more exactness than the English . . . yet, after all, I am of opinion that neither our faults nor their virtues are considerable enough to place them above us.

This was in 1668. By the early eighteenth century Pope, in his Prologue to Addison's *Cato*, found it necessary to appeal to the audience to warm themselves with their own 'native rage':

> Your scene precariously subsists too long
> On French translation and Italian song.

Later in the century Chesterfield was convinced that there was not, and never had been, 'any theatre comparable to the French'. Arthur Young was equally positive:

> Writers, actors, buildings, scenes, decorations, music, dancing, take the whole in a mass and it is unrivalled in London. I write this passage with a lighter heart than I should do were it giving the palm to the French plough.

Garrick had a great success when he acted in Paris, in English, in 1751: Rousseau told him that he had made him weep and laugh, although he had not understood a word. But a few years earlier the Abbé le Blanc claimed that the English themselves recognized the superiority of the general run of French actors:

> Ils en ont eu d'excellents, mais tous ceux du second ordre ont toujours été pitoyables, effet nécessaire du peu do grâces répandu parmi les Anglais.

Apart from a few pleasant comedies, and a few exceptional actors and actresses, it was not really until the end of the nineteenth century that the London stage began to recover its sixteenth- and seventeenth-century glamour. In the 1820s the Marquis de Vermont, in *London and Paris*, was surprised to find English drama 'sunk to so low an ebb' when English literature was otherwise so flourishing: perhaps it was the lack of intimate theatres, the enormous size of Covent Garden and Drury Lane, that were to blame. In the 1860s Taine found that there were no longer any native comedies to be seen in London: 'the authors translate or arrange French pieces'. Matthew Arnold wrote to his mother from Paris, in 1865:

> . . . the theatre here, both for acting and for a study of the language, is just what the English theatre is not, where the acting is detestable, and the mode of speaking is just what one ought *not* to adopt.

Hazlitt, like many Englishmen, was bored by classical French Tragedy, but relished Molière: he thought that the French were better than the English at *serious* comedy. But what particularly struck him was French gravity at the theatre:* 'Their churches are theatres; their theatres are like churches.' It had been the same in the seventeenth century. Dryden makes Neander say:

> . . . we, who are a more sullen people, come to be diverted at our Playes; they who are of an ayery and gay temper come thither to make themselves more serious . . .

Two centuries later George Moore wrote in praise of one, inimitably English, diversion:

> There is one thing in England that is free, that is spontaneous, that reminds me of the blitheness and naturalness of the Conti-

* C.f. p. 58 above.

nent;—but there is nothing French about it, it is wholly and essentially English, and in its communal enjoyment and its spontaneity it is a survival of Elizabethan England—I mean the music-hall . . .

In recent decades both theatres have had their ups and downs, but they have seldom ceased to echo each other. Taine's experience of finding London full of French translations has been a common one for tourists in both directions. There is much less to oppose the two traditions than there used to be, since the French have become less addicted to the unities and the English to bloodshed. Shakespeare is nowadays applauded, almost equally devoutly, on both sides of the Channel.

The dogmatic conflict between the two theatres was—at least symbolically—resolved in the 1820s, when there were two visits by English companies to Paris. On the first occasion, at the Théâtre of the Porte-Saint-Martin in 1822, it was too soon after the allied occupation and the English actors were badly received. The scene was described by Stendhal:

> . . . the whistles and hoots began before the English piece opened and it was impossible to hear a word of it. As soon as the actors appeared, they were assailed with apples and eggs; from time to time people shouted at them: 'Parlez français!' In a word it was a fine triumph for the national honour.

By the time of the next visit, however, the climate had changed. In 1827 an English company (Kemble, Kean, Macready, Miss Smithson) had a tremendous success acting Shakespeare at the Odéon. Berlioz, though knowing no English, found the combination of Shakespeare and Miss Smithson irresistible.

Stendhal himself had passed three weeks in London, where he had seen Kean acting in *Othello* and *Richard III*, in 1821. He had no doubt that the unities were incompatible with the development of a modern drama that would really move audiences. Although the action of *Macbeth* required several months, he argued, 'The compatriots of Fox and Sheridan, who perhaps are not complete idiots' were able to watch it without any feeling of shock:

> The Spectator, so long as he is not a pedant, is simply concerned with the facts and the developing passions that he is invited to watch. Exactly the same thing happens in the head of the Parisian who applauds *Iphigénie en Aulide*, and in that of the Scot who

admires the history of his former kings, Macbeth and Duncan. The only difference is that the well-brought-up Parisian has got into the habit of mocking the other.

Stendhal helped to break down a dogma that had ruled, and divided, for two centuries. The glass of fashion could not reflect freely, until the conflict of form was resolved. There remained the language barrier, which could be crossed, but never dismantled.

SIX

The Mould of Form

POLITICAL AND LITERARY ideas have sometimes crossed the Channel as frivolously as tastes in furniture and dress and had the same kind of ephemeral success. Equally, the traffic in taste between the two countries has at times had deep and lasting effects. But external fashions usually change quicker than internal forms, make a more vivid impact, are more easily copied and leave a shallower mark.

Unlike fashion, political and literary ideas have had to travel through the barriers of religion and language. For centuries the conflict between Roman Catholicism and Protestantism divided the two countries, imposing different religious, political and educational standards. Separated by these standards, even French and English philosophers borrowed relatively little from each other in the field of pure thought. In applied thought, of course, there were often important borrowings; practical success in either country was naturally admired, and coveted, in the other. But there were usually intellectual limits even to these political and scientific debts.

The philosophical gulf already yawned in Voltaire's day. He wrote of Fontenelle's eulogy on Newton in the *Académie des Sciences*:

> On attendait en Angleterre le jugement de M. de Fontenelle comme une déclaration solennelle de la supériorité de la philosophie anglaise; mais, quand on a vu qu'il comparait Descartes à Newton toute la Société royale de Londres s'est soulevée. Loin d'acquiescer au jugement, on a critiqué ce discours. Plusieurs même (et ceux-là ne sont pas les plus philosophes) ont été choqués de cette comparaison, seulement parce que Descartes était Français.

As to the religious gulf, there is a striking passage in Stevenson's *Travels with a Donkey in the Cévennes*. He talked with some French Protestants at Florac and, even in the late nineteenth century, was moved to exclaim:

> I own I met these Protestants with a delight and a sense of coming home. I was accustomed to speak their language, in another and deeper sense of the word than that which distinguishes between French and English; for the true Babel is a divergence upon morals. And hence I could hold more free communication with the Protestants, and judge them more justly than the Catholics.

Language (in the shallower sense of the word) has been both a lesser, and a greater, barrier than religion. It has created less resentment and been more easily crossed; but it is there for good and, if it cannot be crossed, prevents any serious exchange of ideas at all. Even when a foreign language is not itself an insuperable obstacle, the categories of thought that it imposes tend to differ and divide.

The French and English languages are not of course as different from each other as they are from many others. The most Latin of the Germanic languages, English owes a great deal to French, both in its vocabulary and in its word-order. French was after all the educated language of twelfth-century England and, although its use began to decline in the thirteenth century, it was spoken at Court as late as the fifteenth century. This may not have been Parisian French* but, pronunciation apart, it was certainly more French than English.

Educated Englishmen have usually had some knowledge of French, however badly they spoke it. French is the main modern language taught in English schools and at least a little of it sticks. In the earlier centuries, Englishmen had to learn reasonable French if they wanted to converse with foreigners at all. Shakespeare's historical plays, particularly *Henry V*, show a knowledge of French, which he may have got in a Huguenot household in London. Pistol's Boy speaks a little French, though Pistol has none himself, and a fair number of people in the audience must have been able to feel with Katharine of France during her English

* Chaucer's Prioress spoke French:

> . . . ful fayre and fetisly
> After the scole of Stratford atte Bowe,
> For Frenche of Paris was to hire unknowe.

lesson. Several Englishmen of letters stayed in France in the seventeenth and eighteenth centuries and became fluent in the language. Locke could correspond in French; Chateaubriand recalls that, in the Gallophobe 1790s, Hume and Gibbon were blamed by English critics for having imported literary Gallicisms. Some French was part of the equipment of every Englishman of cultivation or fashion; it was essential for diplomatists and useful for soldiers. Cobbett went to France 'for the purpose of learning to speak the French language, having, because it was the language of the military art, studied it by book in America.' At the beginning of the eighteenth century the *Spectator* complained of the in-roads made by the French language during the war and the profusion of French military terms: 'Our Warriors are very Industrious in Propagating the *French* Language. . . .'

There was rather less emphasis on French studies in Victorian education. The wars with Revolutionary and Napoleonic France had lasted long enough to deprive a whole generation of a real chance of learning the language in a French setting. In any event English began to be more widely understood abroad, while more attention began to be paid to German by English scholars. But French governesses were often employed in well-to-do families and the language, if less well spoken than formerly, was still widely read in England. When Chateaubriand spoke to Mrs Trollope of the difficulty that Englishmen must have in judging French literature, she felt that he exaggerated, since many Englishmen had been familiar with the French classics, if not with contemporary French literature, from earliest youth. She thought that Frenchmen were apt to underestimate English knowledge of French because English visitors were forced to use it in Paris, however inexpertly, if they wanted to have any social intercourse. Many could read it well who spoke it haltingly.

Mrs Trollope went on to complain to her readers that far fewer Frenchmen were able to read English and that hardly one in fifty of them would venture to speak it, through fear of ridicule and dislike of incorrect speech. But she added tactfully that the English must pocket their pride and persevere with their poor French, so as to experience the delightful urbanity of French conversation.

Before the eighteenth century English was regarded abroad as a barbarous and insular language and the Frenchman who could even read it was a rare exception. French Ambassadors, and other high-ranking visitors, seldom bothered to learn it at all; they could find enough people ready to talk to them in French, at least at Court. English Dictionaries and Grammars were published in France in the seventeenth century, but they were chiefly used by Huguenots and businessmen. At all times for the English, French culture and travel have opened up a wider world: the French-speaking Englishman has been more of a generalist than a specialist. In France, English studies have more often been a specialized interest, with a specific purpose, commercial or intellectual, in view.

An intellectual reason for learning English—the prestige of English science and English freedom—came into view in the early eighteenth century. Saint-Hyacinthe* wrote: 'None of those who love the sciences should neglect the English language. Truth is not subordinated to the laws in their country . . .' La Fontaine had already commented, in his Fable on the English Fox:

> Les Anglais pensent profondément,
> Leur esprit, en cela, suit leur tempérament,
> Creusant dans les sujets, et forts d'expériences,
> Ils étendent par-tout l'empire des sciences.

Generations later Hazlitt had an anecdote of a French lady married to a remarkably dull Englishman who used to apologize for her husband's silence in company 'by incessantly repeating "*c'est toujours Locke, toujours Newton*", as if these were the subjects that occupied his thoughts'. It was the English reputation for free, and penetrative thought that attracted Voltaire, who made a serious study of the language during his visit from 1726 to 1728.

A century later Stendhal was attracted by the English dramatic tradition and learned to write fluent, if not quite faultless, English. Proust, with his admiration for Ruskin, could apparently read English, even if he could not speak it. An increasing number of Frenchmen learned English for commercial, or snobbish, reasons. Aristocrats had been forced to learn the language during the emigration and tended to keep up the practice in their families after their return. What governesses did for French in England, nannies did for English in France. When nannies began to dwindle, their influence was replaced by a transatlantic one, so that modern Frenchmen speak more, if more American, English than ever before.

* *Mémoires Littéraires* (1716), quoted by Bastide.

Englishmen have always admired the French language for its clarity, elegance and aptness for wit. Perhaps because their own language is smoother than German and Dutch, they are less often struck by its musical softness; yet the Elizabethan Dallington described it as smooth and melodious: 'a tongue d'amours'. Dryden wrote in 1697: 'The French have set up purity for the standard of their language; and a masculine vigour is that of ours.' The Abbé le Blanc in the next century drew much the same contrast. The English language had the advantage over the French of 'energy, abundance and a great freedom', while French was superior in 'clarity, order and politeness'.

Most earlier Frenchmen would have thought it ridiculous to make any comparison between the two languages. Misson wrote dryly of the seventeenth-century English:

> If they believe that their language is the most beautiful in the world, although it is only spoken in their island, they have a still higher opinion of their verses. They never read or recite them, except with a peculiar expression.

One criticism was that English was a lazy language, since the lips needed to be moved so little in speaking it. A more lasting prejudice was recorded by Stendhal: a middle-aged man of letters told him that the English 'cannot have real eloquence, nor really admirable poetry; the nature of their language, not derived from Latin, presents an insurmountable obstacle.' George Moore, who spent several years in France as a young man, found the English language 'coarse and plain' until he read *Marius the Epicurean*.

It is relatively easy, though still a hard labour, to learn enough of a foreign language for day-to-day purposes. But to get to the point of real literary appreciation is of course another thing. The nuances of style are difficult to seize in a foreign language and almost impossible to translate. Voltaire found that fine poetry and topical comedy were particularly hard to render; to judge them properly one must be ready to study on the spot for a longish period. Chateaubriand told Mrs Trollope, in the salon of Madame Récamier, that he doubted whether an Englishman could ever really enjoy Molière or appreciate La Fontaine. He wrote in his *Mémoires d'Outre-Tombe*:

> Nobody, in a living literature, is a competent judge except of works written in his own language. In vain you believe yourself to have a real grasp of a foreign idiom, the nurse's milk is lacking,

as well as the first words that she teaches you at her breast and in your swaddling-clothes; certain accents belong to your native land alone. The English and the Germans have the most baroque notions of our men of letters: they adore what we despise, they despise what we adore; they do not understand Racine, nor La Fontaine, nor even completely Molière. . . . It is maintained that real beauties belong to every age and every country: the beauties of sentiment and thought, yes; the beauties of style, no. Style is not, like thought, cosmopolitan: it has a native land, a sky, a sun of its own.

Yet the foreign reader has one advantage. The less familiar with the literature, the more he is likely to be struck by the characteristics of the language itself. He is like a traveller who, arriving in a strange country, finds a special quality in the atmosphere which the inhabitants take for granted and scarcely notice.

If it is difficult to read a foreign language with discrimination, it is still rarer to write one well. George Moore, who thought that the attitude of a Frenchman's mind was completely opposed to that of an Englishman's, wrote that he had heard of writing and speaking two languages with equal proficiency:

This was impossible to me, and I am convinced that if I had remained two more years in France I should never have been able to identify my thoughts with the language I am now writing in . . .

Similarly Chateaubriand supposed that he would have forgotten his native tongue, and never written a line, if he had married Miss Ives.*

De Madariaga has neatly analysed a fundamental difference between the French and English languages:

An English humorist—nothing inspires English humour like the observation of the French—has said that the French language is that in which it is the most difficult to say the truth. That is unfair . . . But our Englishman was no doubt habituated to *feel* the truth rather than to *think* it, and, consequently, he tended to believe that the French language, in cutting out geometrically limited cubes and pyramids from the formless mass of reality, deprived it of its vital truth. In a word, what troubles the Englishman in the French language, is that it tends naturally towards the abstract style. Thus, abstract and precise, it sins doubly against English tastes, which are vague and concrete.

* C.f. p. 121 above.

It is difficult to judge at all exactly the extent to which the use of a given language shapes and disciplines thought. But anyone who has studied a foreign language knows that there are notions he can no longer express in it, just as there are other notions, hitherto inarticulate, which it enables him to express for the first time. Mathematical reasoning and empirical observation may be more or less independent of linguistic structure. But when it comes to analysing character, describing moods and impressions, or defining political aims, there can be important differences of form and colour between one language and another. In English it is easier to avoid sharp outlines, to leave a problem vaguely stated, than in French. In French it is easier to produce a satisfying verbal formula and to equate the statement of a problem with its solution.

Perhaps this contrast between the languages has something to do with the famous English respect for facts and the famous French respect for ideas. Tocqueville observed that, generally speaking, the English seemed to have 'great difficulty in getting hold of general and undefined ideas. They judge the facts of today perfectly well, but the tendency of events and their distant consequences escape them.' The French weakness was in judging the facts of today. The French Consul in Liverpool had told him a story about some visiting French engineers: '. . . when someone told them a fact, M. Navier, after making some calculations, often said: "The thing is impossible, it does not fit at all with the theory." '

Maurois embroidered on this theme when he suggested that, just because the French took ideas more seriously that the English, they were obliged to cultivate them more soberly:

> With us, ideas are active and dangerous forces which have to be handled with prudence. With the English, action is so well determined through a rigid education, that the verbal clowning of a Shaw remains an inoffensive piece of acrobatics. . . . The divorce of practical life and theoretical thought is so complete that thought finds itself wholly liberated.

If French thought tends to be more theoretical, but also more circumscribed, than English, the construction of the French language is at least partly the cause. But, when one reflects how languages can be manipulated, how they can be made to expand and contract, some further explanation seems needed. In their ability to express facts and thoughts, or to convey colour and emotion, there is more in common between the languages of Gibbon and Montesquieu, say, than between the languages of Montesquieu and Proust or between the languages of Gibbon and James Joyce. Yet at all periods French has been a more exact, while English has often been a more powerful, instrument. The seventeenth-century difference in political/religious systems suggests one reason for this. In a closed, absolute system thought must be developed as a means rather than an end; its aim must be to comprehend, to analyse and to embellish, rather than to explore. Another reason can be traced to a still more basic difference. The French love of art encourages symmetry and logic; the English love of nature encourages freedom and empiricism.

Yet to propose these answers is only to raise fresh questions.

It is pleasant to compare the literature of the two countries, because they have both so obviously been successful. Neither the French nor the English need feel any sense of inferiority about them. This is perhaps the ground on which, at most periods since the Renaissance, Anglo/French combat has been most equal.

The ordinary educated Englishman might admit this more readily than the ordinary educated Frenchman. The French have, or used to have, a streak of cultural chauvinism, just as the English have, or used to have, a streak of political chauvinism. There are Frenchmen who are rather surprised to hear that England has harboured great literary figures other than Shakespeare, Byron, Oscar Wilde and Charles Morgan. But those French who have made any study of English literature will usually concede equality, or at least enough of it not to wound English feelings. Not that the English are particularly touchy where their literature is concerned: they have too much confidence in it. However, it can do no harm to quote a great nineteenth-century French specialist, Taine. He regarded English literature as 'une grande littérature complète'; only ancient Greece and France had, he thought, achieved a similar completeness.

If roughly equal in achievement the two literatures have sometimes been strikingly different in tone. This was certainly the case for much of the seventeenth and nineteenth centuries. At other times there has been more in common: Chaucer was regarded by Taine as 'almost French in spirit, wholly French in style'; the eighteenth century was of course a period of relatively cosmopolitan culture throughout Europe; French literature influenced many late nineteenth- and twentieth-century English writers.*

It is not surprising that English admiration for French writing should have been greatest during these 'cosmopolitan' phases. The late seventeenth and early eighteenth centuries were not, in fact, a particularly rich period in French letters; but the French, who were still living on the prestige of 'le grand siècle', had won a secure reputation for taste and criticism. Pope admitted in his *Imitations of Horace*:

> Late, very late, correctness grew our care,
> When the tired Nation breathed from civil war.
> Exact Racine and Corneille's noble fire
> Show'd us that France had something to admire.

The example of French writers and the authority of French critics, notably Boileau, powerfully affected eighteenth-century English literature, though there was often a touch of sturdy nationalism mixed with the respect felt for French standards.

The response to French influences since the end of the nineteenth century has been more partial, but also more enthusiastic. Swinburne, who could write in French and whose letters are full of references to French writers, is an obvious example; he wrote an elegy on Baudelaire and published a eulogy on *Les Fleurs du Mal* in 1892. Both Kipling and Somerset Maugham confessed how much they owed to Maupassant. Proust's influence has been incalculable. Writers like Gide, Camus and Sartre have had fascinated disciples.

Perhaps the nadir of French literary influence in England was in the early nineteenth century. The long war had developed English self-sufficiency, while the Romantics were in revolt against the classical tradition so long fostered by France. Coleridge and Lamb were ignorant of French culture. De Quincey, who found in the French 'an extraordinary defect in the higher

* Van Tieghem suggests that the notion of 'influence' weakens after about 1880: 'Une mentalité commune se crée qui produit presque simultanément des œuvres littéraires analogues.'

qualities of passion', made what even then must have been an excessive claim:

> If, doubtfully, you except Montaigne and Charron as meditative writers much read by the more thoughtful among our men of the world, and Pascal, as a sort of pet with our religious ascetics, there was never any French writer who established himself as even a limited favourite in England.*

Stendhal, who was a great reader of the *Edinburgh Review*, described it as being 'like most English reviews, not satisfied by Waterloo and desirous of ruining the intellectual prestige of France'.

Even De Quincey, however, seems to have respected French critical writing, which has always been admired in England. Dryden gave the French critics the palm over the English, while two centuries later Matthew Arnold hero-worshipped Sainte-Beuve. Arnold wrote to his mother in 1864:

> I have such a respect for a certain circle of men, perhaps the most truly cultivated in the world, which exists at Paris, that I have more pleasure than I can say in seeing papa brought before them so charmingly and just in the best way to make them appreciate him.

Critical acumen, subtlety of psychological analysis and sense of form: these have usually been for the English the clearest superiorities of French writing. Balzac, though not always edifying enough to be immediately popular in nineteenth-century England, later acquired a big public there; George Moore's reading 'culminated in the Comédie Humaine'. Somerset Maugham feared that his own stories had too much form for the English taste:

> There is evidently something that a number of people do not like in my stories and it is this they try to express when they damn them with the faint praise of competence. I have a notion that it is the definiteness of their form. I hazard this suggestion (perhaps unduly flattering to myself) because this particular criticism has never been made in France where my stories have had with the critics and the public much greater success than they have had in England. The French with their classical sense and their orderly mind, demand a precise form and are exasperated by a work in which the ends are left lying about, themes are propounded and not resolved and a climax is seen and then

* Cf. Clark, *Boileau and the French Classical Critics in England* (pp. 305–6).

eluded. This precision on the other hand has always been slightly antipathetic to the English. Our great novels have been shapeless and this, far from disconcerting their readers, has given them a sense of security.

For the Victorians, French literature had the additional, more ephemeral, charm of forbidden fruit. Lowbrows could amuse themselves with 'French novels'; highbrows could wrestle with more serious works; the satisfaction differed, but the sense of emancipation was the same.

As a rule the English have not warmed to the great seventeenth-century French writers, finding them too controlled, too rhetorical, too sparing of action and sentiment. For most Englishmen the beauties of these writers have been, in Dryden's phrase, those 'of a Statue, but not of a Man'. Even the sympathetic Molière would please them more if he were less cerebral and more tender. Yet Molière has been a favourite, in spite of Chateaubriand's reasonable doubts about whether an Englishman could really enjoy him. Hazlitt's reaction was typical: 'What Englishman does not read Molière with pleasure?' he wrote. But he had less zest for the 'long (and to us tiresome) speeches in French tragedy,' where 'the whole finds its level, like water, in the unembarrassed scope of the French intellect.'

Some English have nevertheless admired the French tragedians, once they have got over the initial shock of finding that their aims and methods were not those of Shakespeare. Pope's tribute to Racine's exactness and Corneille's 'noble fire' was typical enough of his period. A century later Mrs Trollope's admiration of both writers would have satisfied the most classical Frenchman. Lytton Strachey, writing to Virginia Woolf in 1922, trampled on the brink of complete conversion:

> Mr Masefield has produced a very strange little book—an 'adaptation' of Racine's Esther—the most deplorable give-away you ever saw. And the Lit. Sup. treats it quite seriously and implies that Mr M. is a better poet than Racine. We are a nation of barbarians, I fear. The wretched man clearly hadn't the faintest idea what he was up to. Oh! Oh! Style, words, common decency mean nothing to him—or to the Lit. Sup.—nothing. He converts Racine's exquisite silk, length after length of it, into patches of rough canvas with perfect complacency—and the Lit. Sup. is charmed. However, he's sent me back to my old love, and I spent last night in a rapture over Athalie, which I

> had rather forgotten—good gracious me. Reading it, I almost felt a Frenchman, and that there really was nothing like *that* in the world. It took quite an effort to remember King Lear and in fact I'm still rather doubtful whether . . .

But the chief English reproach, or boast, at least until the end of the nineteenth century, was that the French were incapable of lyrical poetry. Dryden thought that the English were as better poets than the French as they were worse critics. Some Englishmen firmly believed that poetry, as they understood it, was not produced in France at all. There is a story (at least symbolically convincing) that André Gide was once put next to A. E. Housman at a Cambridge dinner. As they rose to leave Housman put to him his first and last remark of the evening: 'Tell me, Monsieur Gide, why is it there is no French poetry?' Hazlitt suggested that the English owed their poetry to their discontented humour 'which flings them from cross-grained realities into the region of lofty and eager imaginations'. Unlike the French their imaginations needed the spur of outward objects:

> The French have no poetry, that is no combination of internal feeling with external imagery. . . . Outward objects interfere with and extinguish the flame of their imagination . . . with us they are the fuel that kindles it into a brighter and stronger blaze.

For Taine, too, French poetry could not compete with English. 'When the Frenchman conceives an event or an object, he conceives it rapidly and *distinctly* . . . no race in Europe is less poetic.' The poetic strength of the English came from their sense of the reality of the external world joined to a passionate sensibility. Taine ascribed this 'combination of internal feeling with external imagery' to a Germanic lyrical talent deepened, and made more introspective, by the Norman Conquest:

> The old sensibility, oppressed and perverted, lives and stirs still. The poet subsists under the puritan, under the businessman, under the statesman . . . the English mask of a German head.

Until well into the eighteenth century few Frenchmen knew anything of English imaginative writers. Their respect was reserved for English *savants* and philosophers: Gilbert, Harvey, Bacon, Hobbes, Locke, Newton. Sorbière noted soon after the Restoration: 'De tout temps l'Angleterre a produit d'excellents esprits, qui se sont pleus à l'estude des choses naturelles.' But the great Boileau, in talking to Arthur Maynwaring after the Peace of Rijswijk, 'affected to be as ignorant of the British muse, as if we were as barbarous as the Laplander'. He had to ask another Englishman who Dryden was. He 'acknowledged he had heard a great deal of the merit of our Tragedies but had no notion of our performance in other kinds of poetry, imputing that excellence of ours to sanguinary tempers as Rapin had done.'*

But the fame of Bacon, Locke and Newton, enhanced by the swelling repute of British freedom, heralded a period of much greater French interest. Voltaire discovered that the English poets and tragedians had produced beauties, however irregular, and even daringly suggested that their genius flourished better when it grew wild. Montesquieu had the same impression of rough vigour:

> Leurs écrits satiriques seroient sanglants; et l'on verroit bien des Juvénals chez eux, avant d'avoir trouvé un Horace. . . . Leurs poètes auroient plus souvent cette rudesse originale de l'invention, qu'une certaine délicatesse que donne le goût: on y trouveroit quelque chose qui approcheroit plus de la force de Michel—Ange que de la grâce de Raphaël.

Treading safely in these footsteps the Abbé le Blanc pronounced that many English works had genius, though few had grace.

Montesquieu was not the only Frenchman to be impressed by Swift. It may have been Chateaubriand who really 'discovered' Milton; but Montesquieu had heard of him and so had the Abbé le Blanc. Pope and other eighteenth-century English poets were well known in France, while Richardson and Scott were each very widely read there in his day. In the late 1820s Mme Graslin, in Balzac's *Le Curé de Village*, sought provincial distraction in 'the novels of Walter Scott, the poems of Lord Byron, the works of Schiller and of Goethe'. Byron had an extraordinary vogue which, because of his rebelliousness and exile, did England's reputation as much harm as good. Chateaubriand, who regarded him as the greatest English poet since Milton, felt a curious affinity with him, though they never met. He wrote: '. . . his genius is understood better by us; he will have altars longer in France than in England.' Prosper Mérimée, an Anglomane rather than an Anglophile, felt all Byron's seduction and, in describing his

* Clark, op. cit. (p. 27). Cf p. 150 above.

treatment by English society, wrote of 'this classic land of hypocrisy'.

Shakespeare's genius was dimly perceived in France from time to time, but not fully recognized for two centuries. Towards 1680 the Royal Librarian, Nicolas Clément, noted on a card:

> Will. Shakespeare, *poeta anglicus*. Ce poète anglais a l'imagination assez belle; il pense naturellement, il s'exprime avec finesse; mais ces belles qualités sont obscurcies par les ordures qu'il mêle à ses tragédies.*

Voltaire, when he wrote his *Lettres sur les Anglais*, found Shakespeare great at times, but very uneven and lacking good taste. The Abbé le Blanc thought that English pride in him was exaggerated; he had genius, but his plays 'blessent toutes sortes de bienséances' and he often fell into the 'bas et dans le puéril'. Saurin, in his introduction to *L'Anglomane*, accepted Shakespeare as 'un génie du premier ordre', but wrote of the monstrous absurdities, as well as beauties, in his work. It was not until 1745–6 that any of Shakespeare's plays were translated into French in a free adaptation. It was not until the Romantic movement that they really came into their own.

Summing up his researches in the *Lettres sur les Anglais* Voltaire undervalued Elizabethan tragedy, but was otherwise studiously impartial:

> In conclusion it seems to me that the English have no such good historians as we have, that they have no veritable tragedies, that they have charming comedies, some admirable passages of poetry, and some philosophers who should be the teachers of the human race.
>
> The English have greatly profited from the works of our language; we should borrow from them in our turn, after having lent to them. We have only come, the English and ourselves, after the Italians, who have been our masters in every art, and whom we have in some ways surpassed. I do not know to which of the three nations the preference should be given; but he is fortunate who knows how to feel their different merits.

A few years later the prestige of English letters in France had so far risen since Boileau's day that Chesterfield could ridicule the way in which French authors, chiefly 'the bad ones', envied the

* Quoted by Ascoli, op. cit.

supposed advantages of their English colleagues: 'No wonder, say they, that England produces so many great geniuses; people there may think as they please, and publish what they think. Very true; but who hinders them from thinking as they please?'

One advantage, noted by Voltaire, comes as a surprise. He claimed that letters were more honoured in early eighteenth-century England than in France:

> Ce qui encourage le plus les arts en Angleterre, c'est la considération où ils sont; le portrait du premier ministre se trouve sur la cheminée de son cabinet; mais j'ai vu celui de M. Pope dans vingt maisons.

English nineteenth-century writers, like Thackeray, had quite the reverse experience: a striking instance of the tendency of the two countries to exchange roles periodically, unless Voltaire was misled by the exceptional cultivation of Bolingbroke and his friends.

It would be easy to present the basic difference between French and English literature in terms of classicism and romanticism. These are elusive labels and there are too many French romantic, and English classical, authors. Yet there does seem to have been a general French preference for what is universal, and a general English preference for what is local—and perhaps this contrast (which could also be found in law, government and philosophy) is after all the essence of the classical/romantic conflict.

The English tend to look for a reality of inward feeling or outward sensation in their literature, an essentially local reality of the kind that preoccupies their philosophy. For the French, literature and philosophy are more often ends in themselves, imposing a pattern on experience and less directly derived from it. If Somerset Maugham was right, English novel readers prefer not to have too much art, for fear that it should distort life. The French are readier for life to imitate fiction. Here, once more, is the familiar antithesis between art and nature.

Of course, like all such generalizations, this should not be pushed too far. The English have some feeling for art and sometimes like to look at things universally. The French have feelings and sensations, as well as ideas, and are sometimes attracted by what is local and individual. But a broad distinction remains, corresponding—and perhaps largely traceable—to the distinction between Catholicism and Protestantism. It is also found in political thought and practice.

Until the eighteenth century England was unquestionably more provincial and less polished than France; in some ways it remained so, even after the eighteenth century. But the more backward country had the more rapid political development. Feudalism ceded to monarchy earlier in England than in France; popular institutions developed more steadily; the power of the monarchy was broken sooner and without such drastic social change. In spite of the many differences, there is an extraordinary parallel between the Civil War in England and its aftermath, and the French Revolution and its aftermath some 150 years later. In both cases, in much the same sort of time scale (a total of forty-six years in England and forty-one years in France), rebellion was followed by the execution of the king, by the rule of a dictator, by the restoration of the old royal line, by first a prudent and then a reactionary reign, by a relatively short and painless revolution and by the accession of a king obliged to govern more constitutionally.

But of course the character and effects of this series of events in England were much more parochial than in France. For one thing eighteenth-century France was a more powerful country than seventeenth-century England, held a more central position and was of more interest to the world at large. For another, the French genius for expressing their attitudes in rational and universal terms ensured that, whether they obeyed or rebelled, they did so for reasons that could be applied to humanity as a whole. Louis XIV's monarchy was a conscious work of art, reflecting the ideological rigour of the Counter-Reformation; it impressed as a universal type, whatever difficulties less talented peoples might find in imitating it. The French Revolutionaries, no less inspired by ideological rigour and artistic energy, saw themselves still more clearly as benefactors of mankind. In England, while religious and political theory of course played an important part in the Civil War, statesmen usually had more limited aims and more local instincts. The English (later British) system of government has never been acclaimed as a triumph of design, but as a triumph of adaptation—not so much an artefact as a natural growth.

If freedom has on the whole bulked larger in the British, than in the French, tradition, it is less because the two peoples are different temperamentally than because they evolved politically at different times. In fact, in the sixteenth century, England was the more despotic country of the two. The Tudors got the English to change their religion three times and to swallow regular doses of royal caprice. Most of the French kings of the century could not exercise such power, even had they wished. Brought up in the first Elizabeth's England, Dallington was shocked by the impudent liberty of speech in France, and though he admired Henri IV personally, thought that the French kings were too familiar with their subjects. The same censure colours the contrast between the French and English courts in Chapman's *Boissy d'Ambois*. Equally Dallington criticized the instability and impatience of French diplomacy: '. . . this nation will rather yield the enemie what he demandeth than be troubled with long deliberation.' Nobody would have thought of levelling this charge at the disciplined France of Richelieu or of Louis XIV any more than at Elizabethan England; but early eighteenth-century French writers used exactly the same language about the English diplomacy of their own or recent times.

Visiting England at the beginning of the seventeenth century Sully found an insular self-confidence: 'Si on en croit les Anglois, l'esprit et la raison ne se trouvent que chez eux; ils adorent toutes leurs opinions et méprisent celles de toutes les nations . . .' Later in the century, though still insular and no doubt still pleased with themselves, the English could not ignore the power and lustre of France. They might disapprove of Louis XIV as too absolute, or too Catholic, a ruler; but they could not despise him. The boot was rather on the other foot. The French, appalled by the English treatment of Charles I, became later mildly contemptuous of the way in which they managed their public affairs. It was now a Frenchman's turn (Sorbière's) to remark on the accessibility of the English king (Charles II) and the excessive licence in English thought and conversation. Bossuet's earnest wish was that 'England, too free in her beliefs, too licentious in her feelings, should like us be enchained by those blessed bonds, which prevent human pride from going astray in its thoughts, by making it captive to the authority of the Holy Spirit and the Church.' The more worldly Sorbière was less acutely concerned, because he seems to have felt about the English what Europeans have often tended to feel in developing countries. In spite of their endless discussions on public affairs, the natives were not really dangerous: they 'submit easily to everything, so long as they are well nourished and allowed to talk, and so long as their idleness is not put under too much pressure'. Rather the same colonial note was struck benevolently by Misson:

> On peut dire du Governement d'Angleterre . . . que les Loix en sont très sages et très bonnes, mais mollement exécutées. On a quelquefois aussi des négligences (les François appellent cela des by-and-by). . . . On est un peu plus soigneux et plus diligent en France, sur tout dans les affaires d'Etat.

The English themselves seem to have had some feeling, even in the eighteenth century, that French public administration could give points to their own. 'They order these things better in France . . .' Travellers were invariably impressed by the roads and by the police. Burke was struck by the 'multitude and opulence' of the cities in France, by the 'magnificence of her spacious high roads and bridges', by inland navigation, ports, naval apparatus, fortifications, intensive cultivation, the excellence of manufactures and fabrics, as well as by French charitable and artistic achievements and by the distinction of individual Frenchmen. But, by Burke's time, disapproval of French absolutism had grown and respect for its achievements had weakened. If only the French would become more English! Burke could not believe the government of the *ancien régime* beyond reformation: 'I must think such a government well deserved to have its excellencies heightened, its faults corrected, and its capacities improved into a British constitution.'

The usual verdict of eighteenth-century British writers was that the pre-Revolution French were not as free as they should be, but were nevertheless more humanely governed than most peoples under despotic yoke. Burke described their government as full of abuses, but 'usually, and I think justly, reputed the best of the unqualified or ill-qualified monarchies'. It was 'a despotism rather in appearance than in reality'. The topic of *Lettres de cachet* moved Arthur Young to exclaim: 'Oh, liberty! liberty! And yet this is the mildest government of any considerable country in Europe, our own excepted.' Adam Smith used similar language.*

* *Wealth of Nations*, Bk. IV, Ch. VII: 'The administration of the French colonies . . . has always been conducted with more gentleness and moderation than that of the Spanish and Portuguese. This superiority of conduct is

Horace Walpole wrote in 1789 that the French Government 'was detestable, and might have been much corrected'. But, looking back three years later, he doubted a little whether 'the people of France, till they were told otherwise by the philosophers . . . were a quarter so unhappy as they are at present, especially having had that singular felicity as Frenchmen, of thinking that France was in every point preferable to the rest of the universe.'

Meanwhile, in spite of Horace Walpole's gibe, a devout respect for the free British constitution had become fashionable in France. Voltaire, in the 1730s, wrote enthusiastically how English efforts had finally established 'this wise government where the prince, all-powerful to do good, has his hands tied for doing bad; where the nobles are great without insolence and without vassals, and where the people takes part in the government without confusion.' Montesquieu, whose *De l'esprit des Lois* had ten English translations in twenty-five years, classified the English constitution as a free one, under vestigial absolutist forms. It checked tyranny through its separation of the executive and legislative powers and, through its organization of the legislature on the representative principle, it escaped the demagogy of the ancient democracies. As Tacitus's *Germania* showed (and as English contemporaries of Montesquieu believed) this 'fine system' was originally developed by Germanic tribes in their forests. The English nation was more easily led by its passions than by reason; but its executive power enjoyed prestige abroad, however subject to internal agitation, because it did not seek territorial conquests and had to proceed openly, being obliged to justify its conduct to parliament. 'C'est le peuple du monde qui a le mieux su se prévaloir à la fois de ces trois grandes choses: la religion, le commerce et la liberté.'

Both Voltaire and Montesquieu seem to have come under Bolingbroke's spell; much of what they say, in criticism as well as in praise, reflects his views. The Abbé le Blanc was less convinced of English political advantages. Theoretically, he acknowledged the superiority of the English constitutional form; but in practice faction and revolution had tarnished its excellence. The liberty of the press was estimable, but abused, while states-

suitable both to the character of the French nation, and to . . . the nature of their government, which though arbitrary and violent in comparison with that of Great Britain, is legal and free in comparison with those of Spain and Portugal.'

men had to devote as much energy to defending themselves internally as externally:

> ... every time that their hate for their neighbours has made them conquer their internal divisions they have made themselves formidable to Europe. Unhappily for them, when they are not at war with their enemies, they are so with themselves.

But, at least in progressive circles, these reserves were soon to be swept away. In 1751 the Marquis d'Argenson recorded:

> There blows on us from England a philosophical wind of free and anti-monarchical government; it passes into people's minds and one knows how opinion governs the world.

Mirabeau, who visited England in 1784, favoured a limited monarchy on apparently British lines. In the same year the young La Rochefoucauld reflected the views of his French, as well as his English, friends when he described the British system of government as 'la machine la plus parfaite que les hommes réunis aient faite.' It was democratic, without the abuses of democracy, and monarchical, without the abuses of monarchy. 'It seems to me that it has been well proved that the English government is the most perfect of all.'

The French Revolution had a profound effect in England. At first it was greeted with enthusiasm by liberals, even the most moderate; Rousseau, with his considerable English public, had helped to prepare the ground. But, as the Revolution became bloodier and more aggressive, most Englishmen grew disgusted and alarmed. They came to suspect something intrinsically bloodthirsty and undependable in the French character, just as the French had done in reverse during the Civil War. In each case the execution of the king was the culminating point of shock and dread.

Sir Samuel Romilly, a liberal Member of Parliament and of Huguenot stock, wrote cheerfully to a correspondent on 28 July 1789:

> It will perhaps surprise you, but it is certainly true, that the Revolution had produced a very sincere and very general joy here. It is the subject of all conversations; and even all the newspapers, without one exception, though they are not conducted by the most liberal or philosophic of men, join in sounding forth the praises of the Parisians, and in rejoicing at an event so important for mankind.

Hannah More recalled in 1793:

> What English heart did not exult at the demolition of the Bastille? What lover of his species did not triumph in the warm hope, that one of the finest countries in the world would soon be one of the most free?

One month before the fall of the Bastille Arthur Young had had a rare moment of enthusiasm at Versailles:

> The spectacle of the representatives of 25 millions of people ... rising to the blessings of a freer constitution ... was framed to call into animated feelings, every latent spark, every emotion of a liberal bosom; to banish whatever ideas might intrude of their being a people too often hostile to my own country, and to dwell with pleasure on the glorious idea of happiness to a great nation; of felicity to millions yet unborn.

Three years later, although he had previously admired Paine's writings, Cobbett saw in France 'what republicanism was' and, correcting his principles, foreswore it. Sir Samuel Romilly was now writing sadly: 'How could we ever be so deceived in the character of the French nation as to think them capable of liberty!' Already in 1790 Arthur Young had noticed a change 'in the national character, not only in point of affection for the person of their prince, but also in that of softness and humanity, for which it has been so much admired ...' By 1795 Lord Robert Fitzgerald, who had been at the Paris Embassy from 1789 to 1791, thought that the Revolution had opened men's eyes to 'the real character of Frenchmen ... that horrid mass of infamy, perfidy, and wickedness of every description, which had so long been concealed under the veil of politeness and urbanity ...'

Nobody recalled the process of disillusion more vividly than Wordsworth. When he visited France after his third year at Cambridge he found the country 'standing at the top of golden hours,/And human nature seeming born again'. All was benevolence and welcome; there were 'dances of liberty' down the Rhone:

> All hearts were open, every tongue was loud
> With amity and glee; we bore a name
> Honoured in France, the name of Englishmen,
> And hospitably did they give us hail,
> As their forerunners in a glorious course.

This was a carefree time, when everybody seemed to be of the same mind:

> Bliss was it in that dawn to be alive,
> But to be young was to be very heaven.

Yet it was only during a subsequent visit to France that Wordsworth came to feel politically committed. When he pocketed a stone of the Bastille rubble, it was merely 'in the guise of an enthusiast' and it was with a group of royalist military officers that he later consorted in a town by the Loire. But in time he 'became a patriot', in the revolutionary sense. On returning to England he was deeply shocked to find his country putting forth her strength against France. His feelings were shared by 'all ingenuous youth':

> . . . I rejoiced
> Yea, afterwards—truth most painful to record!—
> Exulted, in the triumph of my soul,
> When Englishmen by thousands were o'erthrown,
> Left without glory on the field, or driven,
> Brave hearts! to shameful fight . . .

The time was one in which 'apostasy from ancient faith/ Seemed but conversion to a higher creed'. But cosmopolitanism failed and ancient faith revived when the French 'become oppressors in their turn', changed a war of self-defence into one of conquest. In 1802, during the brief peace, Wordsworth evoked the vanity of his earlier hopes:

> Jones! as from Calais southward you and I
> Went pacing side by side, this public way
> Streamed with the pomp of a too-credulous day,
> When faith was pledged to new-born liberty. . . .
> And now, sole register that these things were,
> Two solitary greetings have I heard:
> '*Good-morrow, Citizen!*' a hollow word
> As if a dead man spake it! . . .

There was also a revulsion of mood inside France. The revolutionaries were not long content with an English model. Arthur Young talked to two young legislators in 1790: 'In some allusions to the constitution of England, I found they hold it very cheap in regard to political liberty.' Burke wrote in the same year: 'Your leaders in France began by affecting to admire, almost to adore, the British constitution; but as they advanced, they came to look upon it with a sovereign contempt.'

In time the revolutionary fires burned down and it became once more possible for the English to regard the French as normal human beings. But Napoleon inspired the same mixture of admiration and fear in England as Louis XIV had done, together with a sharper disapproval. The First Empire, following so hard on the Revolution, made the English wonder whether the French were really fit for political liberty. The subsequent changes in regime tended to confirm this doubt. Kidd thought that the French were intellectually superior to the English, but less politically successful because they had less social cohesion. This was a typical view for more than a century: the French might resent strong leadership, but they were doomed—and knew they were doomed—to anarchy without it. According to Scythrop, in Peacock's *Nightmare Abbey* (1818):

> A Frenchman is born in harness, ready saddled, bitted, and bridled, for any tyrant to ride. He will fawn under his rider one moment, and throw him and kick him to death the next; but another adventurer springs on his back, and by dint of whip and spur on he goes as before. We may, without much vanity, hope better of ourselves.

Mrs Trollope's view was that republicanism was completely alien to the French character. The great Revolution had taken place in an exceptional moment of intoxication and excitement. Everything that had taken place since then proved that France could not exist as a republic, but needed a king with a capital.

In France English political prestige had benefited from Wellington's campaigns, as it had from Marlborough's a century earlier. It was kept high by English industrial and commercial success. Whatever else might be wrong with the English, they seemed to have a gift, in their political life, for decentralization, stability and ordered liberty. In the 1830s Tocqueville found discontent widespread in England and noted that, in contrast with their former complacency, the English themselves did not realize the excellence of their system. But he only wished that the French would learn from them how to combine centralized government with decentralized administration, since there could be no more effective guarantee of liberty. He contrasted the admirable diversity of English institutions with the demand of the French genius for uniformity 'even in the smallest details'. Another virtue of the English was that, although exclusive, they were able to combine. This was not because they were all cast in the same mould, but because the spirit of individuality, which seemed to be the basis of the English character, inspired strong ambitions and desires that could only be fulfilled through association. In general it was the laws and spirit of English society, not its material advantages, that had created English commercial prosperity: '. . . liberty gives birth to trade.'

Four decades later the economist Leroy-Beaulieu also wrote in praise of decentralization and of the realistic and empirical way in which the British set about things. Taine thought that the British system of government was admirable, though of too local a character always to be exported with success:

> Nous admirons la stabilité du gouvernement anglais, c'est qu'il est l'extrémité et l'épanouissement naturel d'une infinité de fibres vivantes accrochées au sol sur toute la surface du pays.

For Taine the British Government was stable, because the people had natural representatives. It was different in France where bourgeois and worker, noble and peasant, were at loggerheads, and the authorities were rootless officials, who were obeyed but without devotion. The English had civic sense, as their numerous voluntary societies showed; they did not detach themselves from public affairs, but prized them as their own. They were also realistic and practical:

> Un Français rapportera toujours d'Angleterre cette pérsuasion profitable, que la politique n'est pas une théorie de cabinet applicable à l'instant, tout entière et tout d'une pièce, mais une affaire de tact où l'on ne doit procéder que par atermoiements, transactions et compromis.

Halévy echoed these tributes to the civic sense of the English and their capacity for association. He attributed the exceptional stability of English society in the nineteenth century not so much to its free, indeed almost anarchic, institutions as to the moral influence of Methodism and dissent. England was no doubt a 'free country' in the anarchy of her institutions and the jungle of her economic life; but she was free, in a deeper sense, because this religious influence had made her 'the country of voluntary obedience, of spontaneous organization'.

The French sometimes envied the English their political constitution and sometimes not; yet they usually respected it both during and after the nineteenth century. But the charm of discovery receded and, except perhaps in the immediate aftermath of the Second World War, there has been less of a tendency in twentieth-century, than in eighteenth- and nineteenth-century, France to feel that England might have political lessons for her. Between the wars there was a decline of confidence, not so much in English stability as in English vitality. Paul Morand might admire England's indifference to current fashions, her preservation of her special values and her refusal to deify work. But André Siegfried, while recognizing the elegance and repose of 'ce calme traditionnel' and while admitting the persistence of 'des trésors de civisme', thought that the country stood in need of drastic reform. There was too much attachment to old methods, too much mental laziness, perhaps too much preoccupation with what was gentlemanly and not enough 'goût de la lutte'.

Some of this criticism disappeared with the war and with the many changes that have taken place since then. But by now the French economy has more than caught up and, although the English have kept their political stability and their civic sense, they are less noted abroad for social cohesion than they used to be. In spite of the traditional moulds that shape national behaviour practical success in any nation will ultimately be admired and, where possible, imitated. There are different sorts of practical success; but economic performance is more easily quantified and compared than most. In this respect, as in others, the English image has changed since the nineteenth century and no longer inspires the same awe.

One British political institution the French (or at least some French) do, in a sense, covet as much as ever; but, as readers of French picture magazines know, they have almost appropriated it. Perhaps Mrs Trollope was right in suspecting that they were never republicans at heart.

The two political systems, under their frequent revolutions and reforms, offer the same broad contrast between the artistic and the natural, the universal and the local, the absolute and the empirical, as the two literatures. The conflict between Catholicism and Protestantism, once basic to this contrast, has of course become far less strenuous and central. But the educational habits of the two countries, which religion did so much to develop, still tend to keep the contrast alive.

SEVEN

More and Less Cordial

Do THE FRENCH like the English? Do the English like the French? Are they getting to like each other more, or less?

These are really unanswerable questions. Individual Englishmen like or dislike individual Frenchmen, and vice versa. But they cannot properly like or dislike several millions of widely differing people, of whom they have only met a fraction and at best know a small number well. The more they do know, and the better, the less they are likely to have a common feeling towards them based on nationality. An Englishman might say: 'I have known three Frenchmen in my life and found that I could not trust any of them. That is why, although I had no prejudice to start with, I dislike the French.' A Frenchman might say something equally uncomplimentary about the English. But it would be difficult for either of them to make a claim of this kind on the basis of three hundred, or even thirty, acquaintances.

An Englishman could indeed know thirty (hardly three hundred) Frenchmen, all of whom were talkative in company, and a Frenchman could know thirty (hardly three hundred) Englishmen, all of whom were, or seemed, phlegmatic. But national characteristics as striking as these are rare, and often turn out to be more superficial than appears at first. As a rule it is not sober empirical observation that leads people to make up their minds about foreign countries. Sooner or later, usually sooner, they seize on some alien characteristic, or characteristics, which they find attractive or otherwise. Sometimes these are real characteristics; but they are sometimes largely imaginary and, even when not, are often assumed to be more widespread than they in fact are. Thenceforward the whole idea of the foreign country and its people becomes inseparable from the particular thing, or set of things, which have attracted or repelled. Any foreign peg too square for the hole is discarded as a freak: 'You wouldn't take him for a Frenchman.'

Whether intentionally or not, we form an abstract idea of a typical foreigner, just as we do of a typical bureaucrat or a typical artist. Perhaps it is easier to like or dislike an abstraction of this kind, with unflagging zeal, than complex human beings with their unexpected facets and changing moods. We caress our own dolls and stick pins into our own wax images. We know where we are with them.

The feeling of liking or dislike towards the French/English, besides being aimed at an abstraction, can of course be largely impersonal in origin. It may have less to do with them as people than with their countries as places to visit. Or it may reflect the admiration or contempt felt for their religious, political and cultural systems. These feelings will not necessarily be of a piece. Some English visitors to France have relished its beauty, climate, food and wine, without giving the inhabitants any special credit for them. Many Frenchmen, who have found the English personally unattractive, have admired England's political constitution and international role. At some periods the most Francophile Englishmen, while almost adoring France as a shrine of culture, have disapproved of her use of power. But the idea that we have of a country, except when we see it as a monument to a past civilization, is usually more or less in line with our general view of the people who live in it.

Each individual evolves his own attitude towards a foreign people; but he does so against a collective background. Neither subject nor object are simple and personal. When national interests have brought the two countries together, or divided them, each has tended to re-fashion the other's image. Of course this has been most obvious in governmental attitudes; but it has also been true of personal reactions, particularly in wartime. People may be slow to revise their basic conceptions of what foreigners are like, but they view their foibles more or less indulgently as national conflict recedes or revives. To describe England as a 'nation of shopkeepers' was an insult in Napoleonic France; for Voltaire, on the other hand, it would have been a compliment, since he held that commerce had helped to make England strong and free.

Both peoples seem to cling to mythical, or extinct, types in the other, as a kind of reassurance in a perpetually changing world.

These types can become symbols of derision, or affection, as the state of relations requires. A television critic wrote sourly in a French evening newspaper in 1971:

> Nobody in the world but English film stars still believes that the national head-dress of the Frenchman is the Basque beret. In this week's episode of *The Champions*, part of which took place at Paris, we had an orgy of Basque berets, of moth-eaten cafés with parasols, of antique baths and of little schoolboys dressed in aprons. On the antennae of the BBC that has the double advantage of creating 'local colour' and of suggesting that 'niggers begin at Calais'.

Just as the English still cherish, and deride, the beret, the French still deride, and cherish, the bowler hat.

The nineteenth-century English and their early twentieth-century successors often provoked a curious mixture of respect and ridicule in France. Writers in French newspapers still refer to 'nos merveilleux voisins', although both the respect and the ridicule are less keen than they once were. The two emotions have frequently been kept in balance, but one or other tends to come on top when relations are particularly smooth or troubled. There is an example of respect prevailing over ridicule in Maupassant's *Un Duel*, written in the aftermath of the Franco-Prussian War. Two paunchy, enigmatic Englishmen act as a Frenchman's seconds against a German officer; eccentric, not especially winning, they yet turn up trumps in getting their Frenchman back to his train after the German has been killed. Even Anglophobe Frenchmen will sometimes admit that the English can be useful 'in a tight corner'. Maupassant's Englishmen were slow to warm up, but thorough when warmed. General Billotte told André Maurois at the beginning of the last war:

> Je les connais bien, moi, les Anglais: ils sont lents, terriblement lents, mais ils finissent par accoucher. . . . Et puis ils tiennent . . .

Reactions change with time, but they also vary with class. In an interview published in *The Times* on 20 July 1973 the French Minister for Cultural Affairs, M. Maurice Druon, said: 'The élites tend to admire one another and the peoples to despise one another.' M. René Massigli, former Ambassador in London, made the same point in *The Times* Saturday Review Column two years earlier; he wrote of the inter-war years: 'The increased contact between one side of the channel and the other continued to involve the same "élite", but the two peoples went on ignoring one another.'

Although this is certainly true, it seems probable that, at most periods, the admiration and affection of the English 'élite' for France has been stronger and more whole-hearted than that of the French 'élite' for England. On the other hand the English people as a whole has probably been more consistently indifferent, perhaps more consistently antipathetic, to the French than the French people as a whole has been to them.

The feelings of the French élite for England have often been genuinely admiring and sometimes genuinely fond, but they have been complicated by a touch of resentment at parvenu success and by a touch of disdain for Puritanism and insular provincialism. The effect of English governesses and nannies on the French upper class may not always have been happy, though the Comtesse Jean de Pange recalls that she adored her English nurse at the end of the nineteenth century and was brought up to regard England as 'the children's paradise'.

The English élite, both aristocratic and intellectual, has on the whole had fewer reservations. In spite, and even because, of some moral hesitations, Paris has been a Mecca for the fashion and intelligentsia of England. In Miss Mitford's *The Blessing* Sir Conrad Allingham and Mr O'Donovan 'both belonged to that category of English person, not rare among the cultivated classes, and not the least respectable of their race, who can find almost literally nothing to criticize where the French are concerned'.

Popular antipathy to France in England has never affected, or threatened, this kind of Gallomania, although the antipathy was once strong and is not yet quite spent. Saxon resistance to Norman lords and the French language; medieval campaigns in hostile parts of France; suspicion of Popery; Puritan prudery; early scorn for French fashions and refinements; fears of Louis XIV and Napoleon; colonial rivalries: perhaps all these contributed to a sluggish, but tenacious, feeling of enmity, and later of apathy, in the masses. Some of these factors were also present in France and had the same results. But one gets the impression that the Anglophobia of the French masses, though at times more acute and concentrated, was in some ways less general and persistent.

For one thing there has been no parallel in England to the way in which French attitudes have varied regionally. It seems to have been in the parts of France nearest to England that the English have been most, and least, liked. By and large trade has made for friendship. It would not be surprising if this were the case in the Flemish district round Lille; but race does not seem to have been the chief factor. Arthur Young wrote of the merchants of Le Havre in 1788: 'It is no bad prejudice surely to like people that like England; most of them have been there.' Whether because of its wine trade, or because of its occupation by the Plantagenets, there has long been a particular friendship for England in Bordeaux. Edmund Wheatley, in Wellington's army, found the people of Bordeaux 'civil and kind' in 1814; Daninos has written of 'certains Bordelais . . . chez lesquels il est resté un vieux fond d'Aquitaine britannique.' On the other hand Brittany, with its Catholicism and long connection with the French Navy, has been traditionally Anglophobe. Cazamian presumably had Brittany in mind when he wrote of the hereditary *méfiance* felt by the French for the English, particularly in certain provinces.

The French must be more familiar on the south coast, than in the north, of England; yet, if there are provincial differences in the regard of the English for the French, they are certainly not common knowledge. There may be some such difference in the Celtic parts of Britain, but it is racial rather than regional in origin. Thus a Welshman, Charles Morgan, writing to a Frenchman:*

> I always feel that I have a better chance of being instantly understood by a French mind than by an English. The English refusal to count beforehand the cost of their emotions, their extraordinary habit of 'hoping for the best' until the inevitable worst is upon them, their whole attitude towards women, their incapacity to find *pleasure* in art as such, their deadly reticence—all these things make me feel foreign among them.

English feelings about the French tend in any case to be simpler than French feelings about the English. Most Englishmen today who feel strongly on the subject at all are predominantly, sometimes exclusively, Francophile or Francophobe. Many Frenchmen have an odd way of being both Anglophile and Anglophobe at the same time. Daninos makes Major Thompson observe:

* Letter to M. René Lalou of 22 February 1956, reproduced in *Selected Letters of Charles Morgan* (1967), ed. by Eiluned Lewis.

Quand un Français commence par me dire: 'Je vais vous parler franchement: dans ma famille, on a toujours détesté les Anglais . . .', je parierais une bouteille de scotch qu'il me confiera bientôt: 'Au fond, on vous aime bien . . .' Pour un Français, il y a toujours deux Anglais en un seul: le bon (celui du match Oxford-Cambridge) et le mauvais (celui de Fachoda). Cela dépend de son humeur.

Given these complexities of feeling; given the class differences in England and the regional differences in France; given the way in which the national images shift as policies and interests shift; given the unreality of the whole notion of liking or disliking a foreign people: given all this, the difficulty, and perhaps the futility, of the questions at the beginning of this chapter is daunting. Yet perhaps there is no need to probe too deeply. It is at least easy to recognize that, at different periods, *public* cordiality has waxed and waned.

In England, at almost every period, French culture has been respected and French fashions have fascinated. Of course the fascination and respect have not been universal; there has been a recurring grumble, particularly audible in the eighteenth century, of backwoods disapproval. But admiration has been the keynote. During the Napoleonic Wars, and in the days of the British industrial miracle, French culture and fashions both lost some ground; the latter (except in cookery and women's clothes) never quite recovered it. But French art and letters were seldom more in vogue in England than in the half century before the Second World War. Because England was no longer in a subordinate position, their brilliance was less clouded by the resentment that the plain man had tended to feel in earlier centuries.

Conversely, at almost every period, the English, impressed by French culture, have been critical of French politics. But the criticism has been qualified by three distinct moods: a mood of patronizing approval when the French seemed to be trying hard to be moderate and democratic; a mood of uneasy respect when the French were governed more or less absolutely and this was producing dividends; a mood of awed enthusiasm (in progressive circles) when the French were waving, with infectious ardour, their revolutionary torch. Most Englishmen were glad to have been spared 1789, 1830, 1848 and 1870; but there were others who felt deprived and longed to follow, or rival, the French lead.

As I have already suggested, the private feelings of cultivated Englishmen towards the French have more often than not been friendly and sometimes very friendly. There has been comparatively little variation in this warmth, at least since the eighteenth century. The main change has been in the degree of popular hostility, which gradually weakened as English power drew level with French.

Perlin in the middle of the sixteenth century complained that the English 'spit in our face'. Sully, who visited England as a negotiator in 1603, wrote in his memoirs: 'It is certain that the English hate us, and with a hate so strong and so general, that one would be tempted to list it as one of the natural dispositions of this people.' In 1677 the French Ambassador, Courtin, took the same line with Louis XIV: 'The English hate us.' Sully and Courtin presumably had public, as much as private, feelings in mind. But even the mild Misson wrote of the English theatre in 1697:

> If there is something which grieves me in regard to the English theatre, it is that I see there all our people pillaged, copied and at the same time insulted. All the best that they have comes from us, and instead of being grateful to us for our property, they look down on us in the most outrageous way.

Montesquieu, visiting Parliament in early eighteenth-century London, found the French much attacked there and was struck by the extent of the 'terrible jealousy existing between the two nations'. This public jealousy was all too often reflected in the behaviour of the mob. The Swiss, Zimmermann,* wrote of England in the middle of the eighteenth century: 'A foreigner, if not dressed like an Englishman, is in great danger of being assailed with dirt for being thought a Frenchman.' Foote's Englishman, returned from Paris, had an accident in a London street, in his French clothes, and deplored 'the hideous hootings of . . . that murtherous mob, with the barbarous "monsieur in the mud, huzza!"' The Abbé le Blanc noted that English writers 'do not despise us as much as the vulgar population' and admitted that there was an unreasonable hatred on both sides. But the English, whose leaders 'think it is in their interest to make a power that alarms them unpopular', carried their hatred further. Nevertheless, he detected a series of contradictions: 'They hate us and look

* Quoted by Hampson, op. cit., cf. p. 97 above.

down on us: we are the Nation that they receive the most and like the least: they condemn us and imitate us: they adopt our manners by taste and blame them by policy.'

Things gradually improved. There was less popular hostility in the American, than in the Seven Years', War. Horace Walpole wrote in 1778: 'Though at war with France, neither country takes much notice of it.' Dutens recorded of the period 1784–9, in *L'Ami des Etrangers qui voyagent en Angleterre*,* that the French 'come in crowds to England, where they are better received than ever among the nobility: the houses are open to them among the other classes; the people have no longer their old prejudices against a Frenchman.' In 1823 Sir Charles Darnley could claim:

> Fifty years ago, a foreigner no sooner appeared in London than he was followed and abused, and '*French dog*' and other offensive terms applied to him. All this, is now happily changed . . .

Edmund Wheatley, who fought as a junior officer in the Waterloo campaign, thought the French 'far more commendable characters than these heavy, selfish Germans' and believed that most Englishmen liked them in their hearts.

The French Revolution put an end to the brilliant Indian summer of the *entente* between the two aristocracies. But middle-class contacts developed steadily throughout the nineteenth century. These were sometimes hampered by Victorian morality. Mrs Trollope, moving in respectable, *bien-pensant*, circles in Louis Philippe's Paris, found no inferiority in moral standards; in fact ways of thought were altogether much closer than she had expected. But she noticed a difference between French and English notions of what decency and delicacy required. With increasing prosperity, she wrote, the English had more and more managed to avoid seeing, hearing and speaking of unpleasant things. In France, under the surface elegance, much was still primitive. The result was, not an innate crudity of spirit in the French, but some lack of refinement in their words and thoughts.

Mrs Trollope dismissed this as a superficial, rather than a basic, difference: formerly the English themselves had displayed the same crude readiness to call spades spades. In general she was delighted by her stay and enthusiastic about the friendly state of Anglo-French relations. She referred to the Gallomania prevalent in England and thanked God that the days had passed when an

* Quoted by Lockitt, op. cit.

Englishman would think it a proof of patriotism to deny his French neighbours any talents other than bowing and frog-eating. A hard struggle, fought bravely on both sides, had ended in a cordial reconciliation.

Dickens's picture, in *A Tale of Two Cities*, of hunger, misery and arbitrary power under the *ancien régime*, must have affected many of his readers, even in the changed circumstances of the nineteenth century, as a sort of indictment of the French. But, at the end of the book, Carlton foresees 'a beautiful city and a brilliant people rising from this abyss'. It was as 'a brilliant people' that the English middle class of the later nineteenth century tended to regard the French, with an indulgent awareness that their own social and moral soundness was more successful and respectable. Yet there were always English intellectual malcontents, in love with France, who preferred brilliance to soundness or took a different view of what was sound.

The First World War introduced a new English social class to France. André Maurois, in *Les Silences du Colonel Bramble*, made his young French interpreter warm to 'ce petit peuple anglais, au langage véhément, mais aux pensées candides . . . de braves gens, insouciants, courageux et frivoles . . .' A group of drivers and motorcyclists told him that 'they understood people loving France: it was a fine country. All the same there were not enough hedges in the countryside. But they appreciated the housekeeping virtues of the women, the trees along the roads and the terraces of the cafés.'

The Second World War did less to make France known to the average Englishman. However, there were Free French in London and M. Druon found that they benefited 'from affectionate treatment . . .'

A graph of English feelings towards the French would show a more or less steady line at the top for a cultivated minority and at the bottom a slowly, and irregularly, rising line for the majority. A similar graph in France would plot more violent zigzags. A French writer, Jean Jacquart, has observed that French attitudes have tended to oscillate between Anglophobia and Anglomania, seldom pausing at the middle stage of coolly sympathetic understanding. Thus, according to him, the Anglophobia of the reign of Louis XIV was followed by the Anglomania of the eighteenth century and itself followed a period of friendship for England at the beginning of the seventeenth century.

French Anglomanes have not always been Anglophile, in the sense of really enjoying England and the company of Englishmen. But Anglomania could hardly flourish in a climate of total hostility and its successive waves do suggest that there have been marked oscillations in French cordiality, both before and after the eighteenth century. The greatest periods of English prestige in France have been heralded by English victories. The first wave of Anglomania started in the years following the Peace of Utrecht. There was a sour phase just after Waterloo; but a fresh wave of Anglomania soon followed. In very different circumstances there was something like a third wave in the years just after the Second World War.

It was not that the French were attracted by British power as such—they often resented it. But power implied success and this suggested that there might be qualities worth studying or imitating. The English have often had a cultural respect for France at times when she was politically weak. Unless in the 'swinging sixties' of this century this has been much less the case in reverse.

It is important to remember how much seventeenth-century France had outshone seventeenth-century England. In effect the French had scarcely finished looking down on the English before, in the nineteenth century, they had (for a time) to look up to them. This was necessarily a traumatic experience. Perhaps the most genuine friendship between the two countries has been in periods, like the First World War and the years just before the French Revolution, when they have been able to feel most equal.

For much of the seventeenth century the French view of the English was coloured by a pious disapproval of their ungovernability. This was still strong when Voltaire visited England; he wrote: 'The French think that the government of this island is more stormy than the sea that surrounds it . . .' There was an ideological gulf narrower than, but not unlike, the gulf between Communist and capitalist countries today. This was inevitably a barrier to cordial personal relations and there were not many inducements to the French to cross it. Nevertheless, in his study of French seventeenth-century attitudes towards the English, Ascoli concluded:

> Ce qui me frappe c'est que, dans l'ensemble, l'Anglais, de cette analyse, ne ressorte point antipathique; il appelle la curiosité, l'intérêt, on s'efforce de démêler, d'expliquer, plus ou moins justement, son originalité, sa bizarrerie.

It was during the seventeenth century that the English founded the reputation for deep philosophy that they enjoyed in eighteenth-century France. One of the first French experts on England, l'abbé Prévost, wrote an edifying, if improbable, story about a mistress of Charles I, who later became Cromwell's mistress, and finally took to philosophy. Cleveland, her son, is brought up on philosophy by his mother and in due course teaches it to his own son, having reached a haven of suitably philosophic contentment after an eventful career. When he published his play, *l'Anglomane*, Saurin was careful to point out:

> . . . I have not presumed to cast ridicule on the illustrious writers whom England has produced. I admire and respect them; I have only wished to attack the blind enthusiasm of our Anglomanes, the sort of cult that they offer to the English authors, perhaps less in order to exalt them than to degrade our own.

The progress of Anglomania in eighteenth-century France was seldom checked by the continual and world-wide rivalry between the two nations. There were sometimes high tempers and hard feelings, particularly during the Seven Years' War; but, more often than not, the conflict was tempered by mutual esteem. The Abbé le Blanc could write during the Seven Years' War:

> The English in the last War had shown themselves such as I have portrayed them, as humane as they were brave: on several occasions there were seen both on their side and on ours combats of generosity and examples of humanity which did equal honour to the one and the other Nation.*

At the height of the Revolution the English liberal tradition became irrelevant in France and remained so during the Napoleonic years, except as a distant beacon for some of the Emperor's critics. One of them, Mme de Stael, visited England in 1813 and made friends with both Whigs and Tories; she later recalled going to London 'as Muslims go to Mecca'. But these were exalting days for France, or at least for many Frenchmen, and there seems to have been less hostility towards the English than there was towards the French in England. A Quaker gentleman farmer, Morris Birkbeck,† who visited France in the summer of 1814, recorded an amiable reception:

* Cf. Montesquieu on the Hundred Years' War, p. 32 above.

† Quoted by Maxwell, op. cit.

> I do not believe that there is among the French a feeling of jealousy towards us, a sentiment of national rivalship such as I am sorry to see cherished on this side of the water. They have no idea of the English and French being natural foes; the animosity which has been said to prevail between the two nations they refer exclusively to the Governments.

But the military occupation after Waterloo hurt French pride and feelings turned bitter. Mme de Stael herself, though a great admirer of the Duke of Wellington, was deeply pained by what she felt as the humiliation of France; she continually tried to get the Duke to use his influence to secure the withdrawal of foreign troops. Wellington was stung to reply: 'Those who walk may read, and those who read may understand, that France is anything but "soumise à l'influence Anglaise" '; but French opinion held him responsible for the effects of the allied occupation and his unpopularity grew. Although he left France after the Conference of Aix-la-Chapelle in 1818, French hostility to the English remained hot for several years. Sir Charles Darnley found it so in 1823:

> Whether it arises from national jealousy, or from the peculiar hatred engendered by the late war . . . I cannot pretend to say; but no fact is more certain than this, that the English are most unwelcome guests in the circles of the Parisians . . . I fear . . . that at no time was . . . antipathy against the English more violent than at this moment.

Sir Charles referred to a recent representation of Jeanne d'Arc, which was followed by loud vociferations of '*Barbares Anglois! Chiens d'Anglois! Quelle nation barbare!* . . .' Scott, in his Introduction to *Quentin Durward* written at about this time, pictured an old French aristocrat, reserved towards all foreigners and 'particularly shy towards the English' whom he regarded (like Balzac) as 'a haughty, purse-proud people.'

The fierce hostility of the years around 1820 did not last long; but, in spite of the second wave of political and cultural Anglomania that followed, an undercurrent of resentment continued throughout the nineteenth century. Flaubert's *L'Education Sentimentale* shows how this was so under the July monarchy, for all the attempts to foster Anglo-French cordiality. The French might admire England's industrial and political successes, but they could hardly be expected to relish them. Charges of hypocrisy became frequent. In his novel *L'Homme qui Rit*, set in the England of Queen Anne, Victor Hugo puts (quite unhistorically) some words in the mouth of a travelling philosopher/showman which sum up what many nineteenth-century Frenchmen felt about their English contemporaries:

> Hommes et femmes de Londres, me voici. Je vous félicite cordialement d'être anglais. Vous êtes un grand peuple. Vous avez de l'appétit. Vous êtes la nation qui mange les autres. Fonction magnifique. Cette succion du monde classe à part l'Angleterre. Comme politique et philosophie, et maniement des colonies, populations, et industries, et comme volonté de faire aux autres du mal qui est pour soi du bien, vous êtes particuliers et surprenants. Le moment approche où il y aura sur terre deux écriteaux; sur l'un on lira: *Côté des Hommes:* sur l'autre on lira: '*Côté des Anglais.* Je constate ceci à votre gloire . . .

In the closing decades of the century, during the 'Scramble for Africa', this resentment broke out in a torrent of Anglophobia. Lord Dufferin, British Ambassador at Paris in 1893, wrote in a despatch to the Foreign Office: 'I am afraid that I can only describe the sentiments of French people of all classes towards us as that of unmitigated and bitter dislike.' As a small girl, fond of her English nurse, the Comtesse de Pange was deeply upset by the hostility towards England after the Fashoda episode:

> In the Bois de Boulogne, my little friends planted tricolour flags ostentatiously on the sandheaps, crying: 'Down with the English.' The coachmen looked askance at the English nurses . . .

The visit of Edward VII to Paris in May 1903 marked the beginning of a fresh change of mood. By the time of the First World War Proust's Odette, always Anglophile, was no longer obliged to content herself with calling the English 'nos voisins d'outre-Manche' or at best 'nos amis les Anglais', but could describe them as 'nos loyaux alliés'. Even M. de Charlus, with his Germanic sympathies (though perverse admiration for Anglo-Saxon physique), was impressed by England's honourable conduct in entering the war. Cazamian, writing in 1927, said that the 'war left a vision of the Englishman as a "bon camarade" and "loyal soldat improvisé".'

Perhaps it was inevitable that suspicions should revive with peace. There were many apples of discord, particularly in the Middle East. The young French Lieutenant Vincent, in Maurois's *Les Discours du Docteur O'Grady*, made a typical attack on English Policy as a 'mixture of altruistic sermons for our benefit and egoistic imperialism on their own account'. In the inter-war years Maurois found in both countries 'a deep suspicion of the other . . . one of the greatest dangers, for Anglo-French relations, were these meetings of politicians who could not understand each other. France had a taste for precise engagements; the English held them in horror.'

English culture, too, made relatively little impact in France in those years, though André Siegfried described it in 1931 as 'l'une des plus raffinées qui soient.' Writing just after the Second World War Pierre Maillaud recalled of the 1930s:

> It is a remarkable thing that a few years ago . . . the well-travelled man on the Continent still spoke of England as Marco Polo did of China. . . . Indeed, even among the better educated, English culture was making less impression than it had in previous centuries.

The Second World War should have brought the two peoples closer together and to some extent it did. But, even in 'the phoney war', Maurois found a great difference in Anglo-French relations from 1914:

> The staffs got on with each other rather better but, in the military and civilian masses, suspicion and even hostility were constantly kept alive by German propaganda, persistent, insinuating, sarcastic, tenacious, adroit, and appealing to the ancient wrongs of the French: Jeanne d'Arc at the stake, St Helena. O the power of archetypes!

The Battle of Britain, the Blitz and the wartime BBC temporarily recovered for the English in France even more ground than they had lost. But perhaps it was as well that they never fully seized their post-war opportunity in Western Europe. It may have been better that neither they, nor others, should expect too much of human, and national, nature. That mistake, at least, was avoided. The French and the English have continued to react to each other in human and national—and wholly familiar ways.

* * *

The many dissimilarities between the two peoples have sometimes made for liking, and sometimes not, but have always made understanding between them more difficult.

One can speculate endlessly on whether these dissimilarities are chiefly racial, geographic or conventional in origin. The English, often with French encouragement, have tended to regard France as a predominantly Latin country, with the usual Latin charms and weaknesses, though braced by some northern virtues. French writers (like Montesquieu and Taine) have stressed the Germanic origin of the English. Paul Morand, who had served as a young diplomatist in London before the First World War, suggested in 1933 that the Germans were nearer to the hearts of the Anglo-Saxons than the French. But he recognized that England was not solely Germanic:

> London is the result of a compromise, a compromise between earth and water, between Germans and Latins, between the State and the individual, between surprise and habit, between sun and fog.

It may be unscientific to assume differences between peoples other than those that depend on their environments. But one can, after all, distinguish physical characteristics in different races, even when they have long been subject to the same education, climate and food. Emotional characteristics, too, seem sometimes to survive emigration. Roubaud, the doctor in Balzac's *Le Curé de Village*, classified the English medically as 'lymphatic . . . we are generally sanguine or nervous.' The quick vivacity of the French, in comparison with the English, has always been a commonplace and, though it may often have been exaggerated, is easily observed. Chateaubriand recalls how, at the school which he had founded for *émigré* children, Burke liked to watch their vivacity at play. Seeing the way they jumped he would say: 'Our little boys would not do that . . .'

Of course the French have enjoyed a sunnier climate than the English (though this, too, has been exaggerated) and that must have helped to preserve them from Nordic melancholy. But their particular sort of vivacity is not found in all sunny climates. Nor is it a difference in climate that accounts for racial differences inside the British Isles. The many English who have some Highland, Welsh or Irish blood are often conscious of a Celtic strain in themselves, however exclusively they have lived and been educated, in England.

Whether the racial factor is or is not important, it is elusive. The geographical factor is more definite and demonstrable. The English seldom quite realize their own insularity and the way in which it strikes continental peoples. At the height of British power, when Britain was a vast empire as well as a set of islands, this was a confident attitude, global rather than provincial. But it was none the less insular. André Siegfried noted how British customs were 'maintained distinct by insularity' and how the ordinary Englishman preserved, in regard to the Continent, 'the condescending attitude of the colonist towards the native'. Today there are fewer traces of this colonial attitude, but occasional signs of an insular provincialism that in some ways evokes the seventeenth century.

The main conventional, or formal, differences between the French and the English seem basically due to three causes: the earlier development of refined civilization in France; the more rapid and consistent political evolution of England; the supremacy in both countries of different religious faiths.

I have oversimplified some of the effects of these causes in the last chapter. But it is certain that different methods of education, designed to serve different political and religious systems, have induced different habits of thought. The longer and fuller exposure of France to classical civilization may go some way to explain one basic contrast—the French tendency to prefer the artistic and the English tendency to prefer the natural. This has been at the root of many Anglo-French controversies.

But none of these differences, even those of climate in a world of artificial heating, is necessarily immutable. There is plenty of evidence that both peoples have in fact changed considerably throughout their histories. Certainly there have been some noticeable changes in 'the English character' since the Second World War. The bashfulness which James Howell observed in young English travellers in the early seventeenth century was a standard characteristic for centuries, but is a good deal less obvious today.

Many factors—less religious conflict, more mass production, improved communications, standardized culture—are tending to reduce the dissimilarities between the French and the English. But of course local habits and prejudices will remain and national interests will sometimes differ. The language difference will maintain a barrier long after the Channel has effectively ceased to separate. Although there must be an increasing convergence of the two peoples, it will never be rapid or unhesitating.

Yet, even traditionally, there are respects in which the two civilizations have been far closer than they sometimes seemed. It is harder to define these similarities than the dissimilarities; but they have grown naturally from common historical experiences, equivalent achievement and many shared ideas about life and society. Tocqueville could write in 1851: 'So many of my thoughts and feelings are shared by the English, that England has turned into a second native land of the mind for me.' It was not the same mental land as France, but it was land that a French mind could occupy. From a less scholarly viewpoint Pierre Maillaud found 'in England, . . . as in France and nowhere else in the same way, a contentment with life, a quiet humour, which escapes the casual visitor. It emanates from the land and has to be discovered by contact with it.'

Introducing the book from which this passage comes Raymond Mortimer wrote:

> Like M. Maillaud I believe the differences between the English and the French to be much more superficial than their similarities. I hope for a great increase in interchange between our two peoples, because I have noticed that deeper reciprocal knowledge between them almost always makes for warm liking.

Two decades earlier Cazamian had laid more stress on the differences ('In truth we do not understand them; their soul is more distant from us than that of other peoples'). But he too felt that deeper reciprocal knowledge made for liking. He thought that a foreigner going to live in England would find a welcome surprise:

> Assez vite il sent émaner des moeurs, des rapports sociaux, du ton des âmes, une douceur inattendue, une humanité généreuse, une bonté active. La surprise, souvent, n'est pas moins grande pour les Anglais, de trouver chez leur visiteur—un Français par exemple—des qualités de sérieux et d'application suivie au labeur comme au devoir, qu'un ancien préjugé lui refusait en principe. Tant il est vrai que les nations les plus voisines s'ignorent; et que les peuples de la vieille Europe ont encore à se découvrir.

Both England and France lie in a temperate zone, though the one country tips towards the north and the other towards the south. It is a temperate zone mentally as well as climatically. The English have not always remarked on the sense of 'measure' often claimed as a Gallic virtue; the French have sometimes been struck by the excesses, rather than the moderation, of the English. But at least the French would credit the English with some civic, and the English would credit the French with some intellectual, sobriety. Whether they admit it of the other or not, there is an instinctive restraint in the way in which both peoples tend to see the world. They share a sense of what is human and possible, a distaste for what is out of scale, a distrust of emotional depths, a dislike of obscurity and a preference for individual, above collective, values.

This is quite a lot to have in common. Quite enough to justify what President Pompidou said to *The Times* before the last British State Visit to France:

> It seems to me . . . that a long history, a national consciousness nearly a thousand years old, the same traditions of freedom, a certain concept of man and civilization and even our quarrels of long ago, all this endows our relationship with an emotional content.

A study of any relationship is liable to give the impression that it is all-absorbing and exclusive. Of course nothing could be less true in this case. Both the French and the English have been primarily interested in themselves. When they have turned abroad they have often found other partners and enemies. The French have usually felt a greater natural affinity with Mediterranean peoples, the English with Northern Europeans or the peoples of former British colonies. But the emotional interaction of France and England, the exchange of influence between them, has none the less been unique in duration and degree. The Italians, the Spaniards, the Dutch, the Germans and the Americans have all left powerful marks on English life. But none of them have had so many, and such important, dealings with the English, over so long a period, as the French. Equally there is no people that, over the same period, has had a wider or more recurring impact on the French than the English.

Whether this will still be so in the future, nobody can say. Other relationships may loom larger, or the old national distinctions may become provincial if a common European identity is forged. But, whether as states or provinces, France and England will be obliged to stay neighbours. It is difficult to imagine a time when they will not think of each other, more or less cordially, as familiar enemies or baffling friends.

PRINCIPAL SOURCES

(This is an indication of sources, not a detailed bibliography. A list of Anglo-French studies will be found in Baldensperger and Friederich, *Bibliography of Comparative Literature*, 2nd ed., New York, 1960: pp. 55–6; 365–6; 551–3.)

Arnold, Matthew (1822–88): *Letters*

Ascoli, Georges: *La Grande-Bretagne devant l'Opinion Française—Depuis la Guerre de Cent Ans jusqu'à la Fin du XVIe siècle* (1927)
La Grand Bretagne devant l'Opinion Française au XVIIe siecle (1930)

Balzac, Honoré de: *Le Lys dans la Vallée* (1836) and other novels

Bastide, Charles: *Anglais et Français du XVIIe siècle* (1912).

Blanc, L'abbé le: *Lettres d'un François* (1758. 1st ed. 1745).

Bolingbroke, Henry St John, Viscount (1678–1751): *Works*

Bossuet, Jacques Benigne: *Oraison Funèbre de Henriotte-Marie de France Reine de la Grande-Bretagne* (1669)
Oraison funèbre de Henriette-Anne d'Angleterre, Duchesse d'Orléans (1670)

Brogan, D. W.: The Development of Modern France, 1870–1939 (1940)

Burke, Edmund: Reflections on the Revolution in France (1790)
Letter to a Member of the National Assembly (1791)

Byron, George, Lord (1788–1824): *Poems*

Cazamian, Louis: *Ce qu'il faut connaître de l'Ame Anglaise* (1927)

Chateaubriand, René de (1768–1848): *Mémoires d'Outre-Tombe* (published 1848–50)

Chesterfield, Philip, Earl of (1694–1773): *Letters to his Son* (mostly written between 1740–50)

Clark, A. F. B.: *Boileau and the French Classical Critics in England 1660–1830* (1925)

Cobban, Alfred: *The Debate on the French Revolution* 1789–1800 (Ed.) 2nd ed. 1960

Cobbett, William (1761–1835): *The Progress of a Plough-boy to a seat in Parliament as exemplified in the history of the life of*—(ed. W. Reitzel 1933)
Cole, Rev. William: *A Journal of my Journey to Paris in the year 1765*
Cravatiana: *ou Traité Général des Cravates: ouvrage traduit librement de l'Anglais* (1823)
Dagliani, Jean: *Lord Brougham, Inventeur de Cannes*
Dallington, Robert: *The View of France* (1604)
Daninos, Pierre: *Les Carnets du Major Thompson* (1954)
Le Secret du Major Thompson (1956)
Le Major Tricolore (1969)
Dickens, Charles: *A Tale of Two Cities* (1859)
Disraeli, Benjamin: *Coningsby* (1844)
Dryden, John: *Of Dramatick Poesie: An Essay* (1668)
Dumas, Alexandre: *Vingt Ans Après* (1845)
Etherege, Sir George: *The Man of Mode* (1676)
Evelyn, John (1620–1706): *Diary*
Farquhar, George: *The Beaux' Stratagem* (1707)
Fisher, H. A. L.: *History of Europe* (1935)
Fontaine, Jean de la: *Le Renard Anglois* (*Fables*, Book 12, No 23) (1683)
Foote, Samuel: *The Englishman in Paris* (1753)
The Englishman Returned from Paris (1756)
Gaskell, Mrs: *My French Master* (1853)
French Life (1864)
Gautier, Théophile: *Voyages en Angleterre et en Belgigue* (1845)
Militona (1847)
Grant, A. J., and Temperley, Harold: *Europe in the Nineteenth and Twentieth Centuries* (1789–1939) (5th ed., 1947)
Green, J. R. (1837–83): *Letters*
Halévy, Elie: *Histoire du Peuple Anglais au XIXe Siècle* (1912)
Hampson, Norman: *The Enlightenment* (1968)
Hazlitt, William: *Notes of a Journey through France and Italy* (1826)
Hobson, J. A.: *Richard Cobden: The International Man* (1918)
Howell, James: *Instructions for Forreine Travell* (1642)
Hugo, Victor: *L'Homme qui Rit* (1869)
Kidd, Benjamin: *Social Evolution* (1894)
Kipling, Rudyard: *Works* including *France* (1913)
Souvenirs de France (Trans. Louis Gillet, 1936)
La Rochefoucauld, François, Duc de: *Mélanges sur L'Angleterre* (1784)

Leroy-Beaulieu, P.: *De la Colonization chez les Peuples Modernes* (1874)
Leslie, C. R.: *Memoirs of the Life of John Constable* (1843)
Lister, Dr Martin: *A Journey to Paris in the year 1698*
Lockitt, C. H.: *The Relations of French and English Society 1763–1793* (1920)
Longford, Elizabeth: *Victoria* R. *I.* (1964)
Madariaga, Salvador de: *Anglais, Français Espagnols* (15th ed., 1952)
Maillaud, Pierre: *The English Way* (1945)
Maupassant, Guy de: *Boule de Suif* (*Un Duel*) (1880)
Miss Harriet (1884)
Maurois, André: *Les Silences du Colonel Bramble* (1918)
Les Discours du Docteur O'Grady (1922)
Mémoires (1970)
Maxwell, C.: *The English Traveller in France 1698–1815* (1932)
Melville, Lewis: *The Life and Letters of Tobias Smollett 1721–1771*
Mérimée, Prosper (1803–70): *Etudes Anglo-Americaines*
Michelet, Jules: *Sur les Chemins de l'Europe* (1834)
Misson, Maximilien: *Mémoires et observations Faites par un Voyageur en Angleterre* (1698)
Mitford, Nancy: *The Blessing* (1951)
Montaigne, Michel de (1533–92): *Essais*
Montesquieu, Charles de (1689–1755): *Oeuvres* (*Caractères Ethniques, De l'esprit des Lois* (1748), *Notes sur l'Angleterre, etc.*)
Moore, George (1852–1933): *Confessions of a Young Man* (new ed., 1904)
Morand, Paul: 'Les Personnages Anglais dans la Littérature d'Imagination en France du Douzième à la Fin du Dix-huitième siècle', *Anglo-French Review* (September 1920)
Londres (1933)
Musgrove, Clifford: *Regency Furniture* (1961)
Adam and Hepplewhite and other Neo-Classical Furniture (1966)
Palmer, R. E. (ed.): *French Travellers in England 1600–1900*
Pange, Comtesse Jean de: *Comment j'ai vu 1900* (1962)
Pange, Victor de: *Madame de Stael et le duc de Wellington. Correspondance inédite 1815–1817* (1962)
Pepys, Samuel (1633–1703): *Diary*
Perlin, Maistre Etienne: *Description des Royaulmes d'Angleterre et d'Escosse* (1558)

Prévost D'Exiles, L'abbé P.: *The English Philosopher or the history of Mr Cleveland, natural son of Cromwell* (first parts published in 1732)

Proust, Marcel (1871–1922): *A la Recherche du Temps Perdu*

Queval, Jean: *De l'Angleterre* (1956)

Rye, W. B.: *England as seen by Foreigners in the days of Elizabeth and James I* (1865)

Saurin, Bernard Joseph: *L'Anglomane ou l'Orpheline Léguée* (1772)

Scott, Sir Walter: *Quentin Durward* (1823)

Seely, Sir J. R.: *The Expansion of England* (1883)

Shakespeare, William (1564–1616): *King John*
King Henry V
King Henry VI
King Henry VIII

Siegfried, André: *Le Crise Britannique au XXe siècle* (1931)

Smith, Adam: *The Wealth of Nations* (1776–8)

Sorbière, Samuel: *Relation d'un Voyage en Angleterre* (1666)

Spectator (1711–14)

Stanhope, Earl: *Notes of Conversations with the Duke of Wellington: 1831–1851*

Starkie, Enid: *From Gautier to Eliot: The Influence of France on English Literature 1851–1939* (1960)

Stendhal, Henri Beyle (1783–1842): *Racine et Shakespeare* (1823–4)

Sterne, Laurence: *A Sentimental Journey through France and Italy* (1768)

Stevenson, Robert Louis: *Travels with a Donkey in the Cévennes* (1879)

Sully, Maximilien de Béthune, Duc de: *Mémoires* (1638)

Surtees, Robert: *Jorrocks's Jaunts and Jollities* (1838)

Taine, Hippolyte: *Notes sur l'Angleterre* (1872)
Histoire de la Littérature Anglaise (2nd ed., 1866, together with fifth volume on *Les Contemporains* published in 1878)

Tennyson, Alfred, Lord (1809–92): *Poems*

Thackeray, William Makepeace (1811–63): *Works*, including
The Book of Snobs (1846–7)
and
The Adventures of Philip (1861–2)

Thomson, Mark A.: *Essays by and for:*
William III and Louis XIV (1968)

Tieghem, P. van: *Les Influences étrangères sur la Littérature Française 1550–1880* (1961)

Tocqueville, Alexis, Comte de (1805–59): *Journeys to England and Ireland* (ed. J. P. Mayer)

Democracy in America (1835)

Trollope, Frances: *Paris and the Parisians* (1835)

Valles, Julès: *La Rue à Londres* (1884)

Vermont, Marquis de, and Darnley, Sir Charles: *London and Paris, or comparative sketches* (anonymously 'edited') (1823)

Verne, Jules: *Le tour du monde en 80 jours* (1873)

Voltaire, François Marie Arouet de: *Lettres sur les Anglais* (1733–4)

Walpole, Horace (1717–97): *Letters*

Weiner, Margery: *The French Exiles 1789–1815* (1960)

Wheatley, Edmund: *Diary* (1813–17); ed. Christopher Hibbert, 1964

Wilkinson, G. K.: *John Taylor and Son (Cannes) 1864–1964*

Woolfield, Thomas Robinson: *His Life at Cannes, by his nephew* (1890)

Wordsworth, William: *The Prelude* (1805) and other Poems

Young, Arthur: *Travels in France during the years 1787, 1788 and 1789* (ed. C. Maxwell, 1929)

INDEX